Emily

AND the StrangeRs

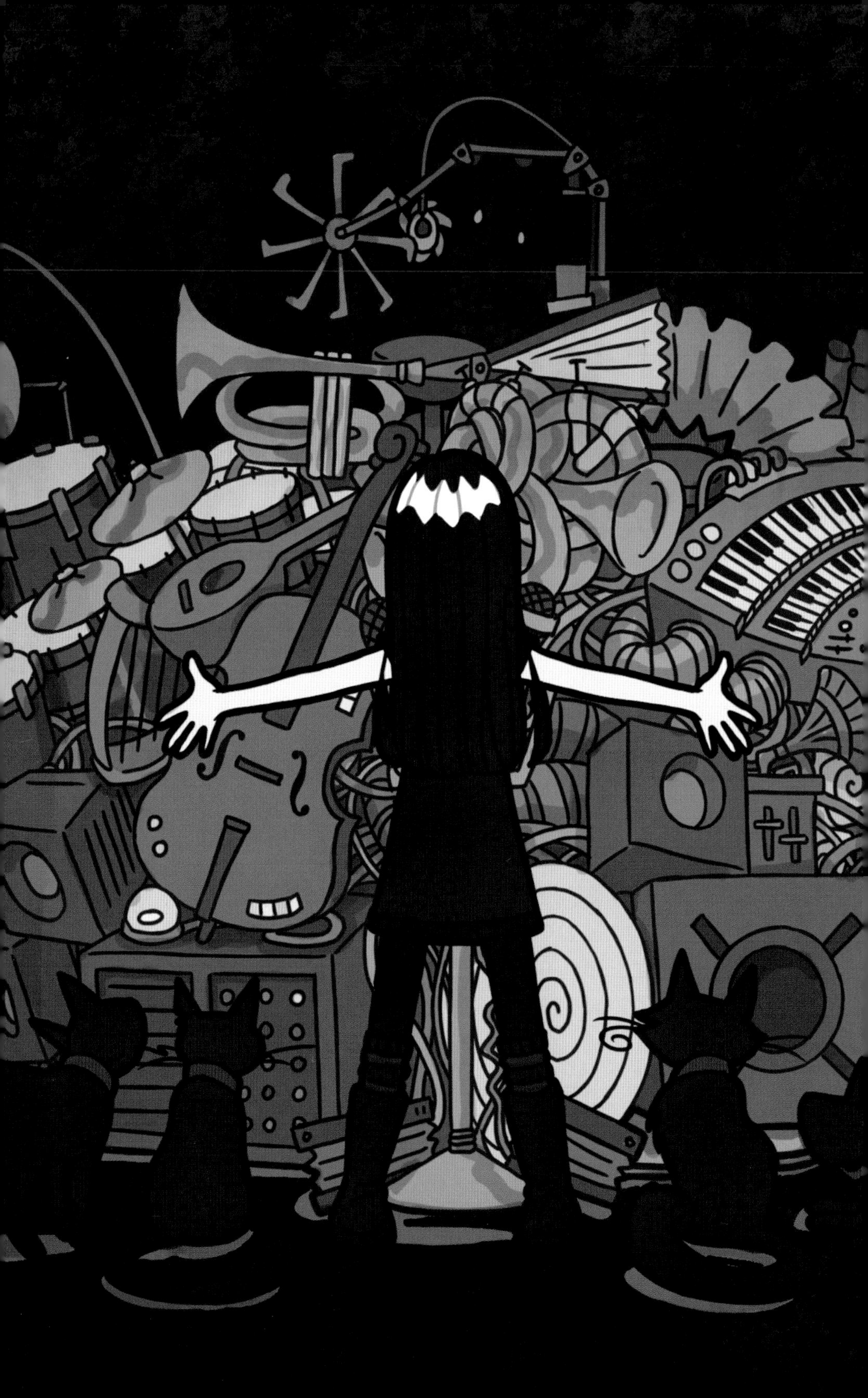

Emily® AND the Strangers

Volume 1
THE BATTLE OF THE BANDS

Created by
ROB REGER

Written by
MARIAH HUEHNER
and **ROB REGER**

Art by
EMILY IVIE

Cover and chapter break art by
EMILY IVIE and **BUZZ PARKER**

DARK HORSE BOOKS

Publisher
Mike Richardson

Collection Editor
Jim Gibbons

Original Series Editors
Rachel Edidin
and Jim Gibbons

Original Series
Assistant Editor
Jemiah Jefferson

Digital Production
Jason Rickerd

Collection Designer
Tina Alessi

Published by Dark Horse Books
A division of Dark Horse Comics, Inc.
10956 SE Main Street
Milwaukie, OR 97222

First edition: May 2014
ISBN 978-1-61655-323-4

1 3 5 7 9 10 8 6 4 2
Printed in China

International Licensing: (503) 905-2377
Comic Shop Locator Service: (888) 266-4226

This volume collects *Emily and the Strangers* #1–#3 from Dark Horse Comics.

MIKE RICHARDSON, President and Publisher   NEIL HANKERSON, Executive Vice President
TOM WEDDLE, Chief Financial Officer   RANDY STRADLEY, Vice President of Publishing
MICHAEL MARTENS, Vice President of Book Trade Sales   ANITA NELSON, Vice President
of Business Affairs   SCOTT ALLIE, Editor in Chief   MATT PARKINSON, Vice President of
Marketing   DAVID SCROGGY, Vice President of Product Development   DALE LaFOUNTAIN,
Vice President of Information Technology   DARLENE VOGEL, Senior Director of Print, Design,
and Production   KEN LIZZI, General Counsel   DAVEY ESTRADA, Editorial Director   CHRIS
WARNER, Senior Books Editor   DIANA SCHUTZ, Executive Editor   CARY GRAZZINI, Director of
Print and Development   LIA RIBACCHI, Art Director   CARA NIECE, Director of Scheduling   TIM
WIESCH, Director of International Licensing   MARK BERNARDI, Director of Digital Publishing

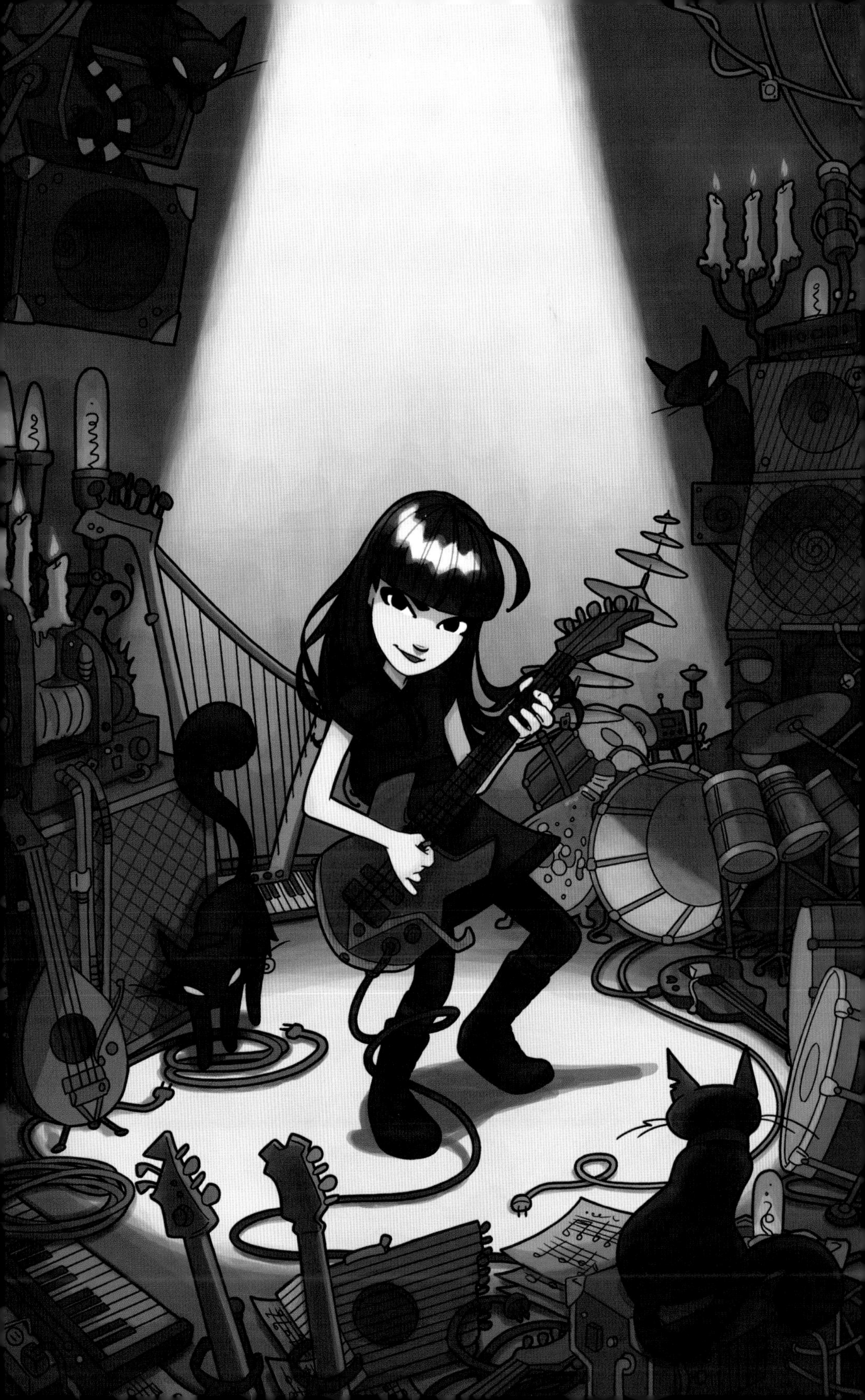

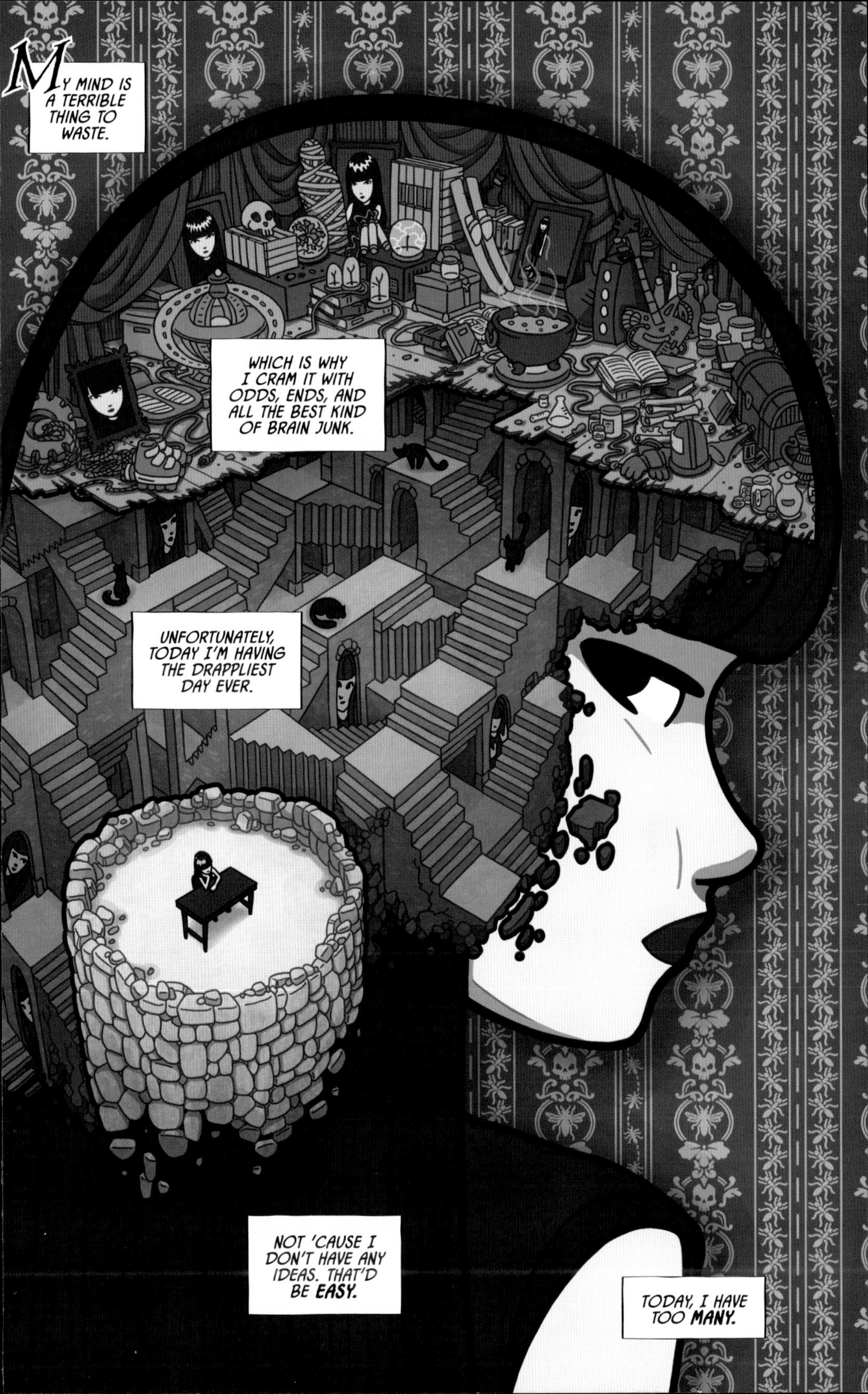
MY MIND IS A TERRIBLE THING TO WASTE.
WHICH IS WHY I CRAM IT WITH ODDS, ENDS, AND ALL THE BEST KIND OF BRAIN JUNK.
UNFORTUNATELY, TODAY I'M HAVING THE DRAPPLIEST DAY EVER.
NOT 'CAUSE I DON'T HAVE ANY IDEAS. THAT'D BE EASY.
TODAY, I HAVE TOO MANY.

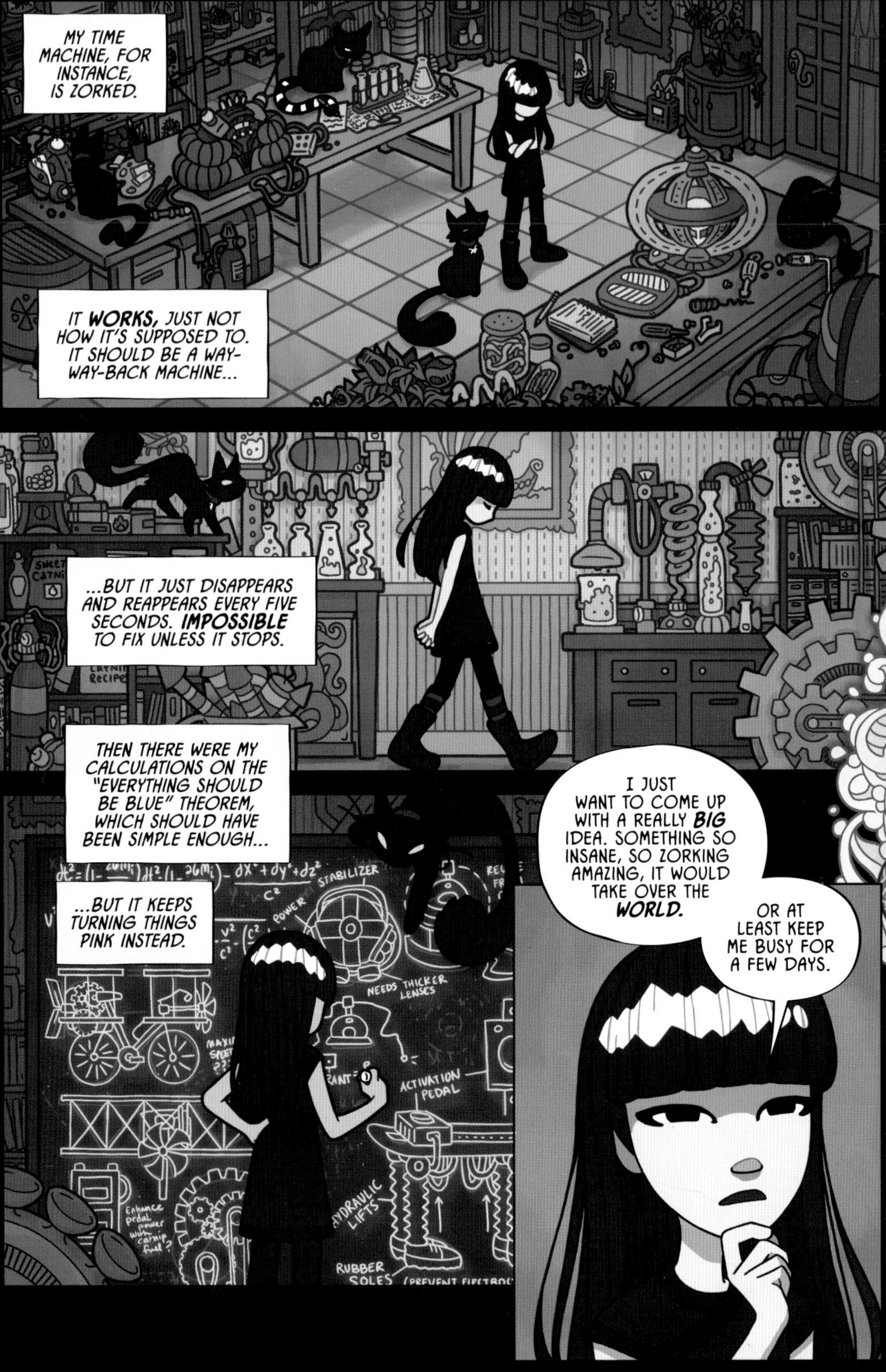
MY TIME MACHINE, FOR INSTANCE, IS ZORKED.
IT **WORKS,** JUST NOT HOW IT'S SUPPOSED TO. IT SHOULD BE A WAY-WAY-BACK MACHINE...
...BUT IT JUST DISAPPEARS AND REAPPEARS EVERY FIVE SECONDS. **IMPOSSIBLE** TO FIX UNLESS IT STOPS.
THEN THERE WERE MY CALCULATIONS ON THE "EVERYTHING SHOULD BE BLUE" THEOREM, WHICH SHOULD HAVE BEEN SIMPLE ENOUGH...
...BUT IT KEEPS TURNING THINGS PINK INSTEAD.
STABILIZER
POWER
NEEDS THICKER LENSES
ACTIVATION PEDAL
HYDRAULIC LIFTS
Enhance pedal power with catnip fuel?
RUBBER SOLES
I JUST WANT TO COME UP WITH A REALLY **BIG** IDEA. SOMETHING SO INSANE, SO ZORKING AMAZING, IT WOULD TAKE OVER THE **WORLD.**
OR AT LEAST KEEP ME BUSY FOR A FEW DAYS.

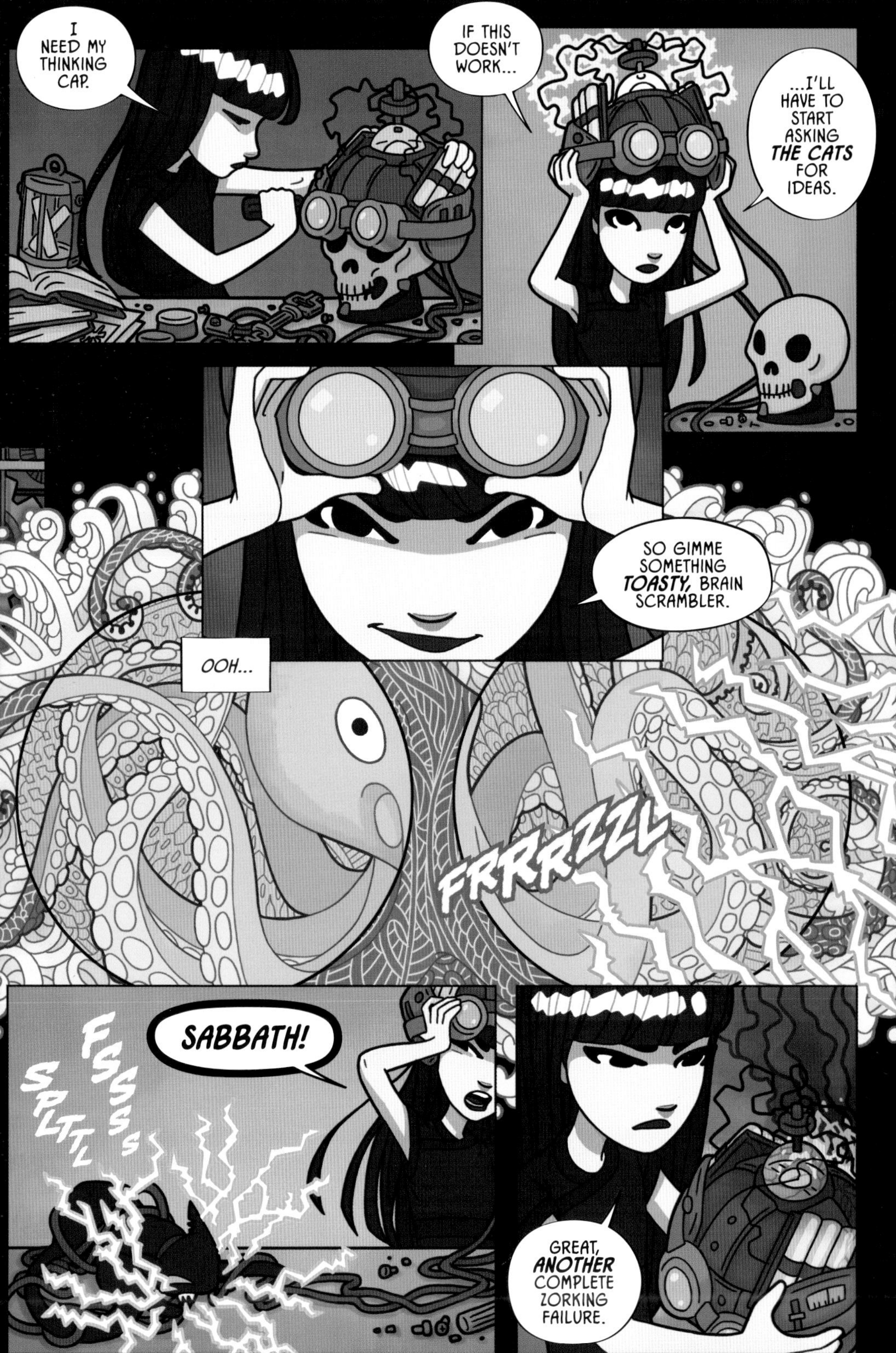

I NEED MY THINKING CAP.
IF THIS DOESN'T WORK...
...I'LL HAVE TO START ASKING ***THE CATS*** FOR IDEAS.
SO GIMME SOMETHING ***TOASTY,*** BRAIN SCRAMBLER.
OOH...
FRRRZZZL
SABBATH!
FSSSSS
SPLTTTL
GREAT, ***ANOTHER*** COMPLETE ZORKING FAILURE.

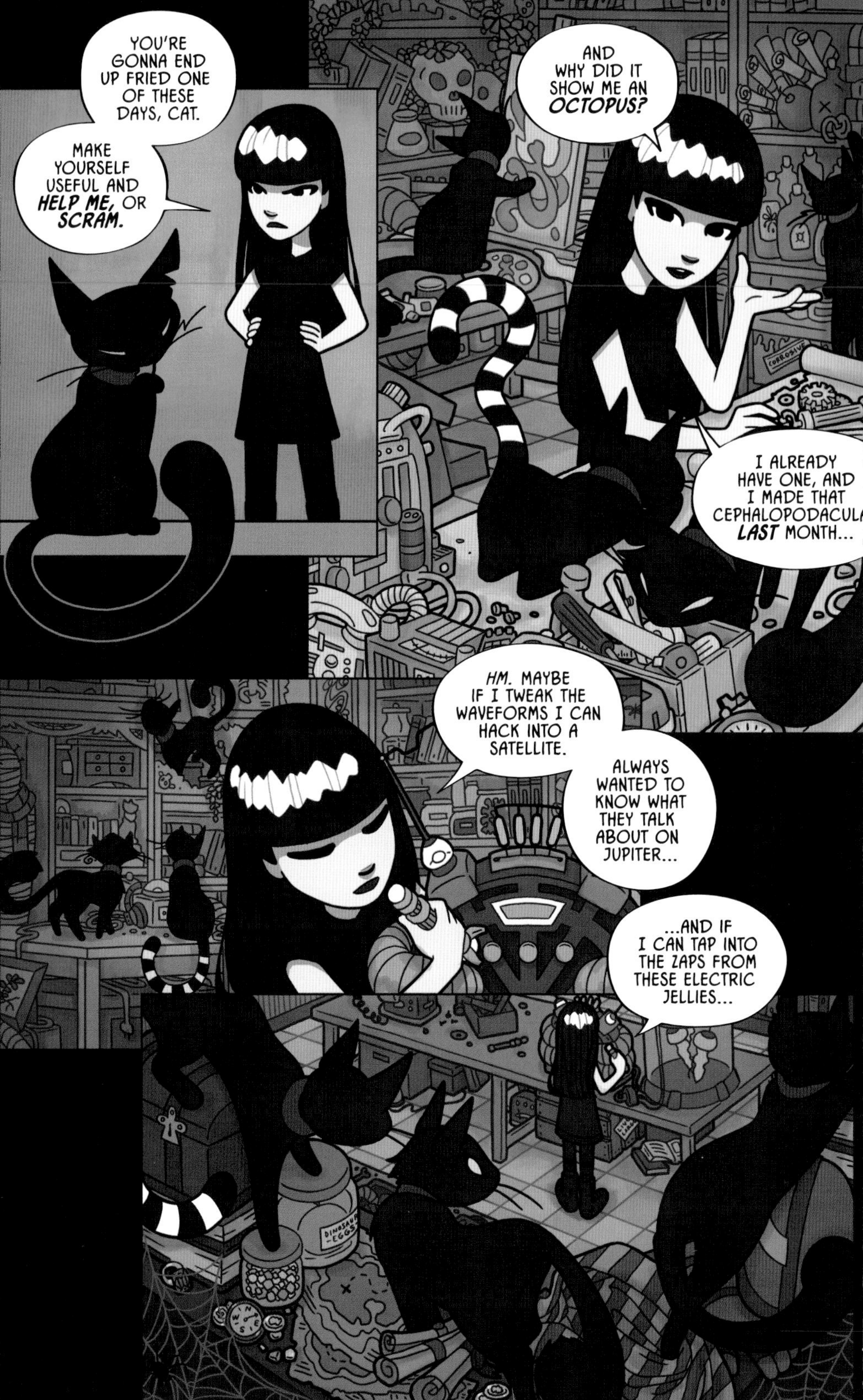
YOU'RE GONNA END UP FRIED ONE OF THESE DAYS, CAT.
MAKE YOURSELF USEFUL AND **HELP ME,** OR **SCRAM.**
AND WHY DID IT SHOW ME AN ***OCTOPUS?***
I ALREADY HAVE ONE, AND I MADE THAT CEPHALOPODACULA
LAST MONTH...
HM. MAYBE IF I TWEAK THE WAVEFORMS I CAN HACK INTO A SATELLITE.
ALWAYS WANTED TO KNOW WHAT THEY TALK ABOUT ON JUPITER...
...AND IF I CAN TAP INTO THE ZAPS FROM THESE ELECTRIC JELLIES...

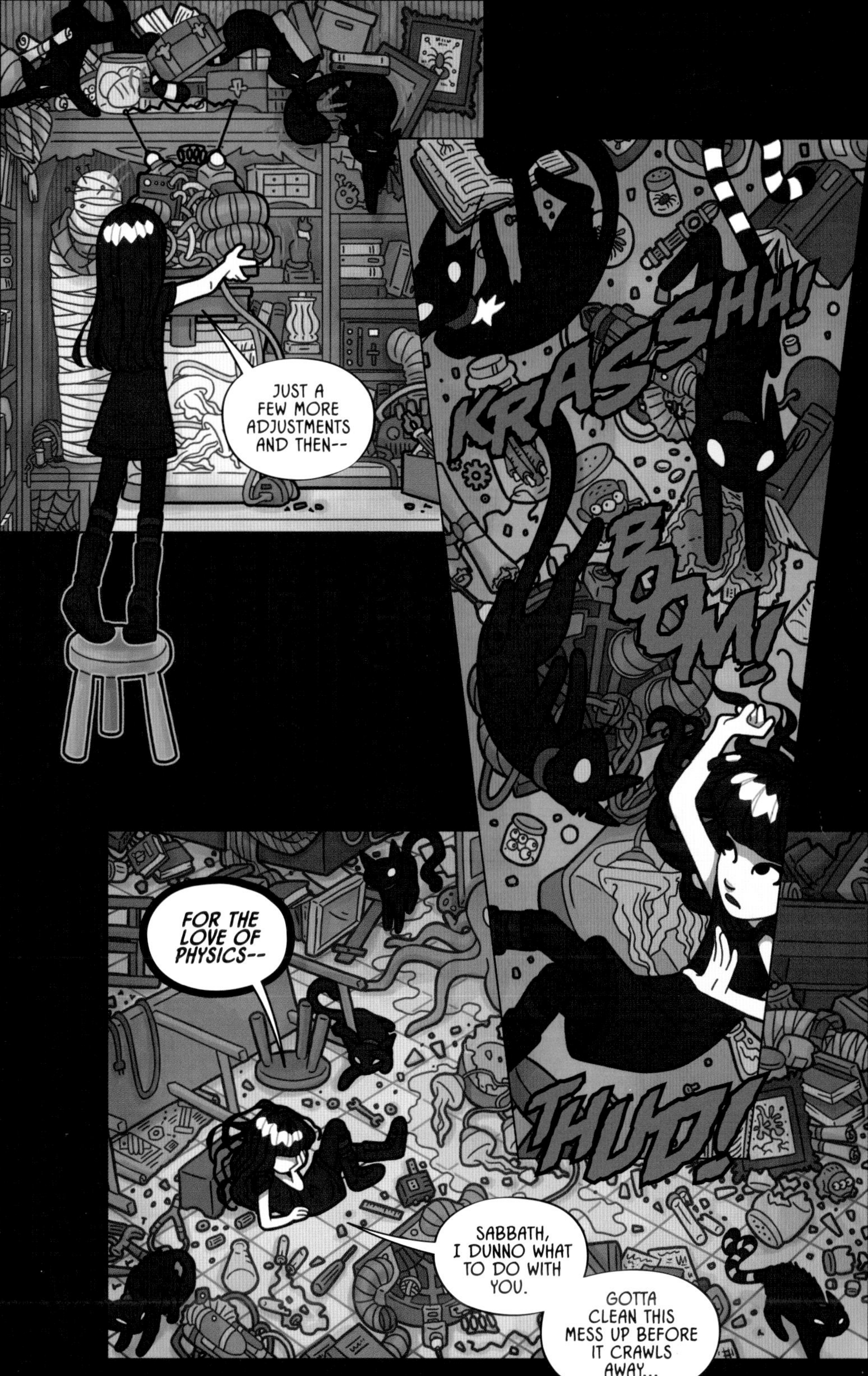

JUST A FEW MORE ADJUSTMENTS AND THEN--
KRASSHH!
BOOM!
THUD!
FOR THE LOVE OF PHYSICS--
SABBATH, I DUNNO WHAT TO DO WITH YOU.
GOTTA CLEAN THIS MESS UP BEFORE IT CRAWLS AWAY...

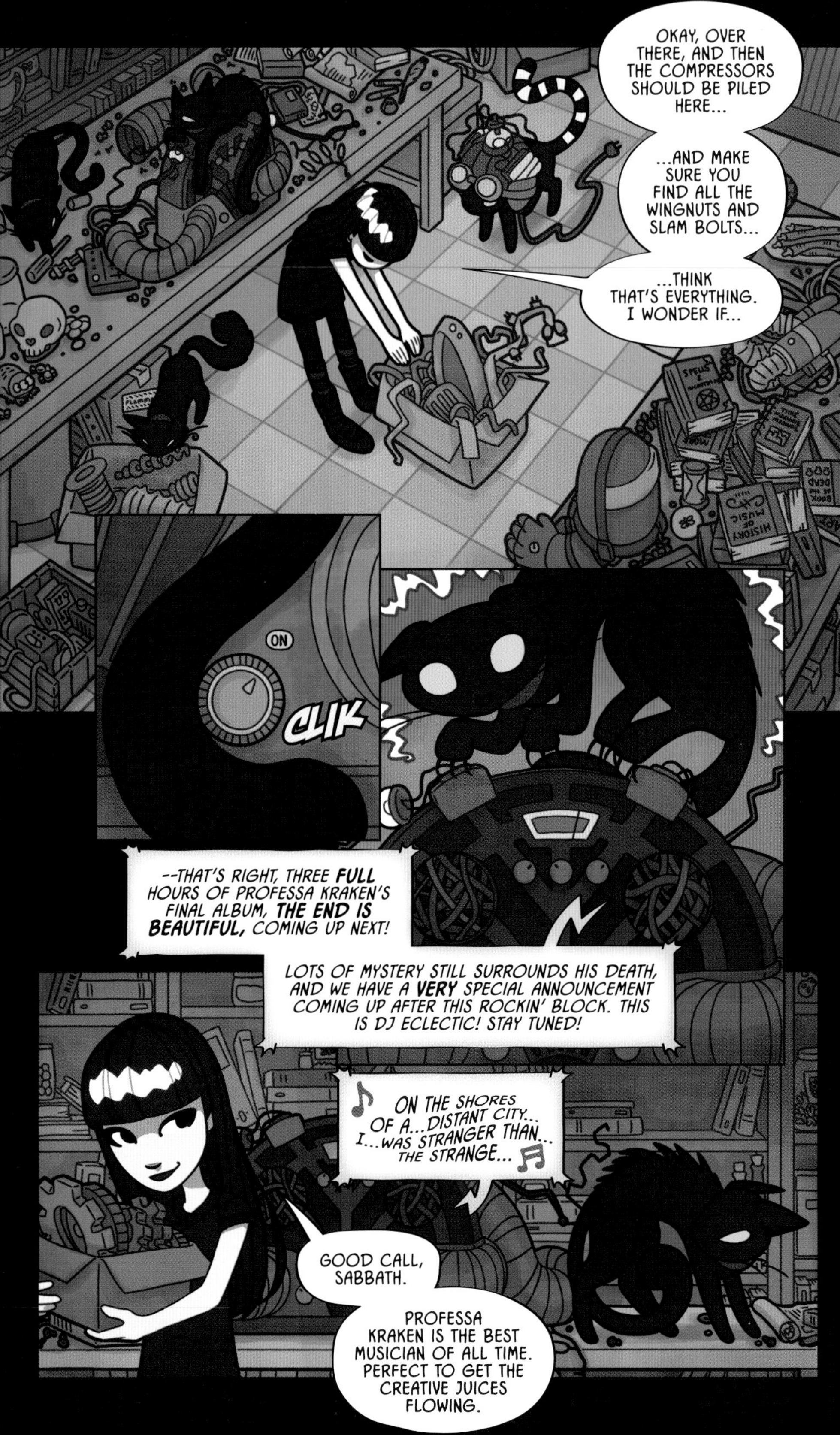

OKAY, OVER THERE, AND THEN THE COMPRESSORS SHOULD BE PILED HERE...
...AND MAKE SURE YOU FIND ALL THE WINGNUTS AND SLAM BOLTS...
...THINK THAT'S EVERYTHING. I WONDER IF...
SPELLS & INCANTATIONS
HISTORY OF MUSIC
BOOK OF THE DEAD
ON
CLIK
--THAT'S RIGHT, THREE FULL HOURS OF PROFESSA KRAKEN'S FINAL ALBUM, THE END IS BEAUTIFUL, COMING UP NEXT!
LOTS OF MYSTERY STILL SURROUNDS HIS DEATH, AND WE HAVE A VERY SPECIAL ANNOUNCEMENT COMING UP AFTER THIS ROCKIN' BLOCK. THIS IS DJ ECLECTIC! STAY TUNED!
ON THE SHORES OF A... DISTANT CITY... I... WAS STRANGER THAN... THE STRANGE...
GOOD CALL, SABBATH.
PROFESSA KRAKEN IS THE BEST MUSICIAN OF ALL TIME. PERFECT TO GET THE CREATIVE JUICES FLOWING.

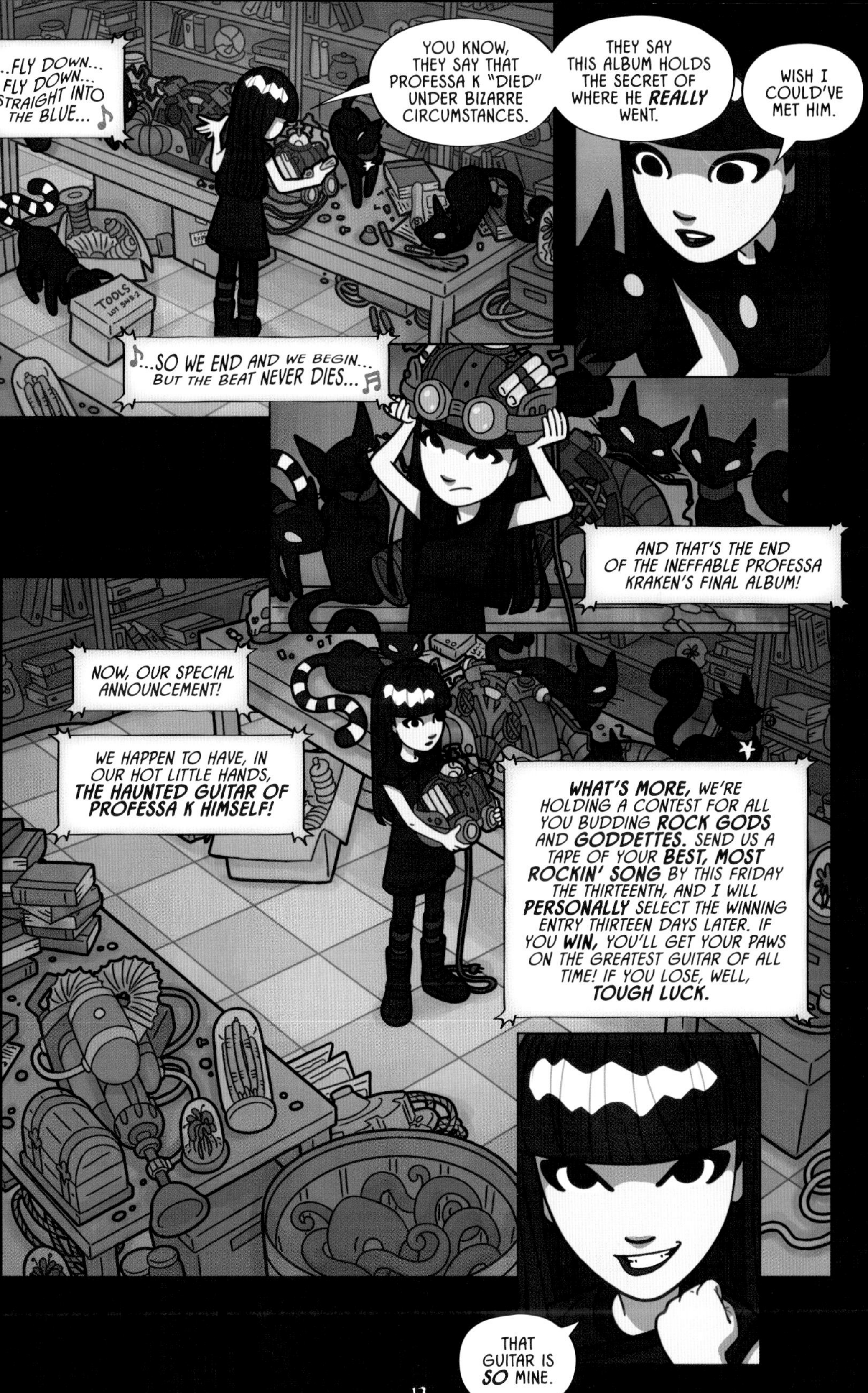
...FLY DOWN... FLY DOWN... STRAIGHT INTO THE BLUE...
YOU KNOW, THEY SAY THAT PROFESSA K "DIED" UNDER BIZARRE CIRCUMSTANCES.
THEY SAY THIS ALBUM HOLDS THE SECRET OF WHERE HE REALLY WENT.
WISH I COULD'VE MET HIM.
...SO WE END AND WE BEGIN... BUT THE BEAT NEVER DIES...
AND THAT'S THE END OF THE INEFFABLE PROFESSA KRAKEN'S FINAL ALBUM!
NOW, OUR SPECIAL ANNOUNCEMENT!
WE HAPPEN TO HAVE, IN OUR HOT LITTLE HANDS, THE HAUNTED GUITAR OF PROFESSA K HIMSELF!
WHAT'S MORE, WE'RE HOLDING A CONTEST FOR ALL YOU BUDDING ROCK GODS AND GODDETTES. SEND US A TAPE OF YOUR BEST, MOST ROCKIN' SONG BY THIS FRIDAY THE THIRTEENTH, AND I WILL PERSONALLY SELECT THE WINNING ENTRY THIRTEEN DAYS LATER. IF YOU WIN, YOU'LL GET YOUR PAWS ON THE GREATEST GUITAR OF ALL TIME! IF YOU LOSE, WELL, TOUGH LUCK.
THAT GUITAR IS SO MINE.

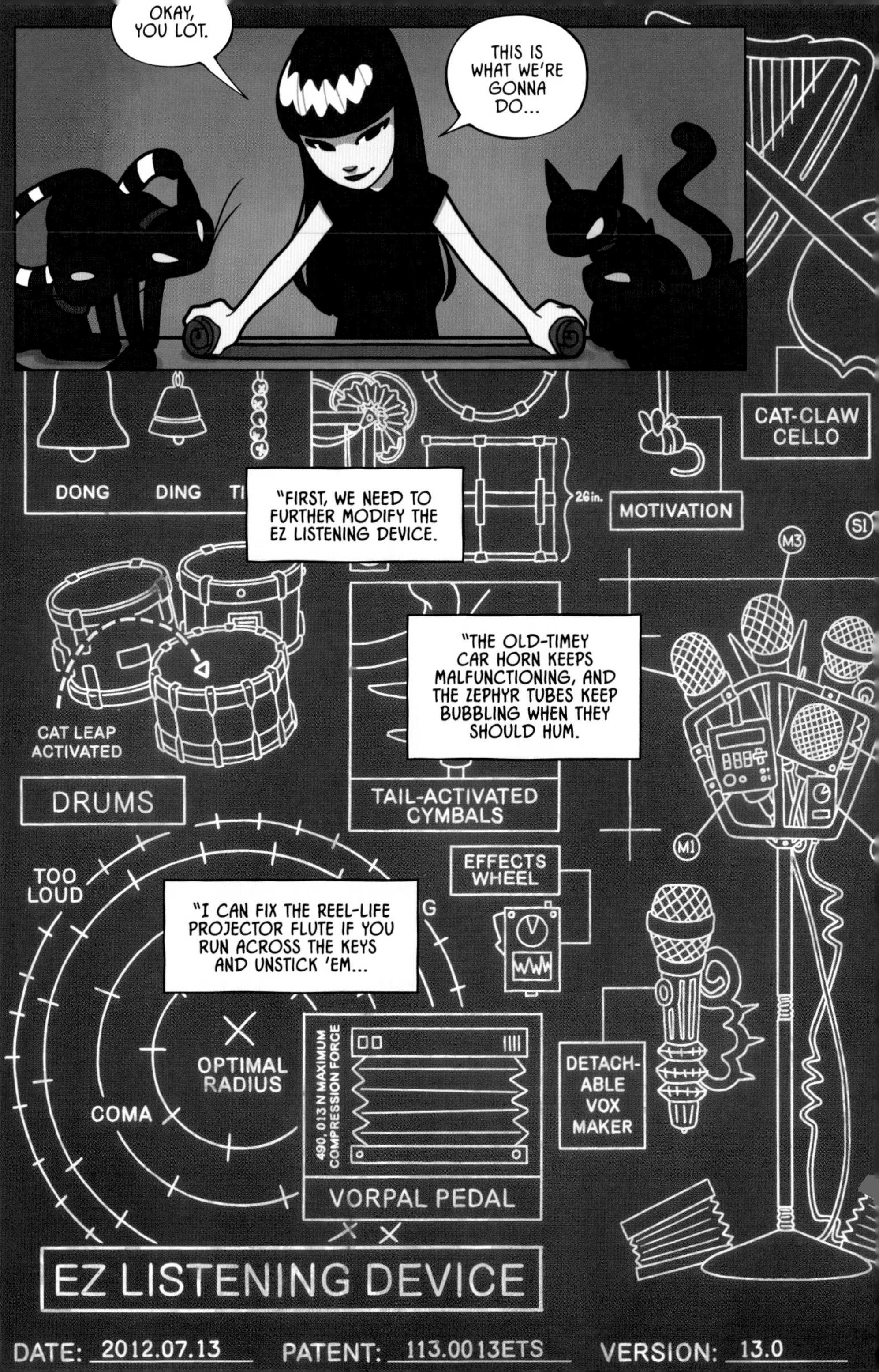
OKAY, YOU LOT.
THIS IS WHAT WE'RE GONNA DO...
CAT-CLAW CELLO
DONG
DING
MOTIVATION
26in.
"FIRST, WE NEED TO FURTHER MODIFY THE EZ LISTENING DEVICE.
M3
S1
"THE OLD-TIMEY CAR HORN KEEPS MALFUNCTIONING, AND THE ZEPHYR TUBES KEEP BUBBLING WHEN THEY SHOULD HUM.
CAT LEAP ACTIVATED
DRUMS
TAIL-ACTIVATED CYMBALS
M1
EFFECTS WHEEL
TOO LOUD
"I CAN FIX THE REEL-LIFE PROJECTOR FLUTE IF YOU RUN ACROSS THE KEYS AND UNSTICK 'EM...
OPTIMAL RADIUS
COMA
490, 013 N MAXIMUM COMPRESSION FORCE
VORPAL PEDAL
DETACH-ABLE VOX MAKER
EZ LISTENING DEVICE
DATE: 2012.07.13
PATENT: 113.0013ETS
VERSION: 13.0

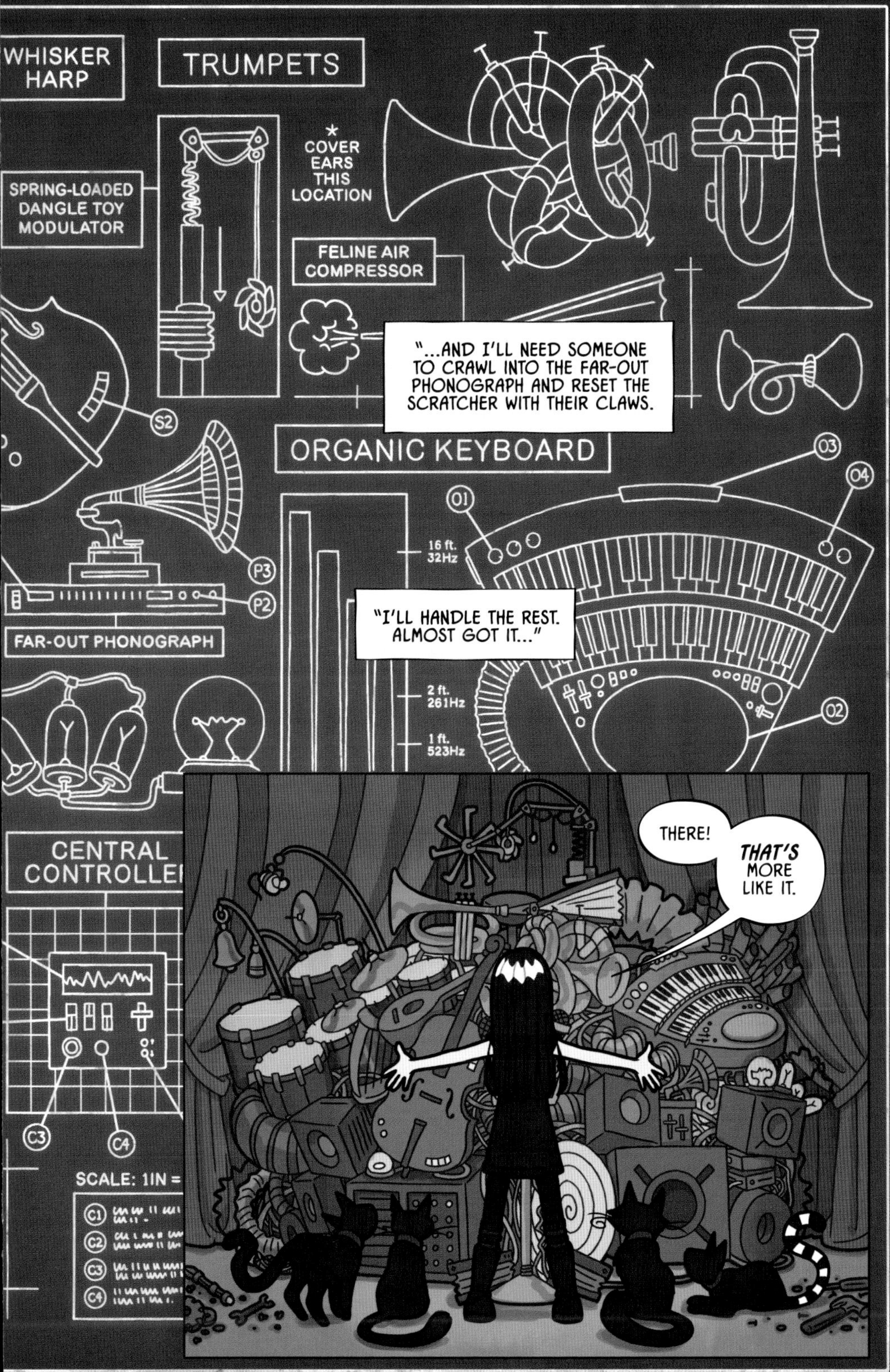

WHISKER HARP
TRUMPETS
SPRING-LOADED DANGLE TOY MODULATOR
* COVER EARS THIS LOCATION
FELINE AIR COMPRESSOR
"...AND I'LL NEED SOMEONE TO CRAWL INTO THE FAR-OUT PHONOGRAPH AND RESET THE SCRATCHER WITH THEIR CLAWS.
ORGANIC KEYBOARD
S2
O3
O4
O1
16 ft. 32Hz
P3
P2
FAR-OUT PHONOGRAPH
"I'LL HANDLE THE REST. ALMOST GOT IT..."
2 ft. 261Hz
1 ft. 523Hz
O2
CENTRAL CONTROLLER
C3
C4
SCALE: 1IN =
C1
C2
C3
C4
THERE!
THAT'S MORE LIKE IT.

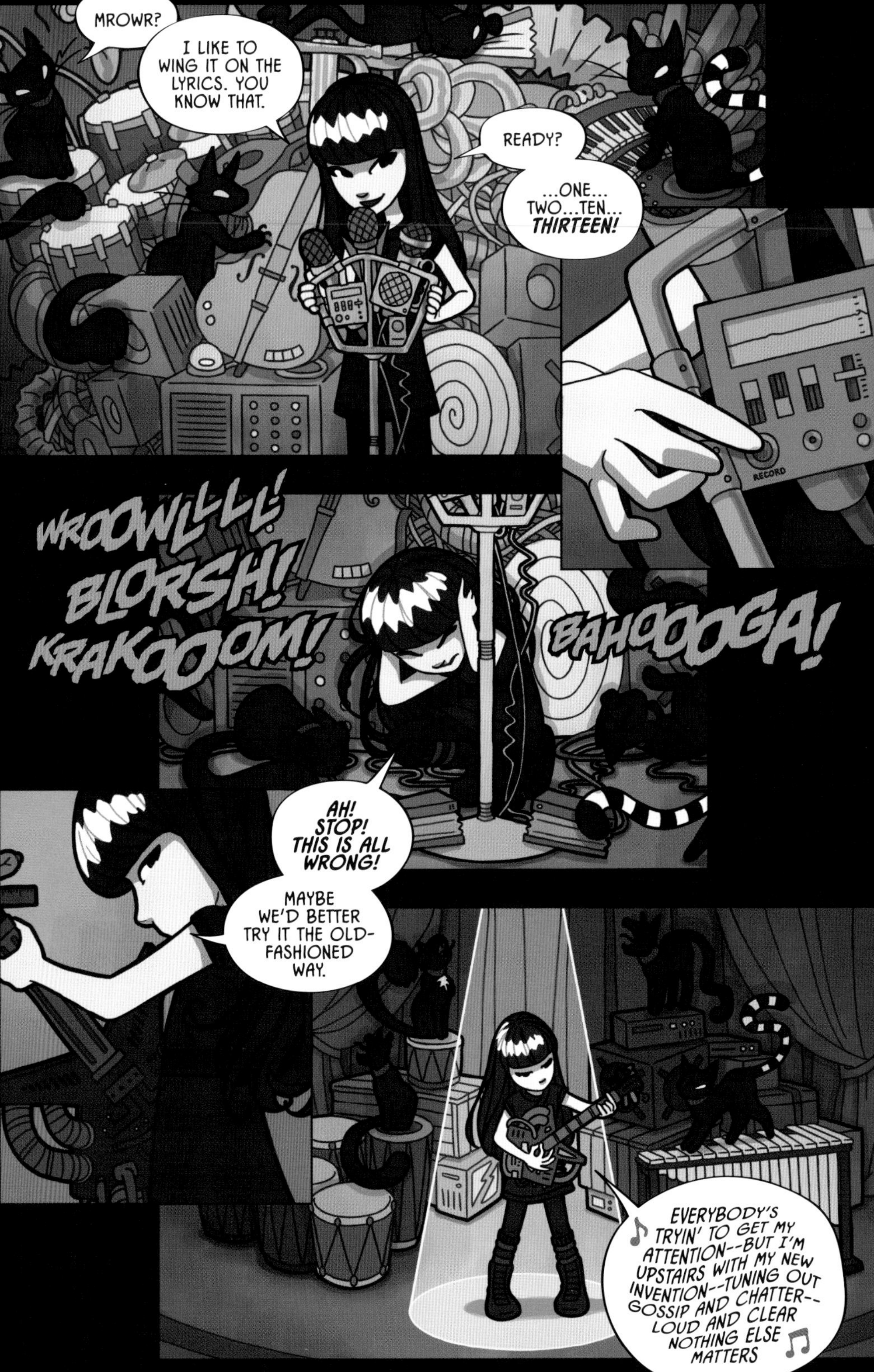
MROWR?
I LIKE TO WING IT ON THE LYRICS. YOU KNOW THAT.
READY?
...ONE... TWO...TEN... THIRTEEN!
RECORD
WROOWLLLL!
BLORSH!
KRAKOOOM!
BAHOOOOGA!
AH! STOP! THIS IS ALL WRONG!
MAYBE WE'D BETTER TRY IT THE OLD-FASHIONED WAY.
EVERYBODY'S TRYIN' TO GET MY ATTENTION--BUT I'M UPSTAIRS WITH MY NEW INVENTION--TUNING OUT GOSSIP AND CHATTER--LOUD AND CLEAR NOTHING ELSE MATTERS

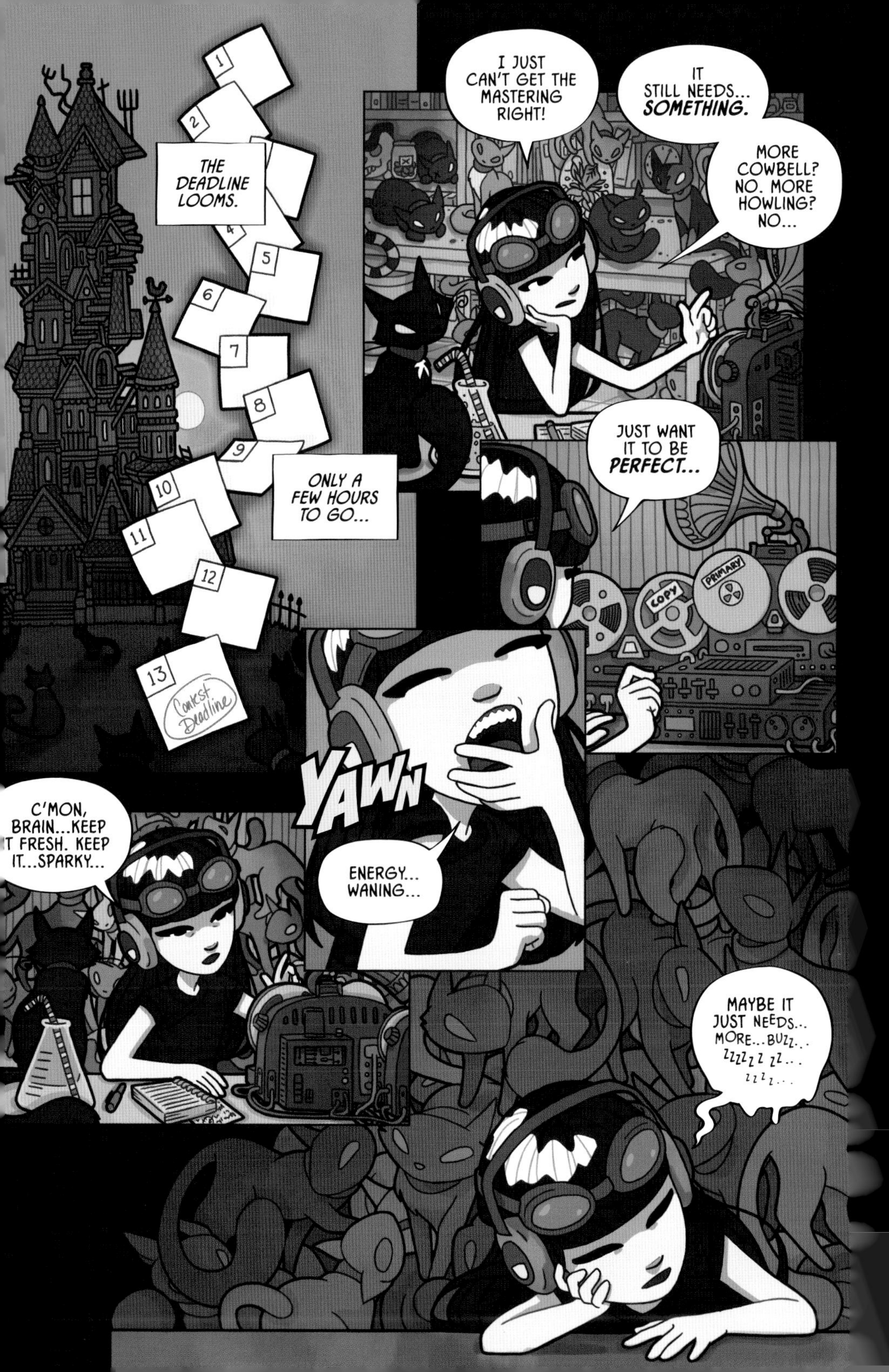

THE DEADLINE LOOMS.
1
2
4
5
6
7
8
9
10
11
12
13
Contest Deadline
ONLY A FEW HOURS TO GO...
I JUST CAN'T GET THE MASTERING RIGHT!
IT STILL NEEDS... SOMETHING.
MORE COWBELL? NO. MORE HOWLING? NO...
JUST WANT IT TO BE PERFECT...
COPY
PRIMARY
YAWN
C'MON, BRAIN...KEEP IT FRESH. KEEP IT...SPARKY...
ENERGY... WANING...
MAYBE IT JUST NEEDS... MORE...BUZZ... ZZZZZ Z ZZ... ZZZZ...

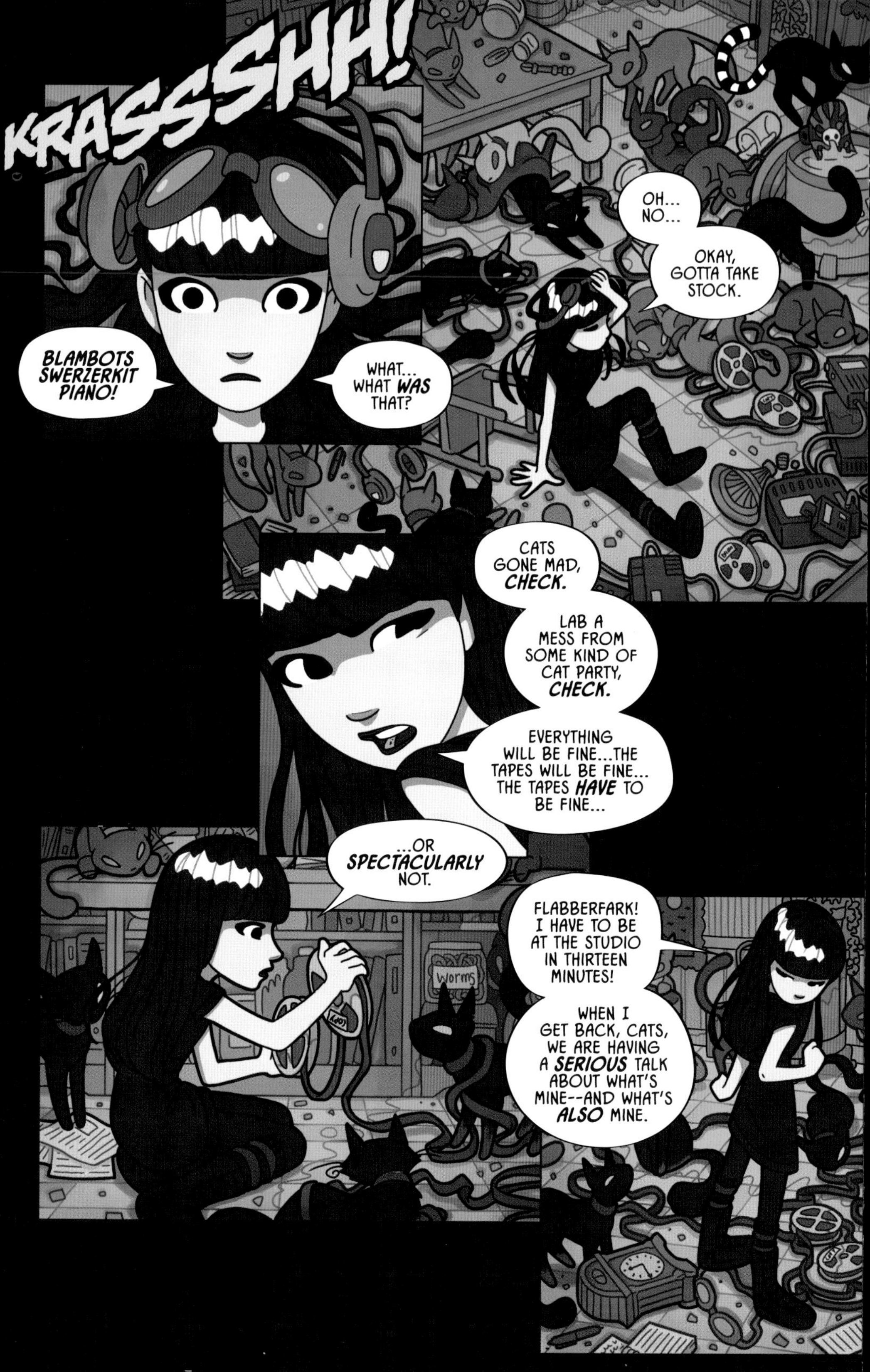
KRASSSHH!
BLAMBOTS SWERZERKIT PIANO!
WHAT... WHAT WAS THAT?
OH... NO...
OKAY, GOTTA TAKE STOCK.
CATS GONE MAD, CHECK.
LAB A MESS FROM SOME KIND OF CAT PARTY, CHECK.
EVERYTHING WILL BE FINE...THE TAPES WILL BE FINE... THE TAPES HAVE TO BE FINE...
...OR SPECTACULARLY NOT.
Worms
FLABBERFARK! I HAVE TO BE AT THE STUDIO IN THIRTEEN MINUTES!
WHEN I GET BACK, CATS, WE ARE HAVING A SERIOUS TALK ABOUT WHAT'S MINE--AND WHAT'S ALSO MINE.

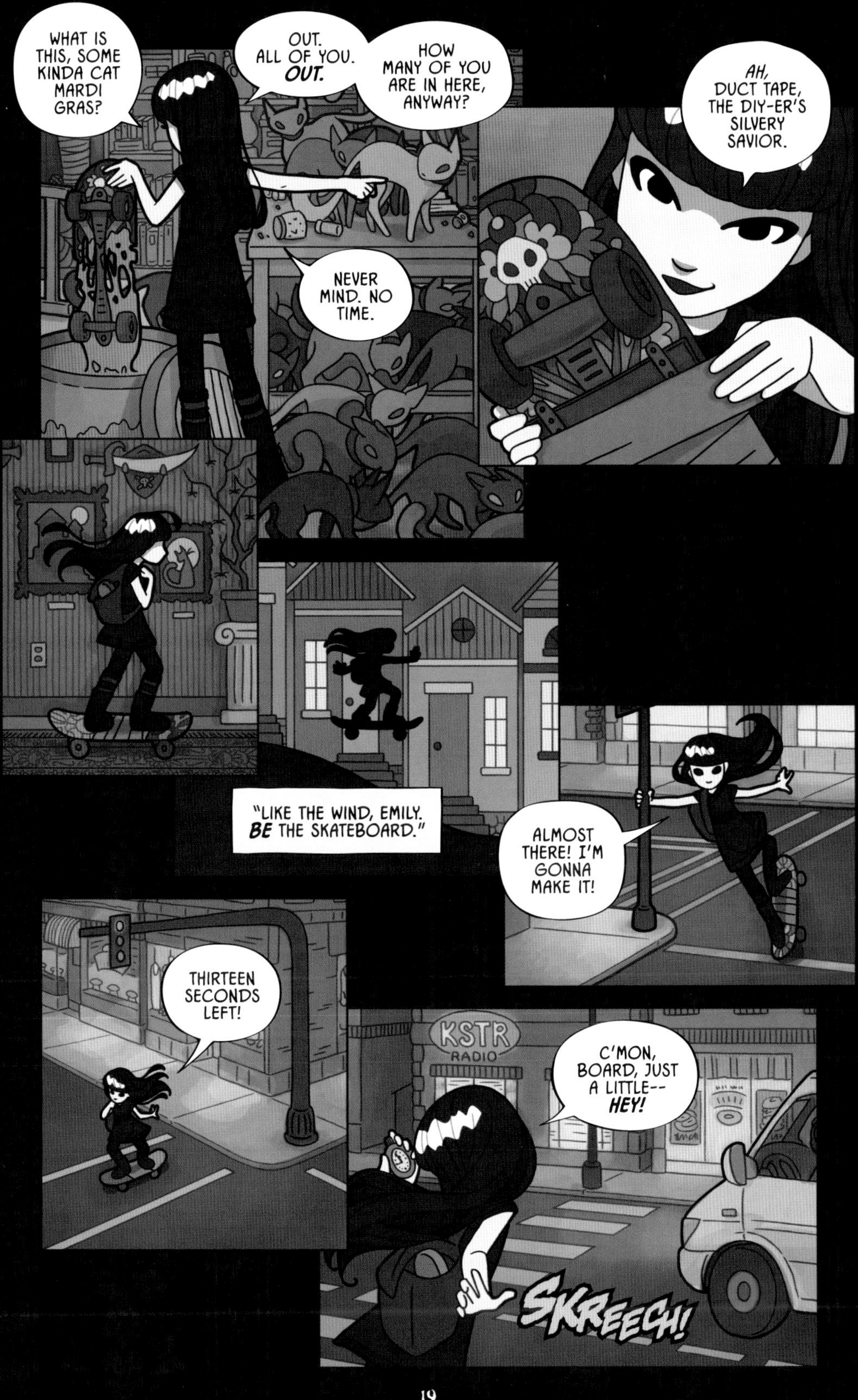
WHAT IS THIS, SOME KINDA CAT MARDI GRAS?
OUT. ALL OF YOU. *OUT.*
HOW MANY OF YOU ARE IN HERE, ANYWAY?
NEVER MIND. NO TIME.
AH, DUCT TAPE, THE DIY-ER'S SILVERY SAVIOR.
"LIKE THE WIND, EMILY. *BE* THE SKATEBOARD."
ALMOST THERE! I'M GONNA MAKE IT!
THIRTEEN SECONDS LEFT!
KSTR RADIO
C'MON, BOARD, JUST A LITTLE-- *HEY!*
SKREECH!

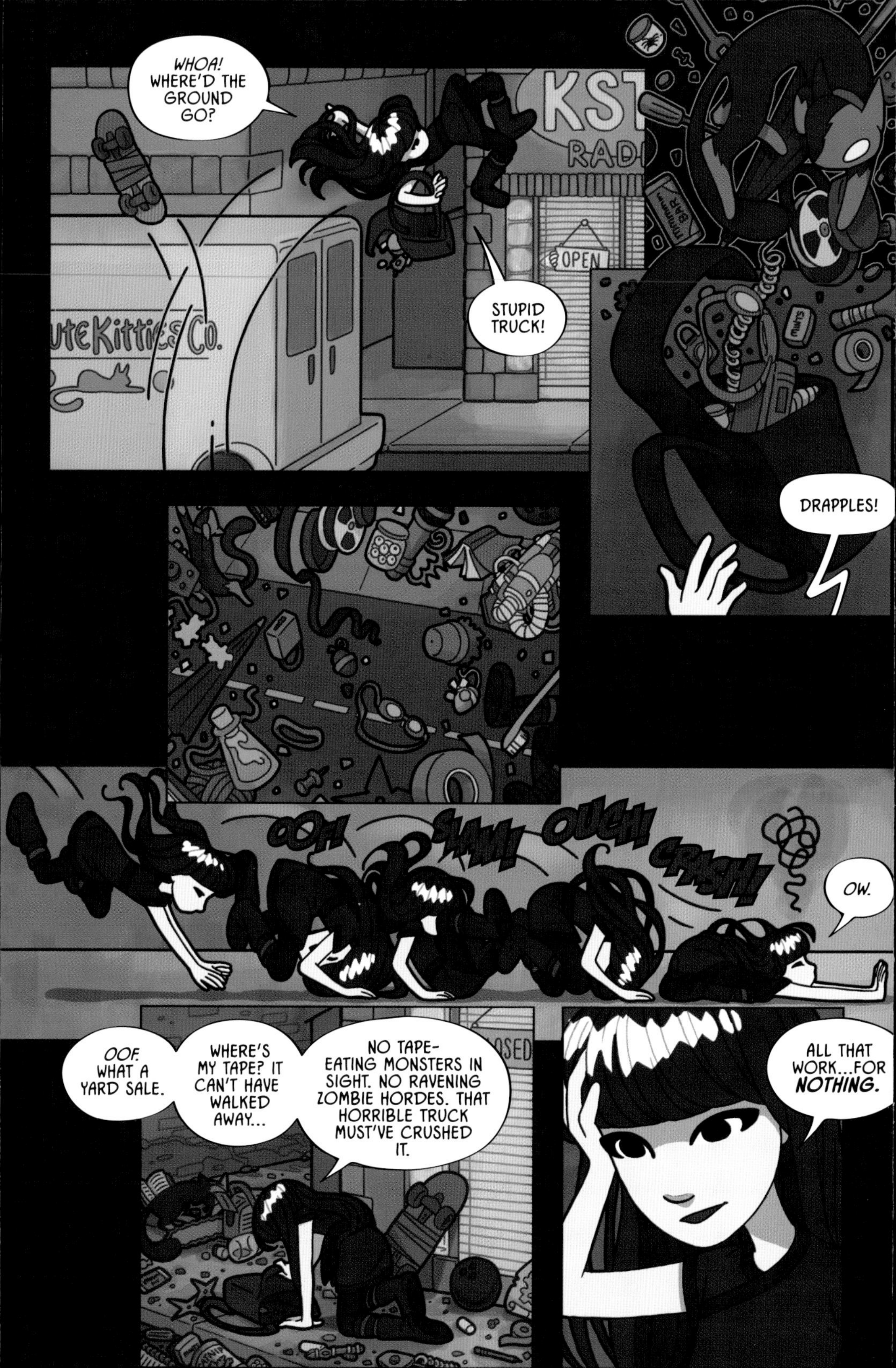

WHOA! WHERE'D THE GROUND GO?
KST RADI
OPEN
CUTE KITTIES CO.
STUPID TRUCK!
DRAPPLES!
OOF!
SLAM!
OUCH!
CRASH!
OW.
OOF. WHAT A YARD SALE.
WHERE'S MY TAPE? IT CAN'T HAVE WALKED AWAY...
NO TAPE-EATING MONSTERS IN SIGHT. NO RAVENING ZOMBIE HORDES. THAT HORRIBLE TRUCK MUST'VE CRUSHED IT.
ALL THAT WORK...FOR ***NOTHING.***

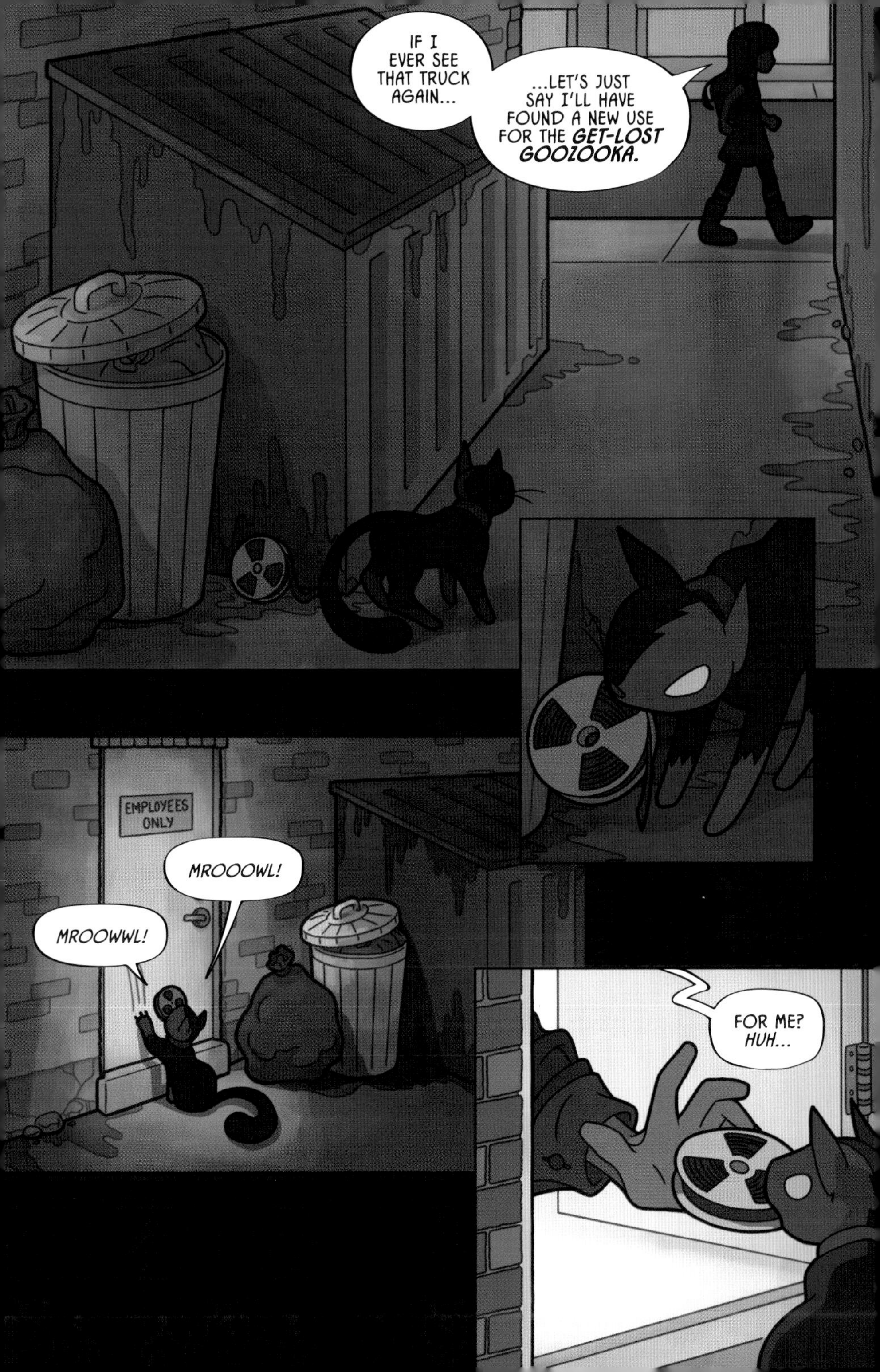
IF I EVER SEE THAT TRUCK AGAIN...
...LET'S JUST SAY I'LL HAVE FOUND A NEW USE FOR THE ***GET-LOST GOOZOOKA.***
EMPLOYEES ONLY
MROOOWL!
MROOWWL!
FOR ME? *HUH...*

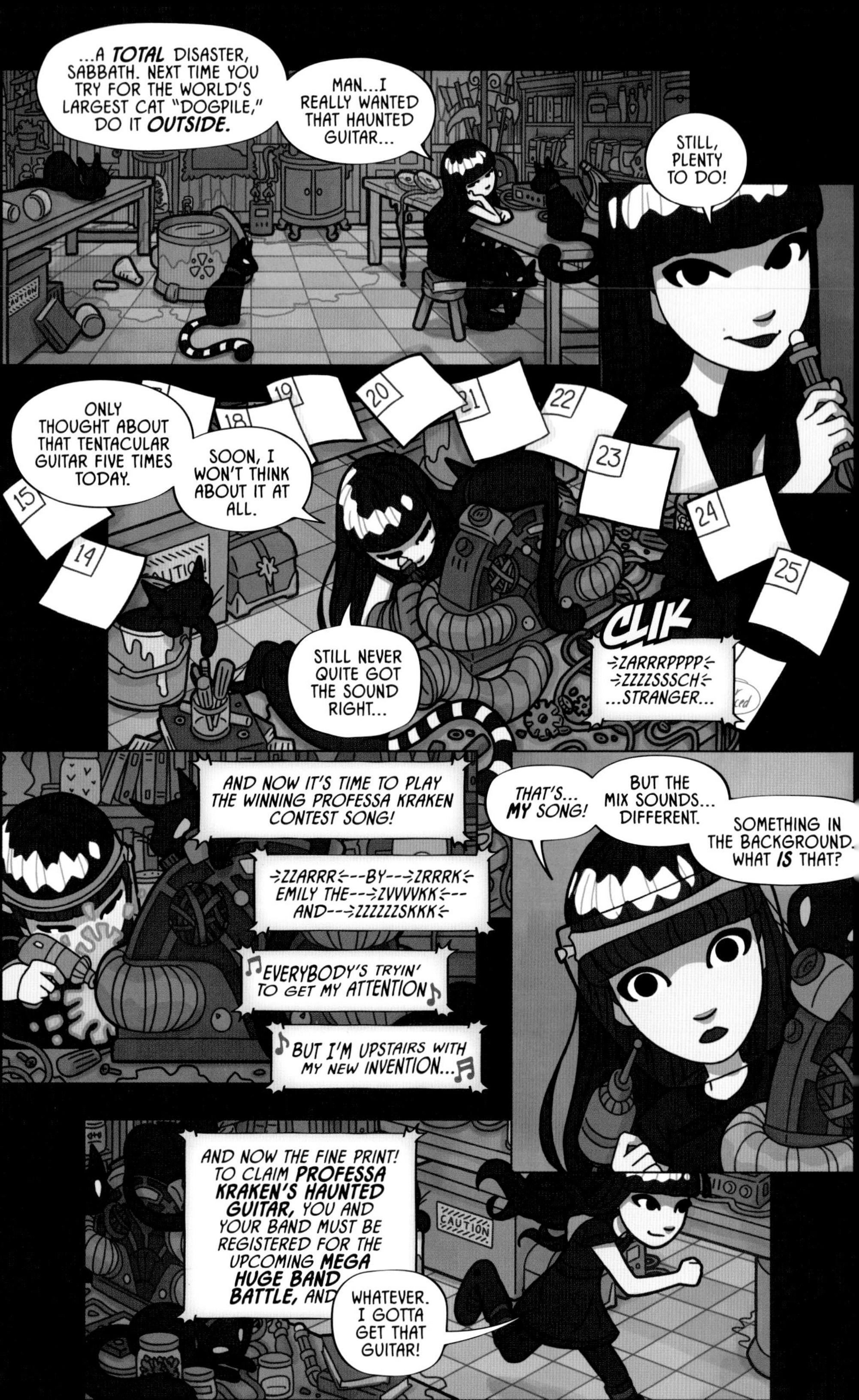
...A TOTAL DISASTER, SABBATH. NEXT TIME YOU TRY FOR THE WORLD'S LARGEST CAT "DOGPILE," DO IT OUTSIDE.
MAN...I REALLY WANTED THAT HAUNTED GUITAR...
STILL, PLENTY TO DO!
ONLY THOUGHT ABOUT THAT TENTACULAR GUITAR FIVE TIMES TODAY.
SOON, I WON'T THINK ABOUT IT AT ALL.
14
15
18
19
20
21
22
23
24
25
STILL NEVER QUITE GOT THE SOUND RIGHT...
CLIK
ZARRRPPPP ZZZZSSSCH ...STRANGER...
AND NOW IT'S TIME TO PLAY THE WINNING PROFESSA KRAKEN CONTEST SONG!
ZZARRR--BY--ZRRRK EMILY THE--ZVVVVKK-- AND--ZZZZZZSKKK
EVERYBODY'S TRYIN' TO GET MY ATTENTION
BUT I'M UPSTAIRS WITH MY NEW INVENTION...
THAT'S... MY SONG!
BUT THE MIX SOUNDS... DIFFERENT.
SOMETHING IN THE BACKGROUND. WHAT IS THAT?
AND NOW THE FINE PRINT! TO CLAIM PROFESSA KRAKEN'S HAUNTED GUITAR, YOU AND YOUR BAND MUST BE REGISTERED FOR THE UPCOMING MEGA HUGE BAND BATTLE, AND
WHATEVER. I GOTTA GET THAT GUITAR!
CAUTION

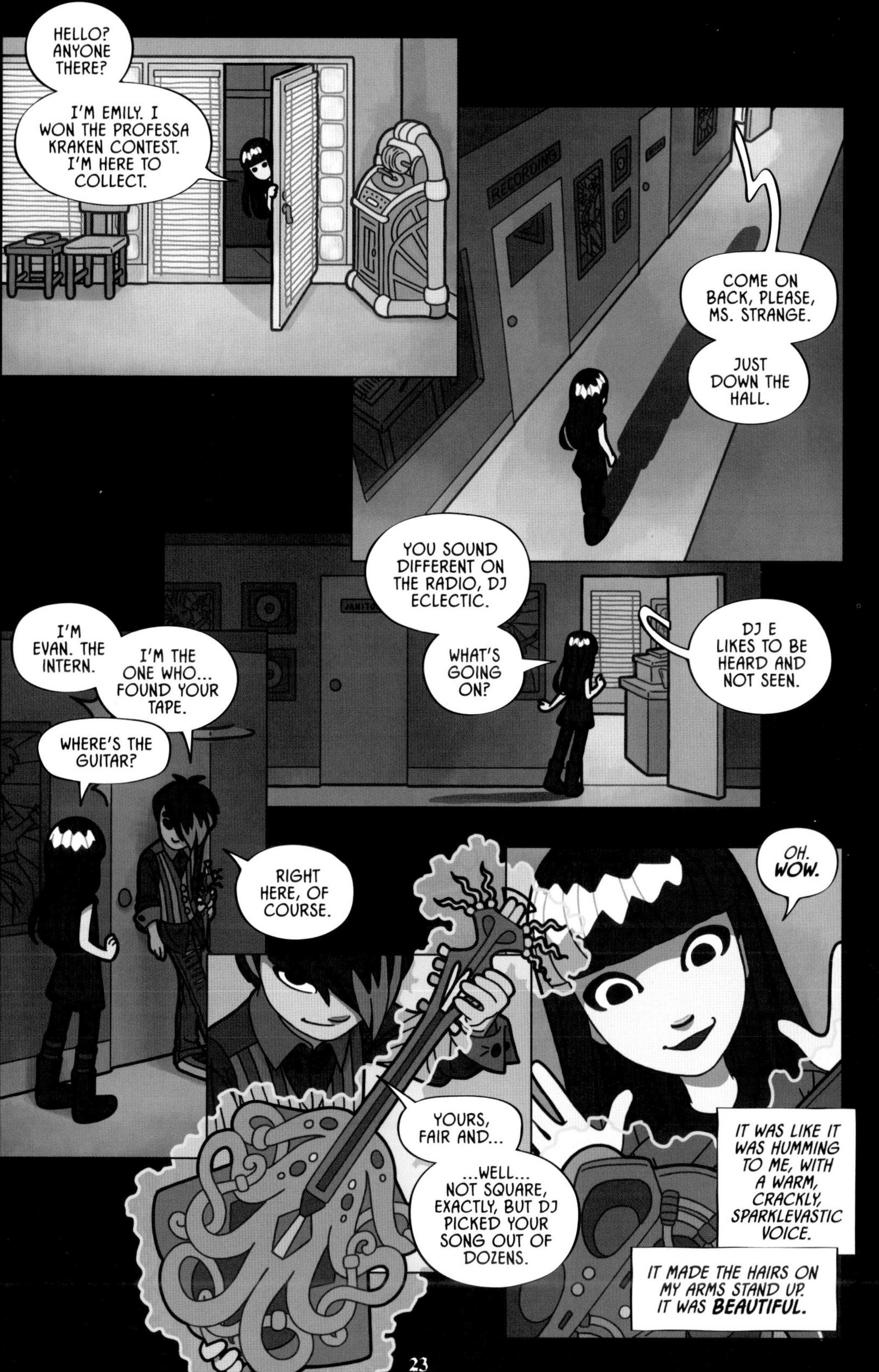
HELLO? ANYONE THERE?
I'M EMILY. I WON THE PROFESSA KRAKEN CONTEST. I'M HERE TO COLLECT.
RECORDING
COME ON BACK, PLEASE, MS. STRANGE.
JUST DOWN THE HALL.
YOU SOUND DIFFERENT ON THE RADIO, DJ ECLECTIC.
WHAT'S GOING ON?
DJ E LIKES TO BE HEARD AND NOT SEEN.
I'M EVAN. THE INTERN.
I'M THE ONE WHO... FOUND YOUR TAPE.
WHERE'S THE GUITAR?
RIGHT HERE, OF COURSE.
OH. **WOW.**
YOURS, FAIR AND...
...WELL... NOT SQUARE, EXACTLY, BUT DJ PICKED YOUR SONG OUT OF DOZENS.
IT WAS LIKE IT WAS HUMMING TO ME, WITH A WARM, CRACKLY, SPARKLEVASTIC VOICE.
*IT MADE THE HAIRS ON MY ARMS STAND UP. IT WAS **BEAUTIFUL.***

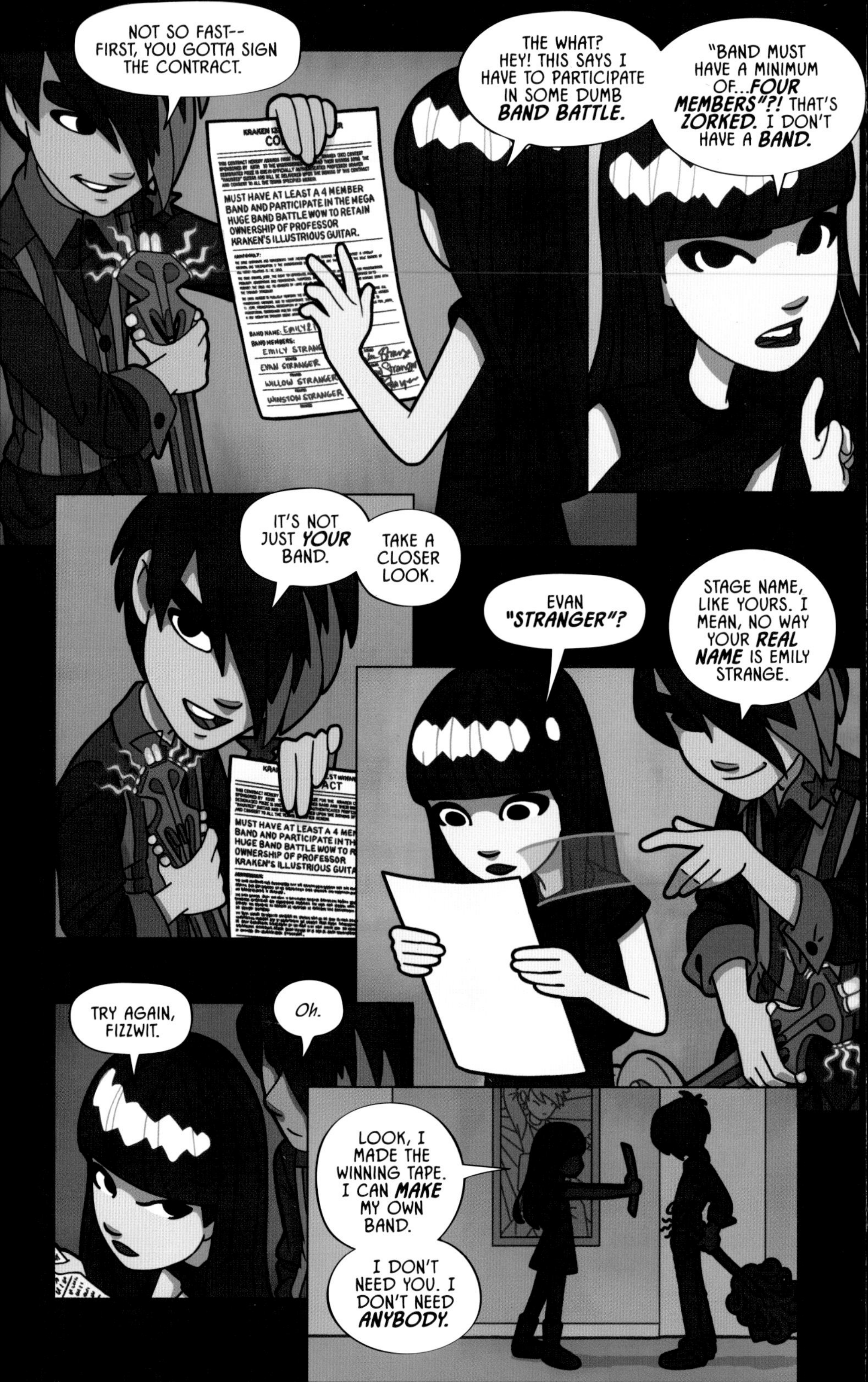
NOT SO FAST-- FIRST, YOU GOTTA SIGN THE CONTRACT.
MUST HAVE AT LEAST A 4 MEMBER BAND AND PARTICIPATE IN THE MEGA HUGE BAND BATTLE WOW TO RETAIN OWNERSHIP OF PROFESSOR KRAKEN'S ILLUSTRIOUS GUITAR.
BAND MEMBERS:
EMILY STRANGER
EVAN STRANGER
WILLOW STRANGER
WINSTON STRANGER
THE WHAT? HEY! THIS SAYS I HAVE TO PARTICIPATE IN SOME DUMB BAND BATTLE.
"BAND MUST HAVE A MINIMUM OF...FOUR MEMBERS"?! THAT'S ZORKED. I DON'T HAVE A BAND.
IT'S NOT JUST YOUR BAND.
TAKE A CLOSER LOOK.
EVAN "STRANGER"?
STAGE NAME, LIKE YOURS. I MEAN, NO WAY YOUR REAL NAME IS EMILY STRANGE.
TRY AGAIN, FIZZWIT.
Oh.
LOOK, I MADE THE WINNING TAPE. I CAN MAKE MY OWN BAND.
I DON'T NEED YOU. I DON'T NEED ANYBODY.

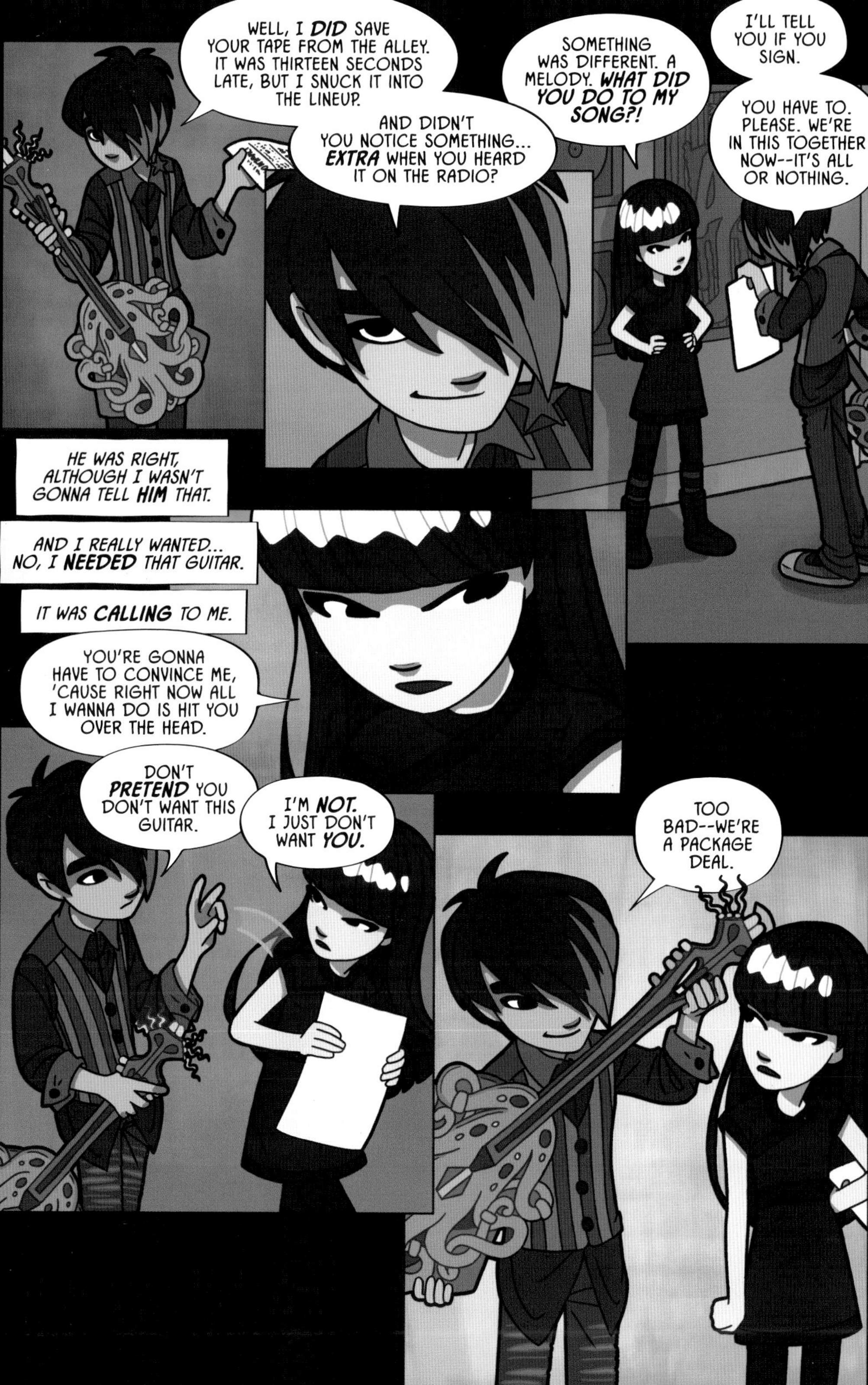
WELL, I DID SAVE YOUR TAPE FROM THE ALLEY. IT WAS THIRTEEN SECONDS LATE, BUT I SNUCK IT INTO THE LINEUP.
AND DIDN'T YOU NOTICE SOMETHING... EXTRA WHEN YOU HEARD IT ON THE RADIO?
SOMETHING WAS DIFFERENT. A MELODY. WHAT DID YOU DO TO MY SONG?!
I'LL TELL YOU IF YOU SIGN.
YOU HAVE TO. PLEASE. WE'RE IN THIS TOGETHER NOW--IT'S ALL OR NOTHING.
HE WAS RIGHT, ALTHOUGH I WASN'T GONNA TELL HIM THAT.
AND I REALLY WANTED... NO, I NEEDED THAT GUITAR.
IT WAS CALLING TO ME.
YOU'RE GONNA HAVE TO CONVINCE ME, 'CAUSE RIGHT NOW ALL I WANNA DO IS HIT YOU OVER THE HEAD.
DON'T PRETEND YOU DON'T WANT THIS GUITAR.
I'M NOT. I JUST DON'T WANT YOU.
TOO BAD--WE'RE A PACKAGE DEAL.

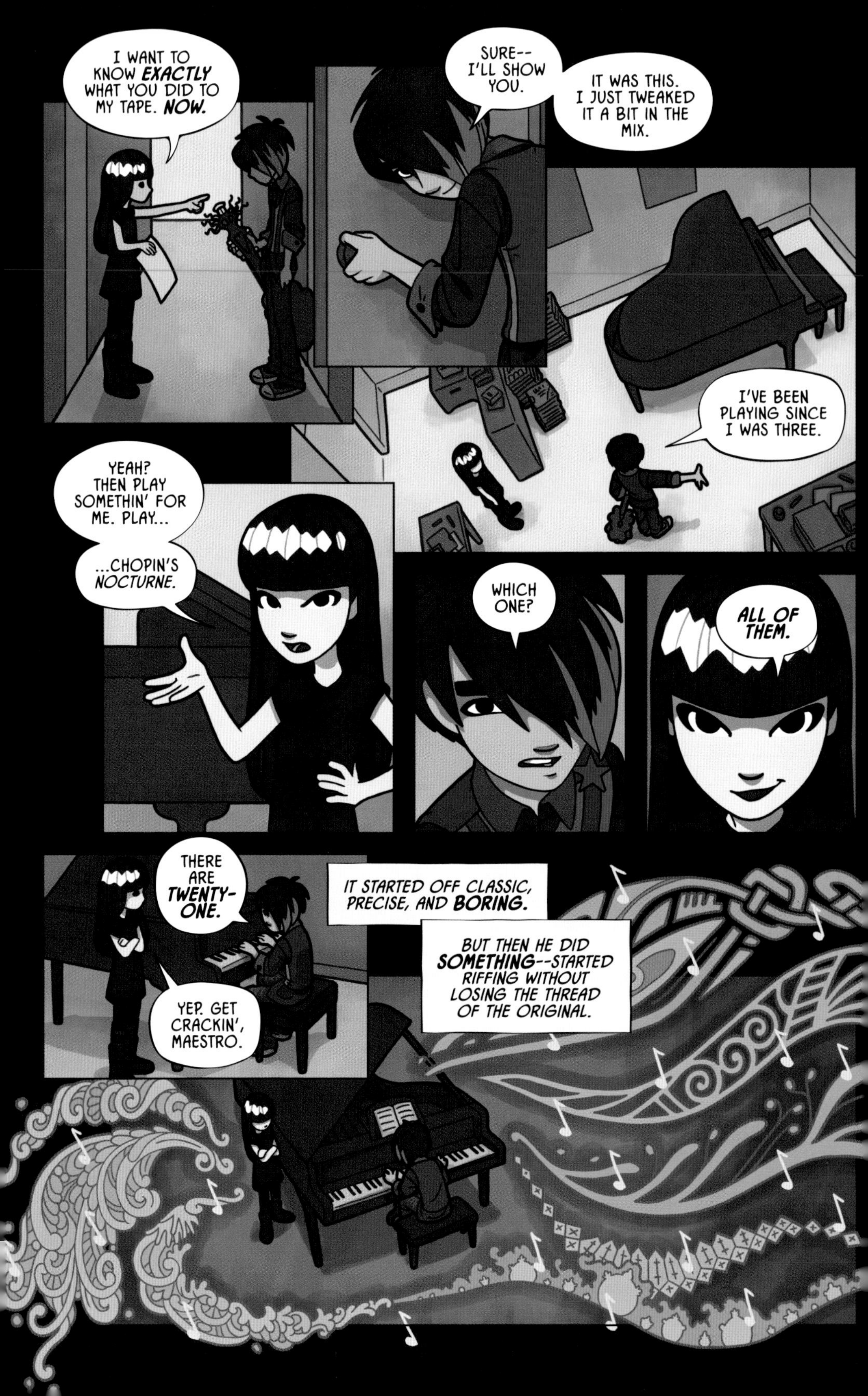
I WANT TO KNOW **EXACTLY** WHAT YOU DID TO MY TAPE. **NOW.**
SURE-- I'LL SHOW YOU.
IT WAS THIS. I JUST TWEAKED IT A BIT IN THE MIX.
I'VE BEEN PLAYING SINCE I WAS THREE.
YEAH? THEN PLAY SOMETHIN' FOR ME. PLAY...
...CHOPIN'S *NOCTURNE*.
WHICH ONE?
ALL OF THEM.
THERE ARE ***TWENTY-ONE.***
YEP. GET CRACKIN', MAESTRO.
IT STARTED OFF CLASSIC, PRECISE, AND ***BORING.***
BUT THEN HE DID ***SOMETHING****--STARTED RIFFING WITHOUT LOSING THE THREAD OF THE ORIGINAL.*

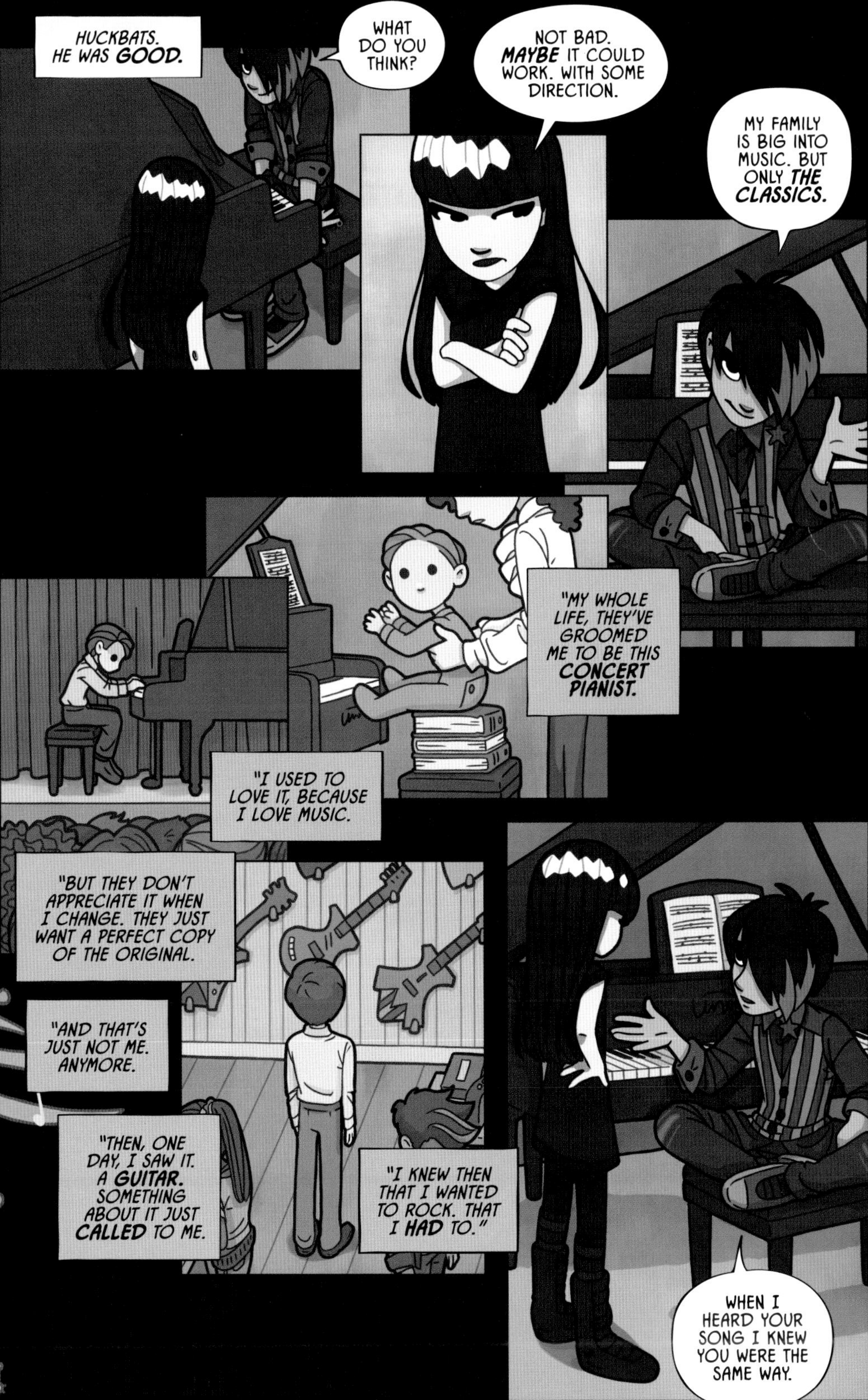
HUCKBATS. HE WAS **GOOD.**
WHAT DO YOU THINK?
NOT BAD. ***MAYBE*** IT COULD WORK. WITH SOME DIRECTION.
MY FAMILY IS BIG INTO MUSIC. BUT ONLY ***THE CLASSICS.***
"MY WHOLE LIFE, THEY'VE GROOMED ME TO BE THIS **CONCERT PIANIST.**
"I USED TO LOVE IT, BECAUSE I LOVE MUSIC.
"BUT THEY DON'T APPRECIATE IT WHEN I CHANGE. THEY JUST WANT A PERFECT COPY OF THE ORIGINAL.
"AND THAT'S JUST NOT ME. ANYMORE.
"THEN, ONE DAY, I SAW IT. A **GUITAR.** SOMETHING ABOUT IT JUST **CALLED** TO ME.
"I KNEW THEN THAT I WANTED TO ROCK. THAT I **HAD** TO."
WHEN I HEARD YOUR SONG I KNEW YOU WERE THE SAME WAY.

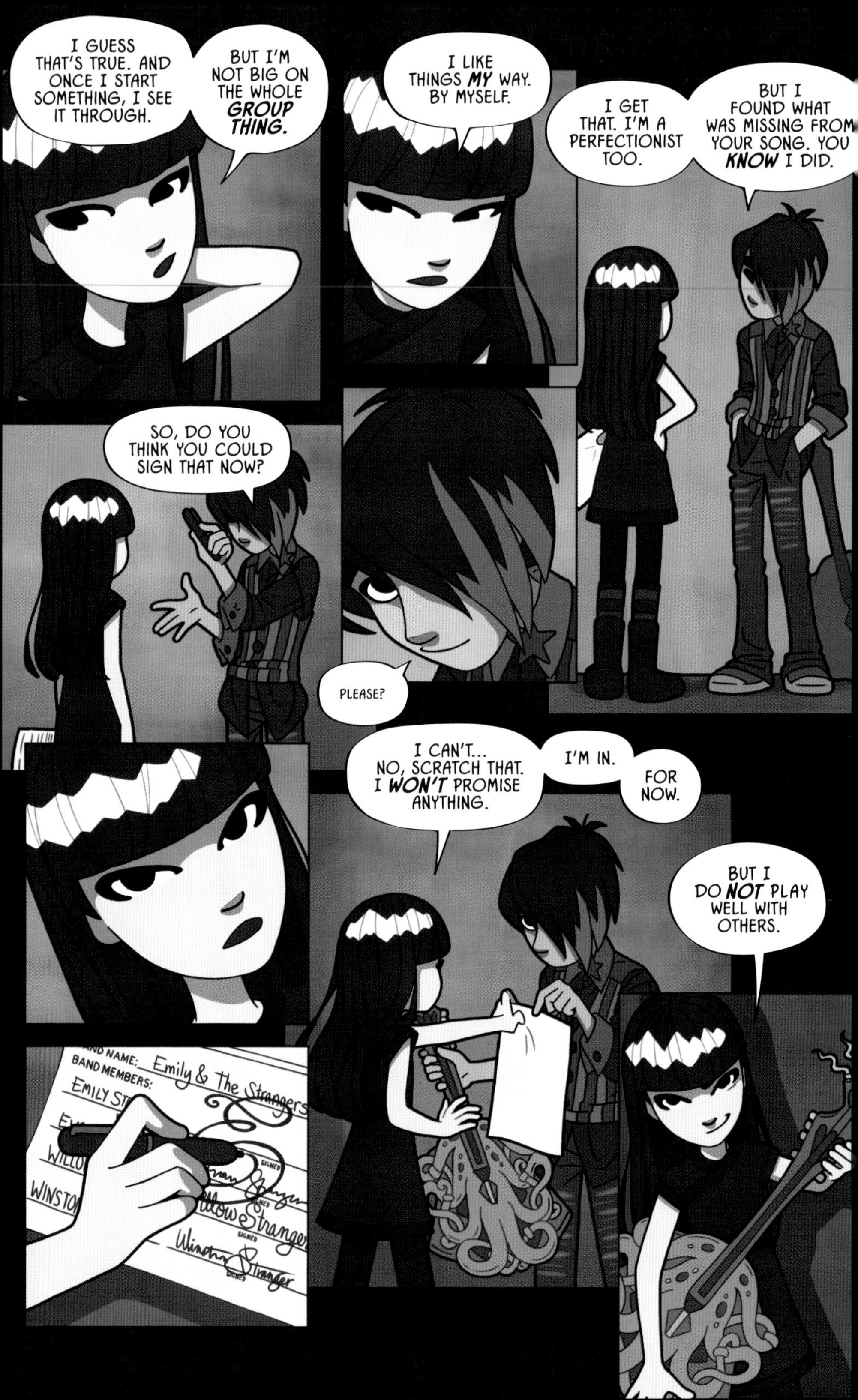

I GUESS THAT'S TRUE. AND ONCE I START SOMETHING, I SEE IT THROUGH.
BUT I'M NOT BIG ON THE WHOLE ***GROUP THING.***
I LIKE THINGS ***MY*** WAY. BY MYSELF.
I GET THAT. I'M A PERFECTIONIST TOO.
BUT I FOUND WHAT WAS MISSING FROM YOUR SONG. YOU ***KNOW*** I DID.
SO, DO YOU THINK YOU COULD SIGN THAT NOW?
PLEASE?
I CAN'T... NO, SCRATCH THAT. I ***WON'T*** PROMISE ANYTHING.
I'M IN.
FOR NOW.
BUT I DO ***NOT*** PLAY WELL WITH OTHERS.
BAND MEMBERS:
Emily & The Strangers

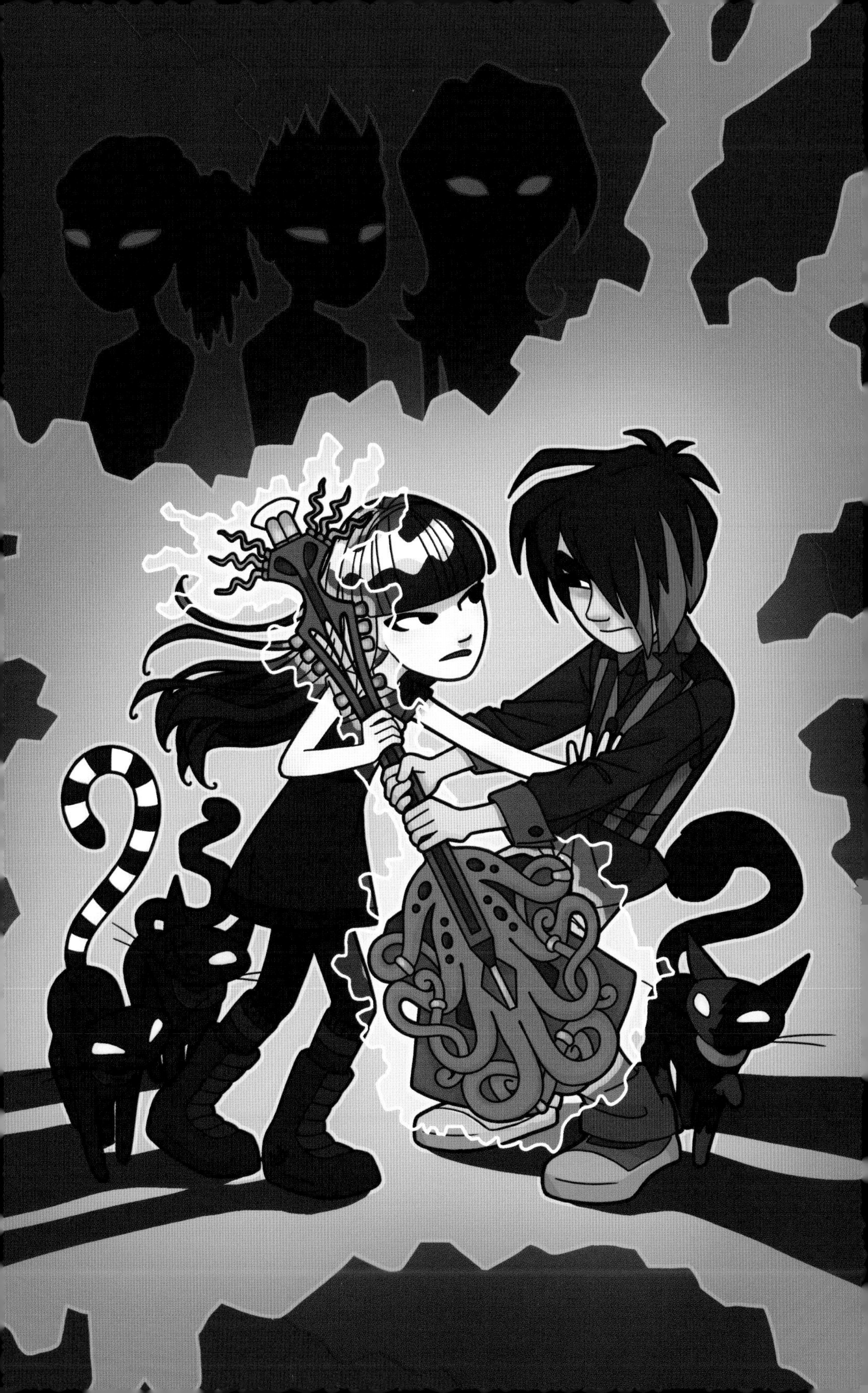

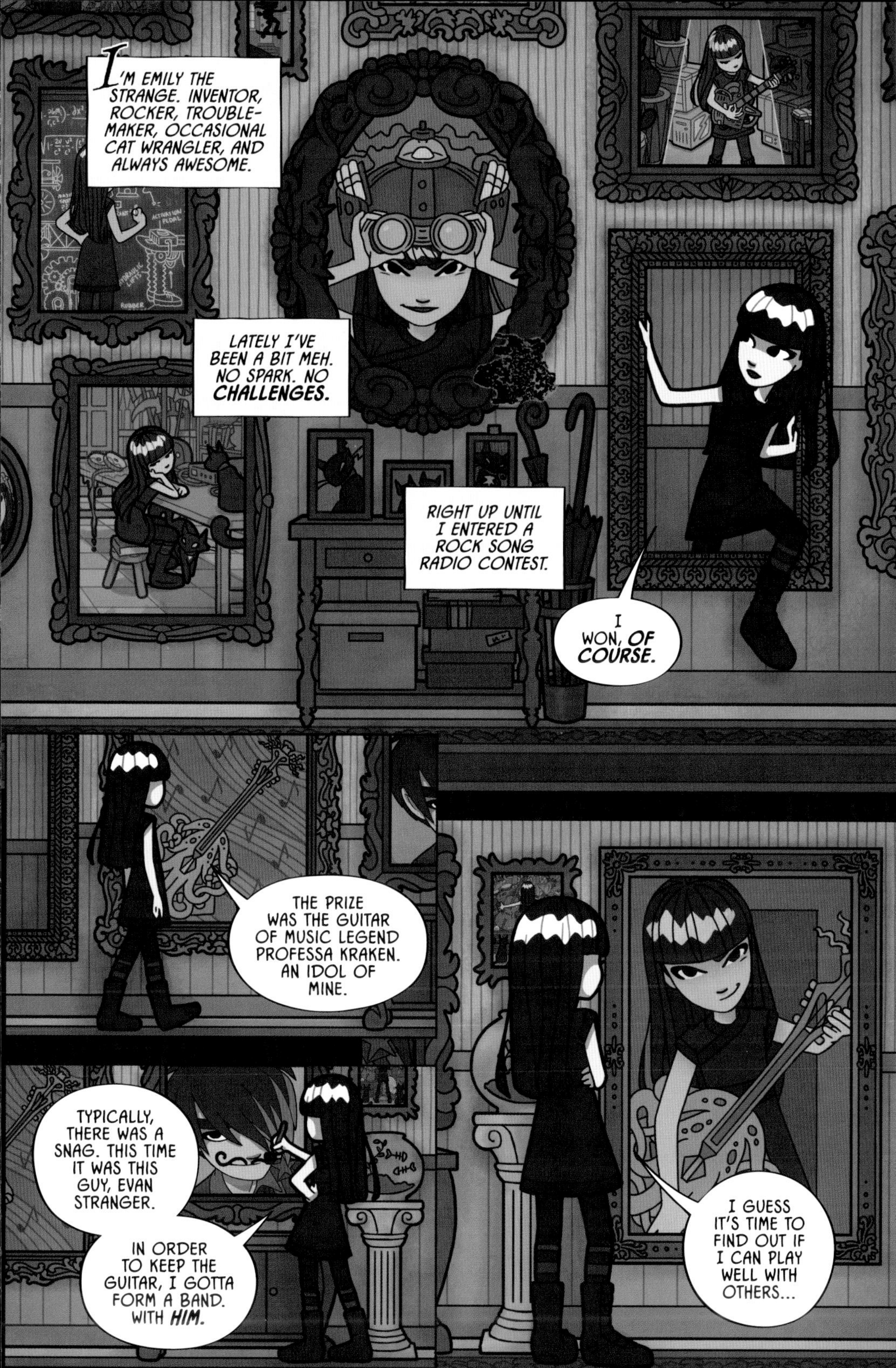
I'M EMILY THE STRANGE. INVENTOR, ROCKER, TROUBLE-MAKER, OCCASIONAL CAT WRANGLER, AND ALWAYS AWESOME.
LATELY I'VE BEEN A BIT MEH. NO SPARK. NO CHALLENGES.
RIGHT UP UNTIL I ENTERED A ROCK SONG RADIO CONTEST.
I WON, OF COURSE.
THE PRIZE WAS THE GUITAR OF MUSIC LEGEND PROFESSA KRAKEN. AN IDOL OF MINE.
TYPICALLY, THERE WAS A SNAG. THIS TIME IT WAS THIS GUY, EVAN STRANGER.
IN ORDER TO KEEP THE GUITAR, I GOTTA FORM A BAND. WITH HIM.
I GUESS IT'S TIME TO FIND OUT IF I CAN PLAY WELL WITH OTHERS...

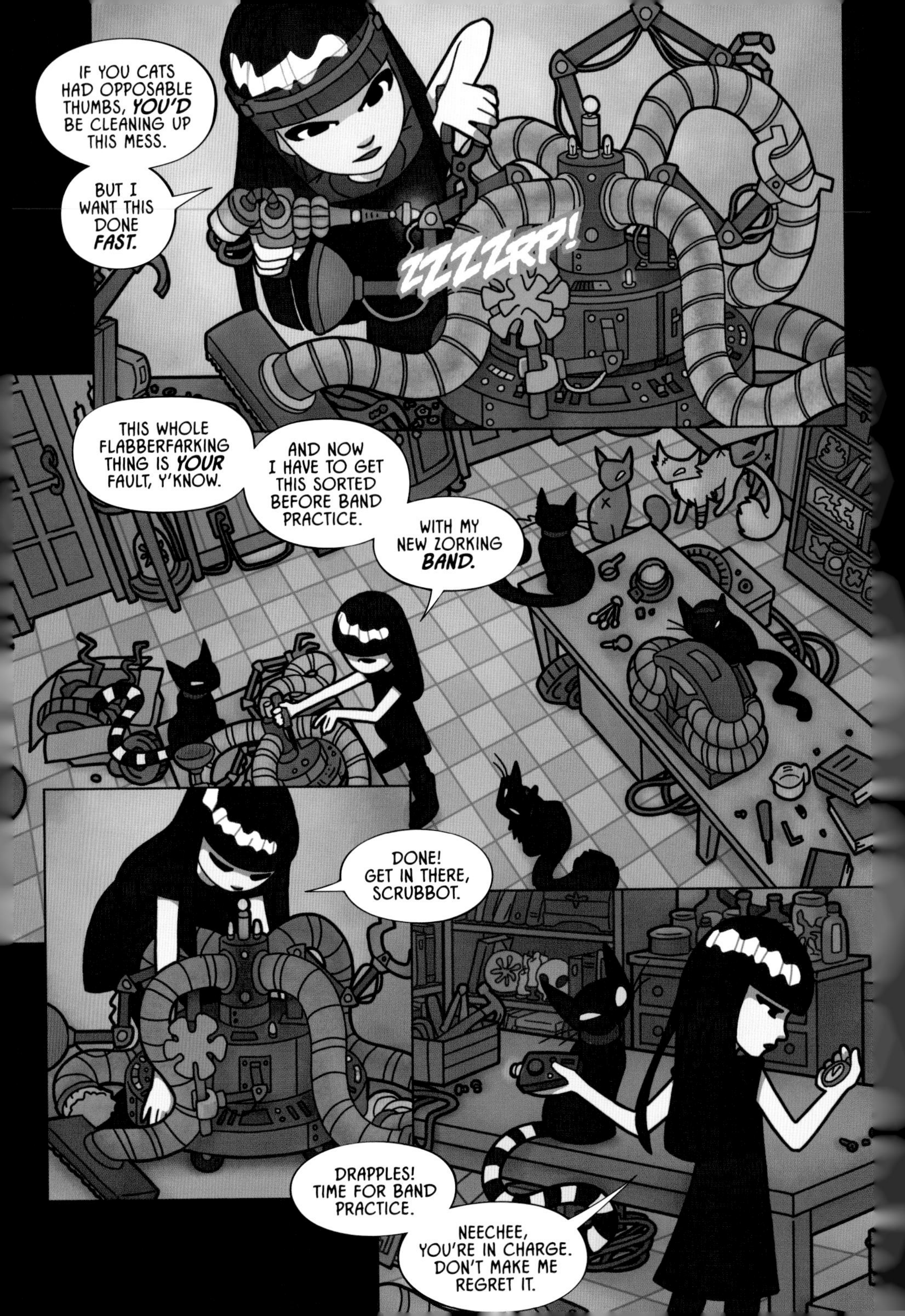
IF YOU CATS HAD OPPOSABLE THUMBS, *YOU'D* BE CLEANING UP THIS MESS.
BUT I WANT THIS DONE *FAST.*
ZZZZZRP!
THIS WHOLE FLABBERFARKING THING IS *YOUR* FAULT, Y'KNOW.
AND NOW I HAVE TO GET THIS SORTED BEFORE BAND PRACTICE.
WITH MY NEW ZORKING *BAND.*
DONE! GET IN THERE, SCRUBBOT.
DRAPPLES! TIME FOR BAND PRACTICE.
NEECHEE, YOU'RE IN CHARGE. DON'T MAKE ME REGRET IT.

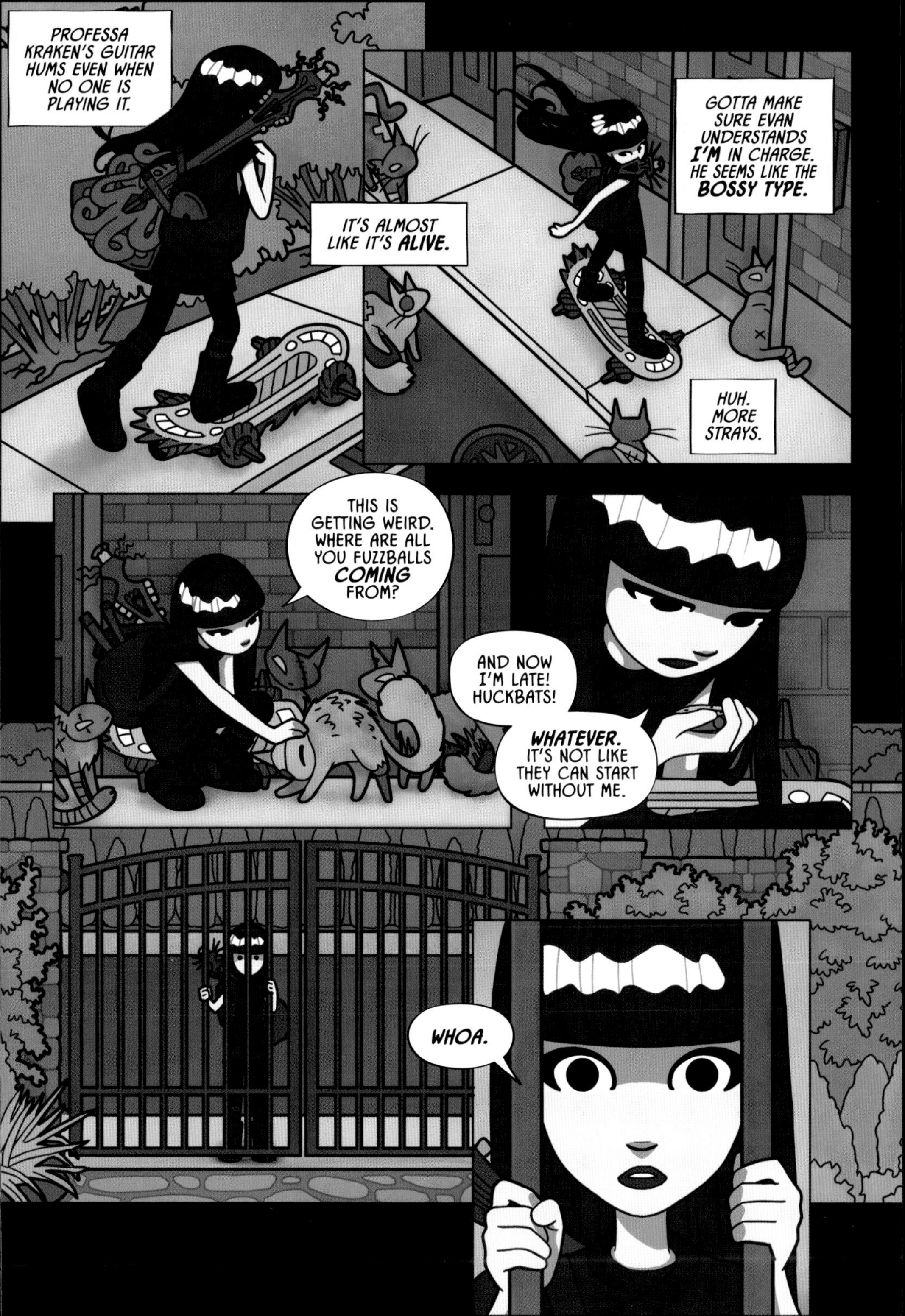
PROFESSA KRAKEN'S GUITAR HUMS EVEN WHEN NO ONE IS PLAYING IT.
IT'S ALMOST LIKE IT'S **ALIVE.**
GOTTA MAKE SURE EVAN UNDERSTANDS ***I'M*** IN CHARGE. HE SEEMS LIKE THE ***BOSSY TYPE.***
HUH. MORE STRAYS.
THIS IS GETTING WEIRD. WHERE ARE ALL YOU FUZZBALLS ***COMING*** FROM?
AND NOW I'M LATE! HUCKBATS!
WHATEVER. IT'S NOT LIKE THEY CAN START WITHOUT ME.
WHOA.

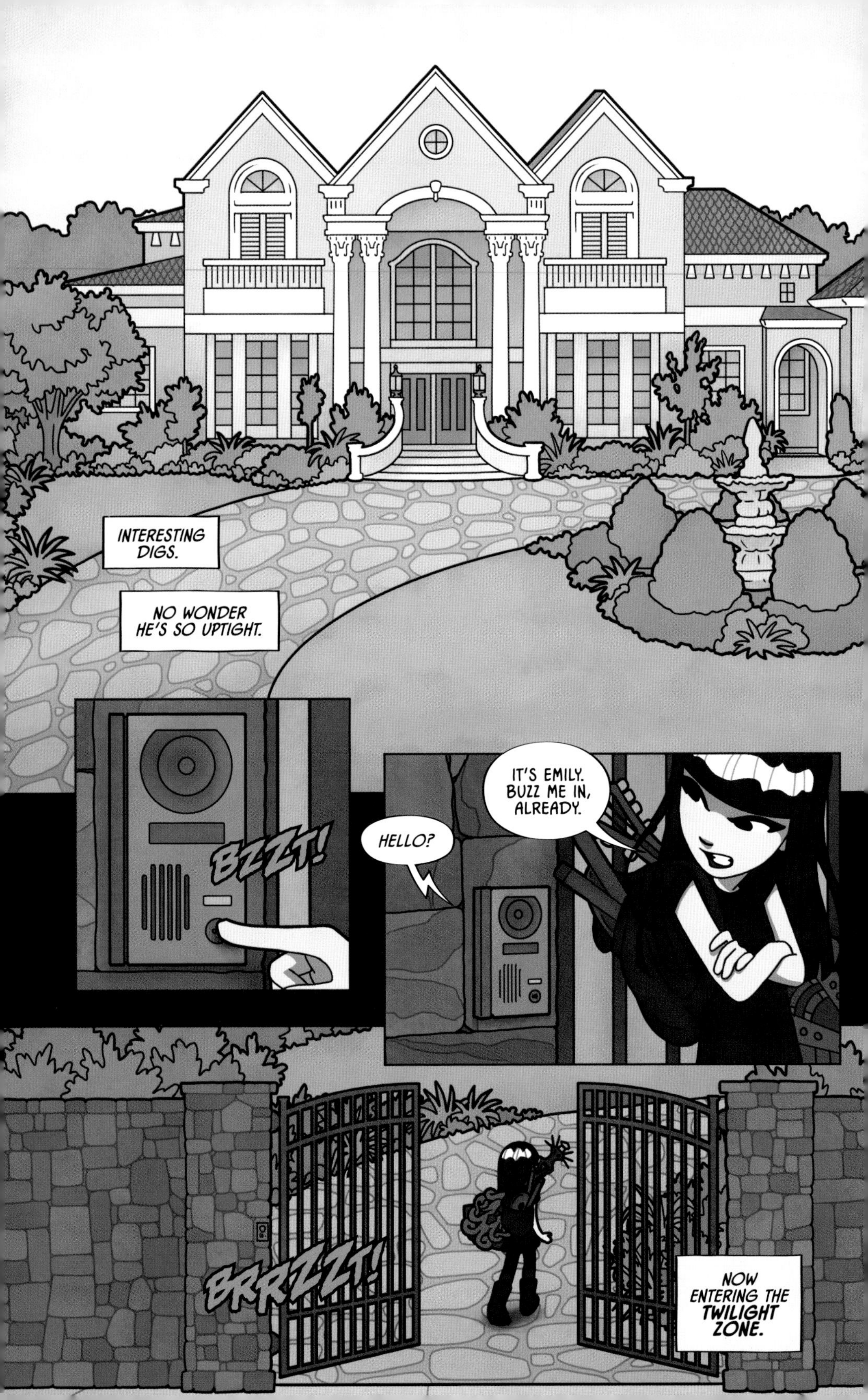
INTERESTING DIGS.
NO WONDER HE'S SO UPTIGHT.
BZZT!
HELLO?
IT'S EMILY. BUZZ ME IN, ALREADY.
BRRZZZT!
NOW ENTERING THE TWILIGHT ZONE.

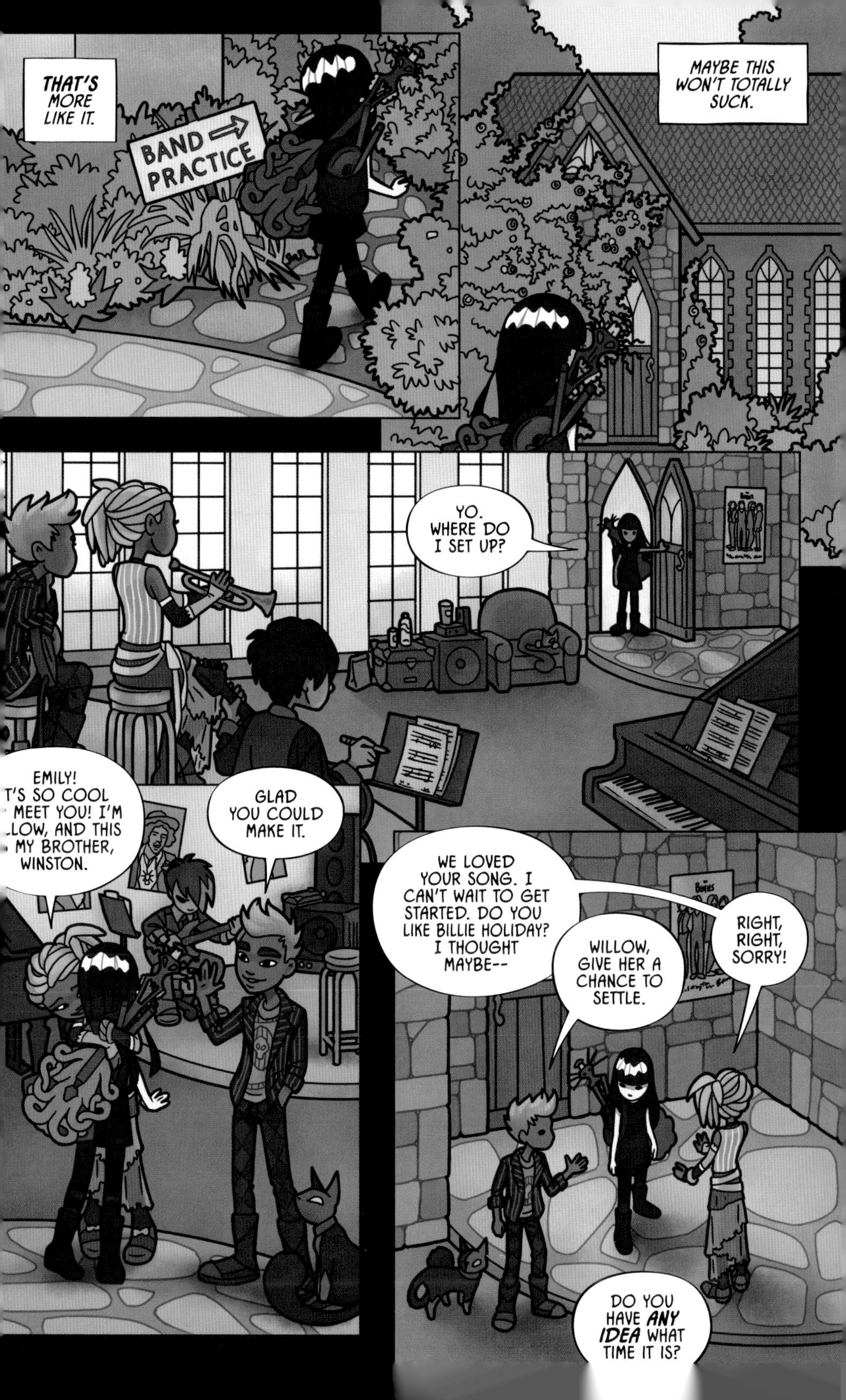
THAT'S MORE LIKE IT.
BAND PRACTICE
MAYBE THIS WON'T TOTALLY SUCK.
YO. WHERE DO I SET UP?
EMILY! T'S SO COOL MEET YOU! I'M LOW, AND THIS MY BROTHER, WINSTON.
GLAD YOU COULD MAKE IT.
WE LOVED YOUR SONG. I CAN'T WAIT TO GET STARTED. DO YOU LIKE BILLIE HOLIDAY? I THOUGHT MAYBE--
WILLOW, GIVE HER A CHANCE TO SETTLE.
RIGHT, RIGHT, SORRY!
DO YOU HAVE ***ANY IDEA*** WHAT TIME IT IS?

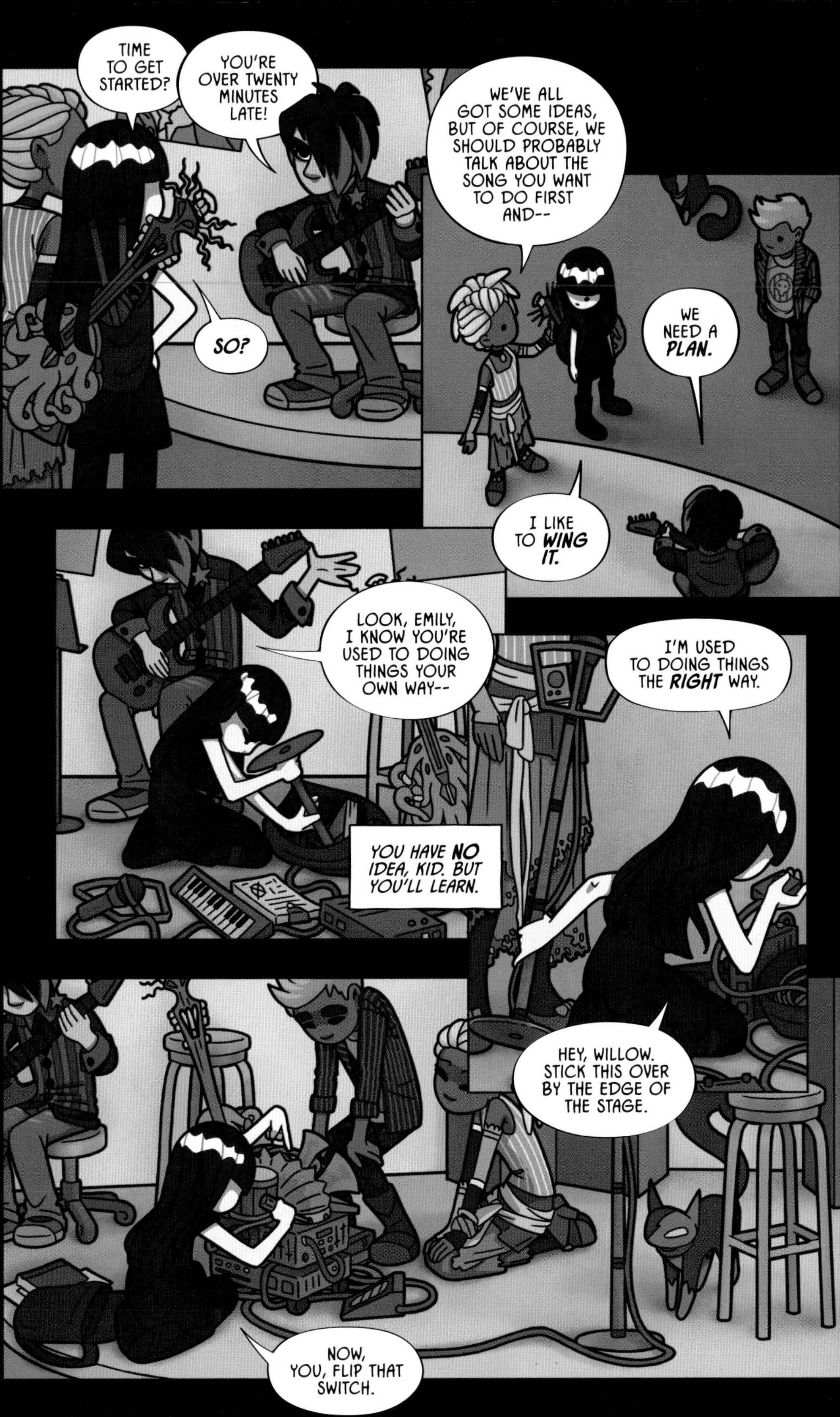
TIME TO GET STARTED?
YOU'RE OVER TWENTY MINUTES LATE!
SO?
WE'VE ALL GOT SOME IDEAS, BUT OF COURSE, WE SHOULD PROBABLY TALK ABOUT THE SONG YOU WANT TO DO FIRST AND--
WE NEED A PLAN.
I LIKE TO WING IT.
LOOK, EMILY, I KNOW YOU'RE USED TO DOING THINGS YOUR OWN WAY--
I'M USED TO DOING THINGS THE RIGHT WAY.
YOU HAVE NO IDEA, KID. BUT YOU'LL LEARN.
HEY, WILLOW. STICK THIS OVER BY THE EDGE OF THE STAGE.
NOW, YOU, FLIP THAT SWITCH.

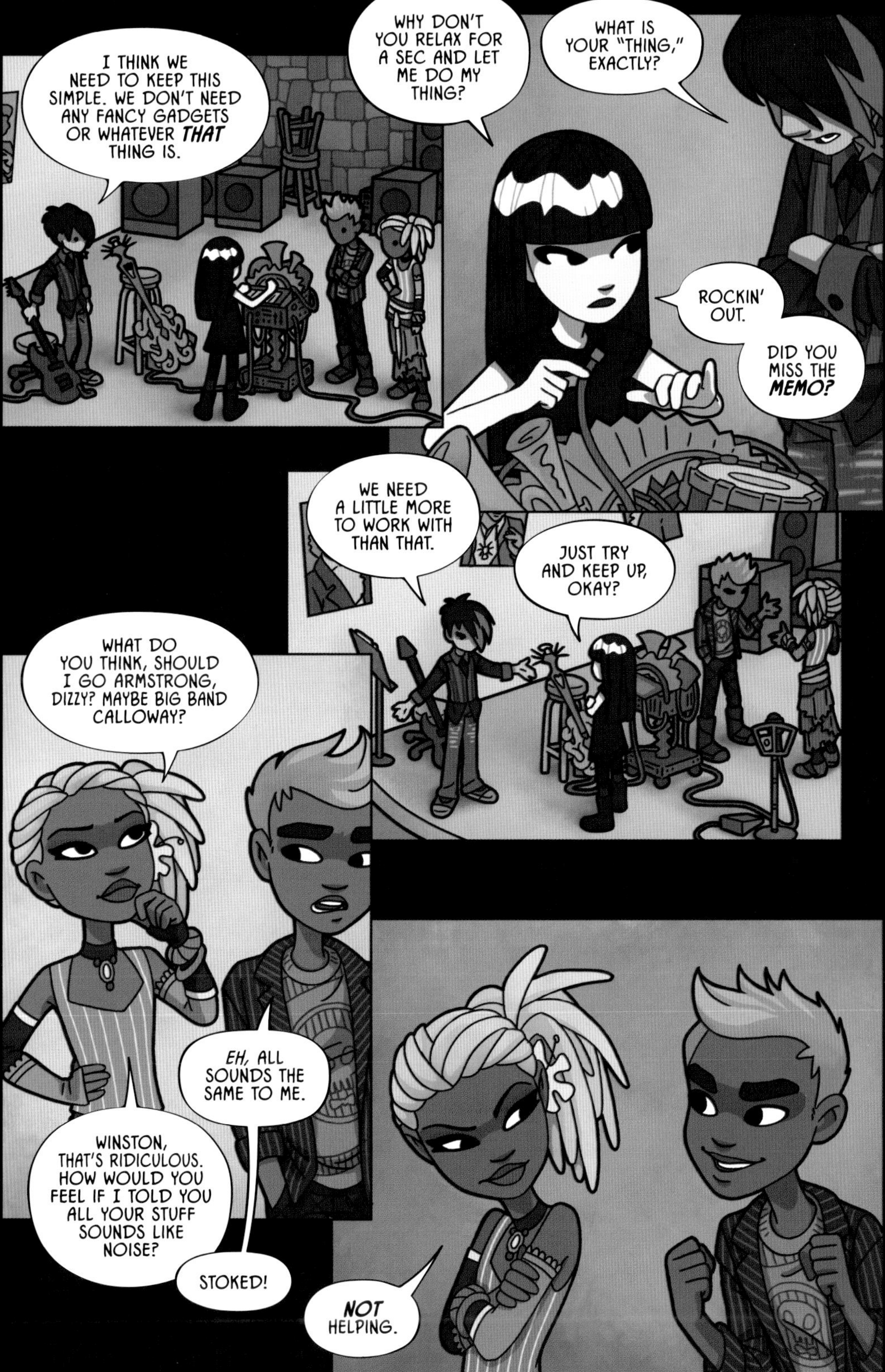
I THINK WE NEED TO KEEP THIS SIMPLE. WE DON'T NEED ANY FANCY GADGETS OR WHATEVER *THAT* THING IS.
WHY DON'T YOU RELAX FOR A SEC AND LET ME DO MY THING?
WHAT IS YOUR "THING," EXACTLY?
ROCKIN' OUT.
DID YOU MISS THE *MEMO?*
WE NEED A LITTLE MORE TO WORK WITH THAN THAT.
JUST TRY AND KEEP UP, OKAY?
WHAT DO YOU THINK, SHOULD I GO ARMSTRONG, DIZZY? MAYBE BIG BAND CALLOWAY?
EH, ALL SOUNDS THE SAME TO ME.
WINSTON, THAT'S RIDICULOUS. HOW WOULD YOU FEEL IF I TOLD YOU ALL YOUR STUFF SOUNDS LIKE NOISE?
STOKED!
NOT HELPING.

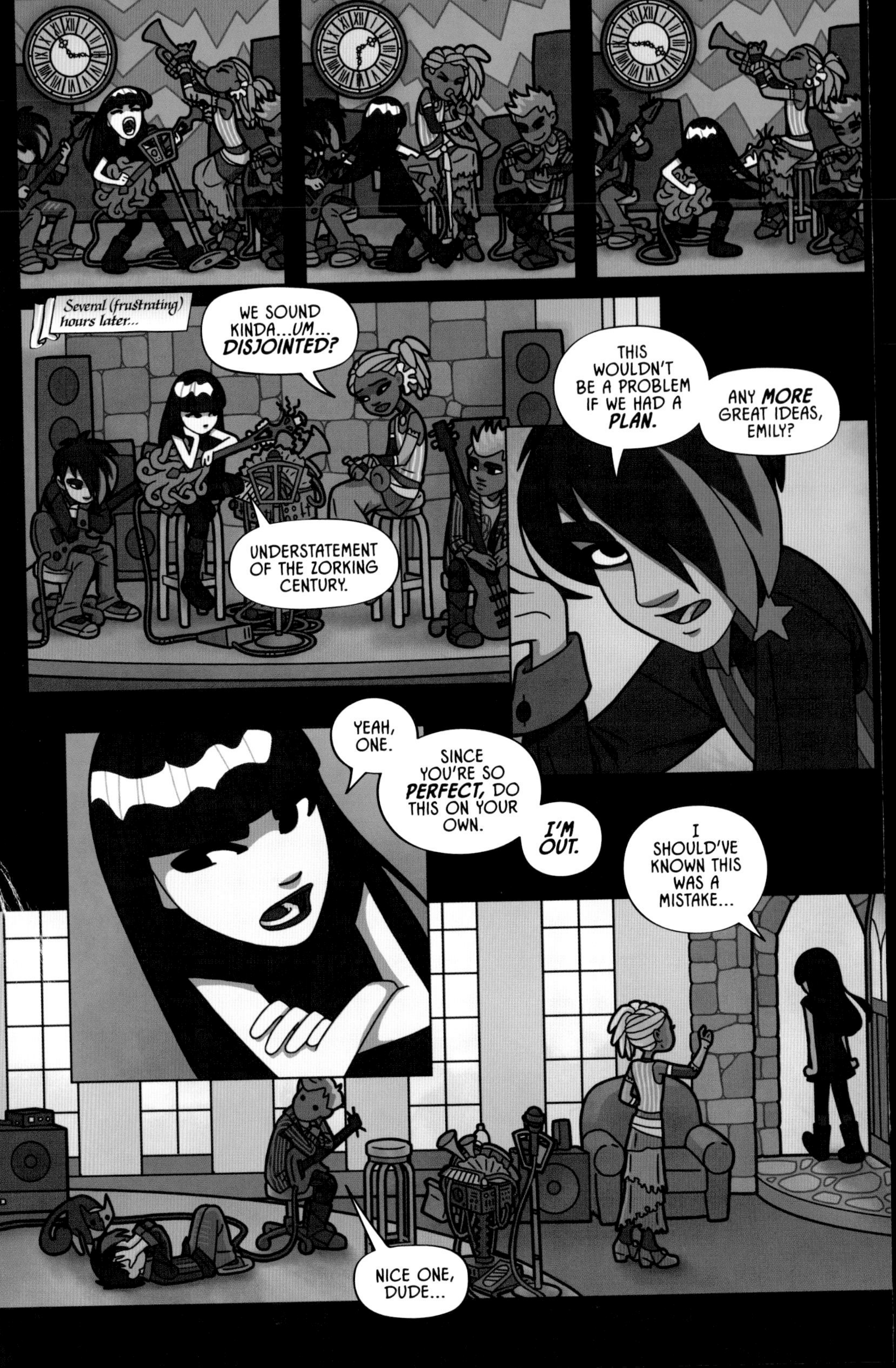
Several (frustrating) hours later...
WE SOUND KINDA...UM... DISJOINTED?
UNDERSTATEMENT OF THE ZORKING CENTURY.
THIS WOULDN'T BE A PROBLEM IF WE HAD A PLAN.
ANY MORE GREAT IDEAS, EMILY?
YEAH, ONE.
SINCE YOU'RE SO PERFECT, DO THIS ON YOUR OWN.
I'M OUT.
I SHOULD'VE KNOWN THIS WAS A MISTAKE...
NICE ONE, DUDE...

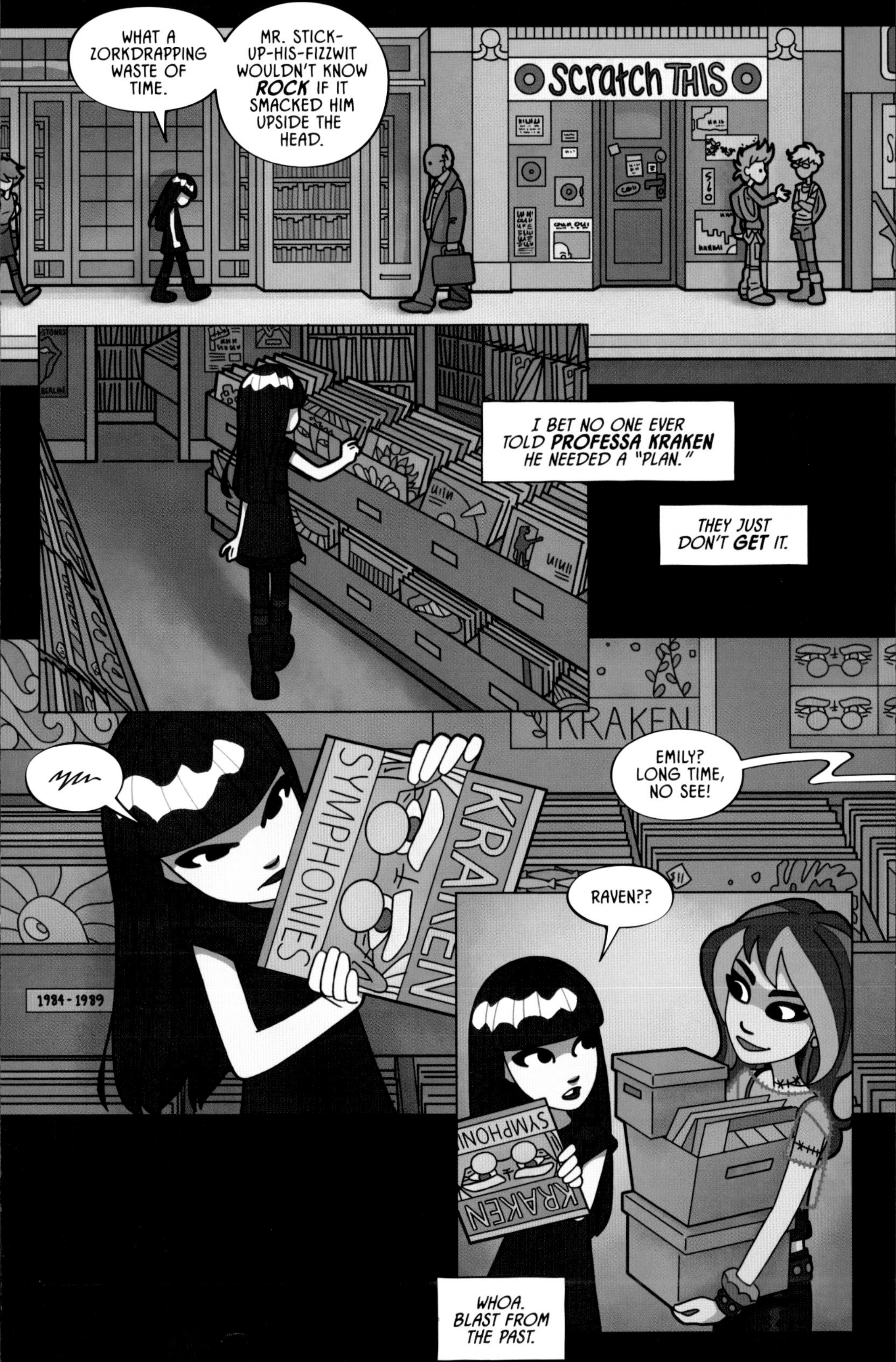
WHAT A ZORKDRAPPING WASTE OF TIME.
MR. STICK-UP-HIS-FIZZWIT WOULDN'T KNOW ROCK IF IT SMACKED HIM UPSIDE THE HEAD.
SCRATCH THIS
I BET NO ONE EVER TOLD PROFESSA KRAKEN HE NEEDED A "PLAN."
THEY JUST DON'T GET IT.
KRAKEN
KRAKEN SYMPHONIES
1984 - 1989
EMILY? LONG TIME, NO SEE!
RAVEN??
WHOA. BLAST FROM THE PAST.

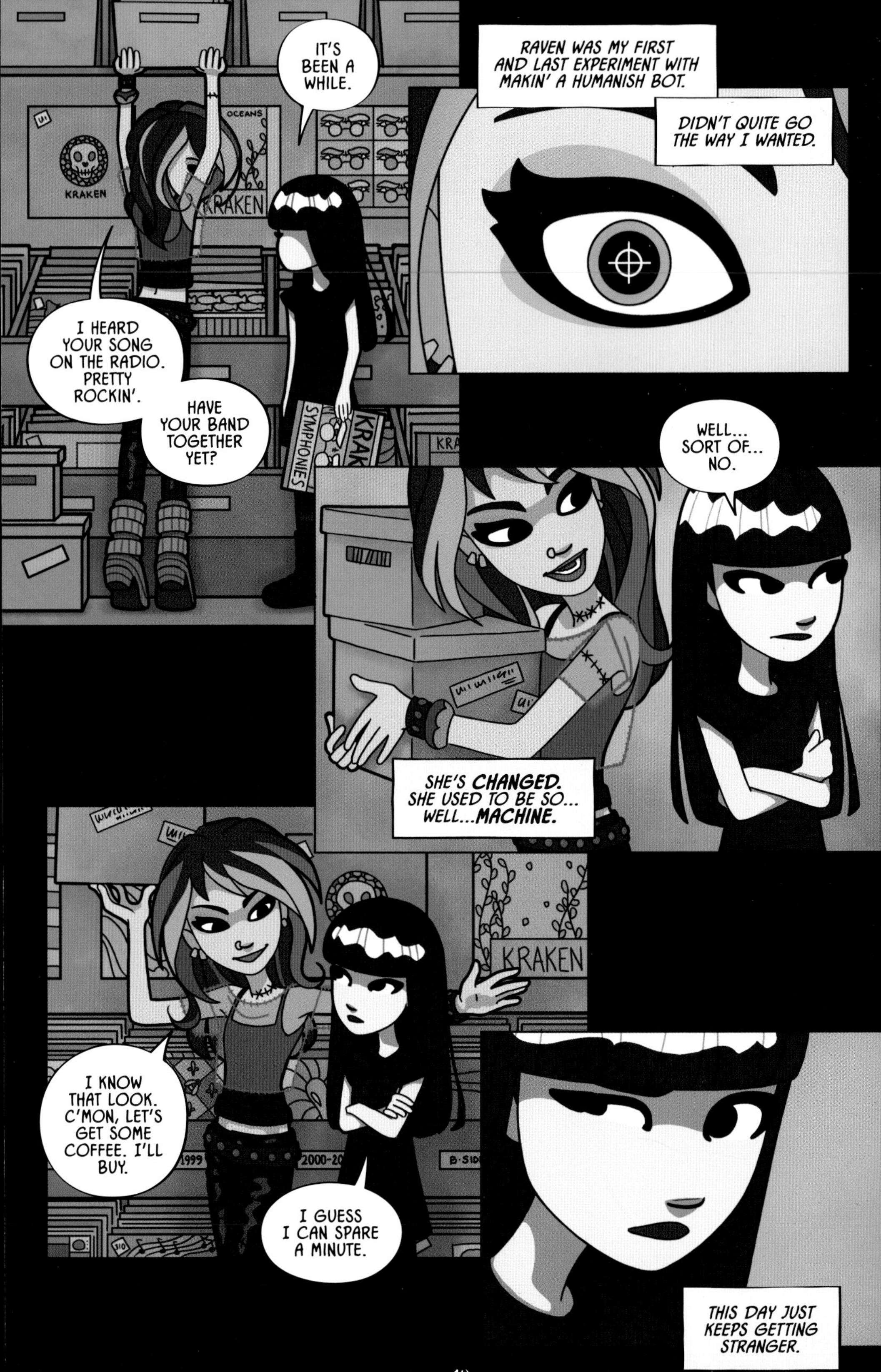
IT'S BEEN A WHILE.
I HEARD YOUR SONG ON THE RADIO. PRETTY ROCKIN'.
HAVE YOUR BAND TOGETHER YET?
RAVEN WAS MY FIRST AND LAST EXPERIMENT WITH MAKIN' A HUMANISH BOT.
DIDN'T QUITE GO THE WAY I WANTED.
WELL... SORT OF... NO.
SHE'S CHANGED. SHE USED TO BE SO... WELL...MACHINE.
I KNOW THAT LOOK. C'MON, LET'S GET SOME COFFEE. I'LL BUY.
I GUESS I CAN SPARE A MINUTE.
THIS DAY JUST KEEPS GETTING STRANGER.
KRAKEN
OCEANS
SYMPHONIES
1999
2000-20
B·SID

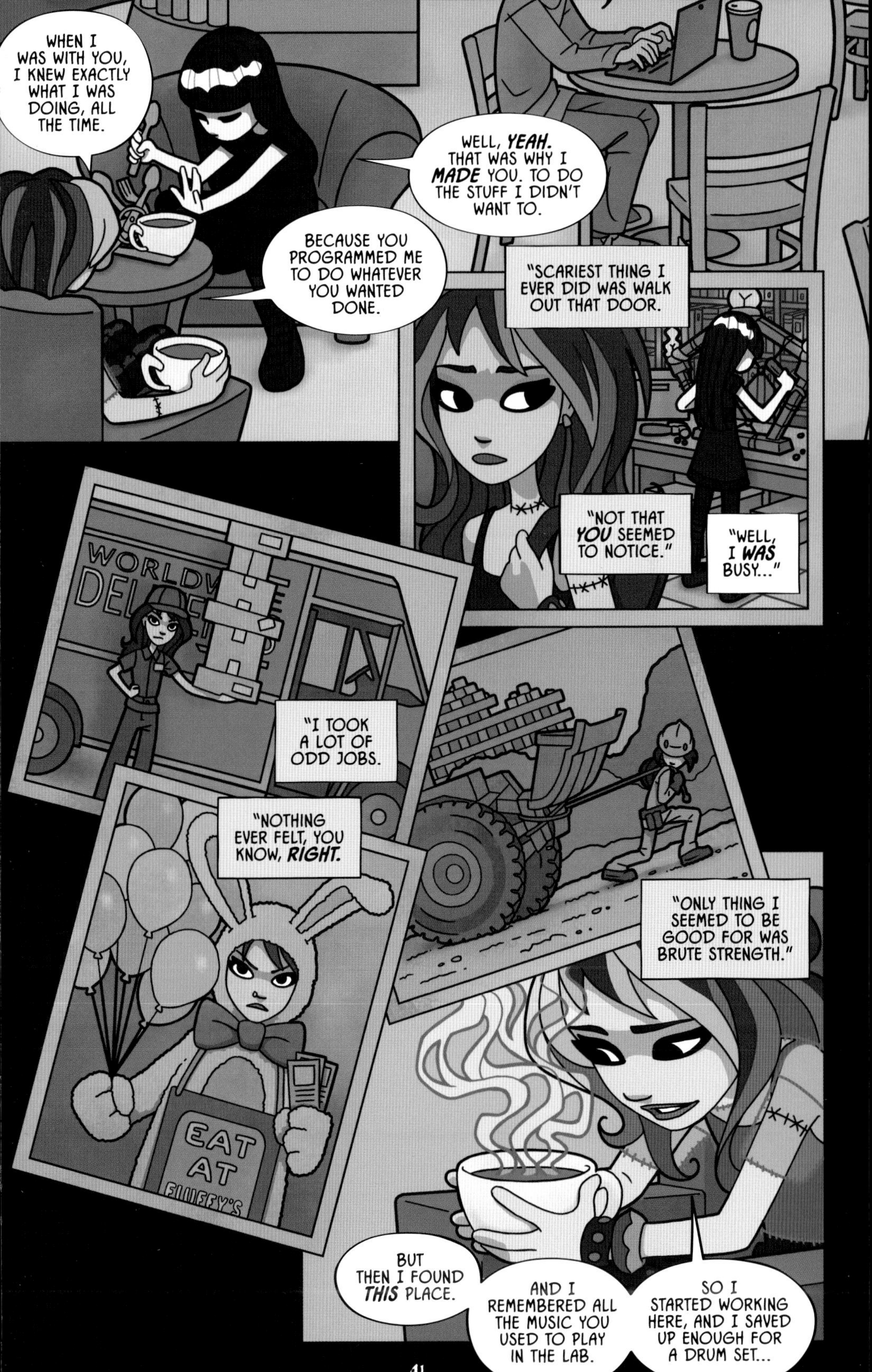
WHEN I WAS WITH YOU, I KNEW EXACTLY WHAT I WAS DOING, ALL THE TIME.
WELL, *YEAH.* THAT WAS WHY I *MADE* YOU. TO DO THE STUFF I DIDN'T WANT TO.
BECAUSE YOU PROGRAMMED ME TO DO WHATEVER YOU WANTED DONE.
"SCARIEST THING I EVER DID WAS WALK OUT THAT DOOR.
"NOT THAT *YOU* SEEMED TO NOTICE."
"WELL, I *WAS* BUSY..."
WORLDW DEL
"I TOOK A LOT OF ODD JOBS.
"NOTHING EVER FELT, YOU KNOW, *RIGHT.*
EAT AT FLUFFY'S
"ONLY THING I SEEMED TO BE GOOD FOR WAS BRUTE STRENGTH."
BUT THEN I FOUND *THIS* PLACE.
AND I REMEMBERED ALL THE MUSIC YOU USED TO PLAY IN THE LAB.
SO I STARTED WORKING HERE, AND I SAVED UP ENOUGH FOR A DRUM SET...

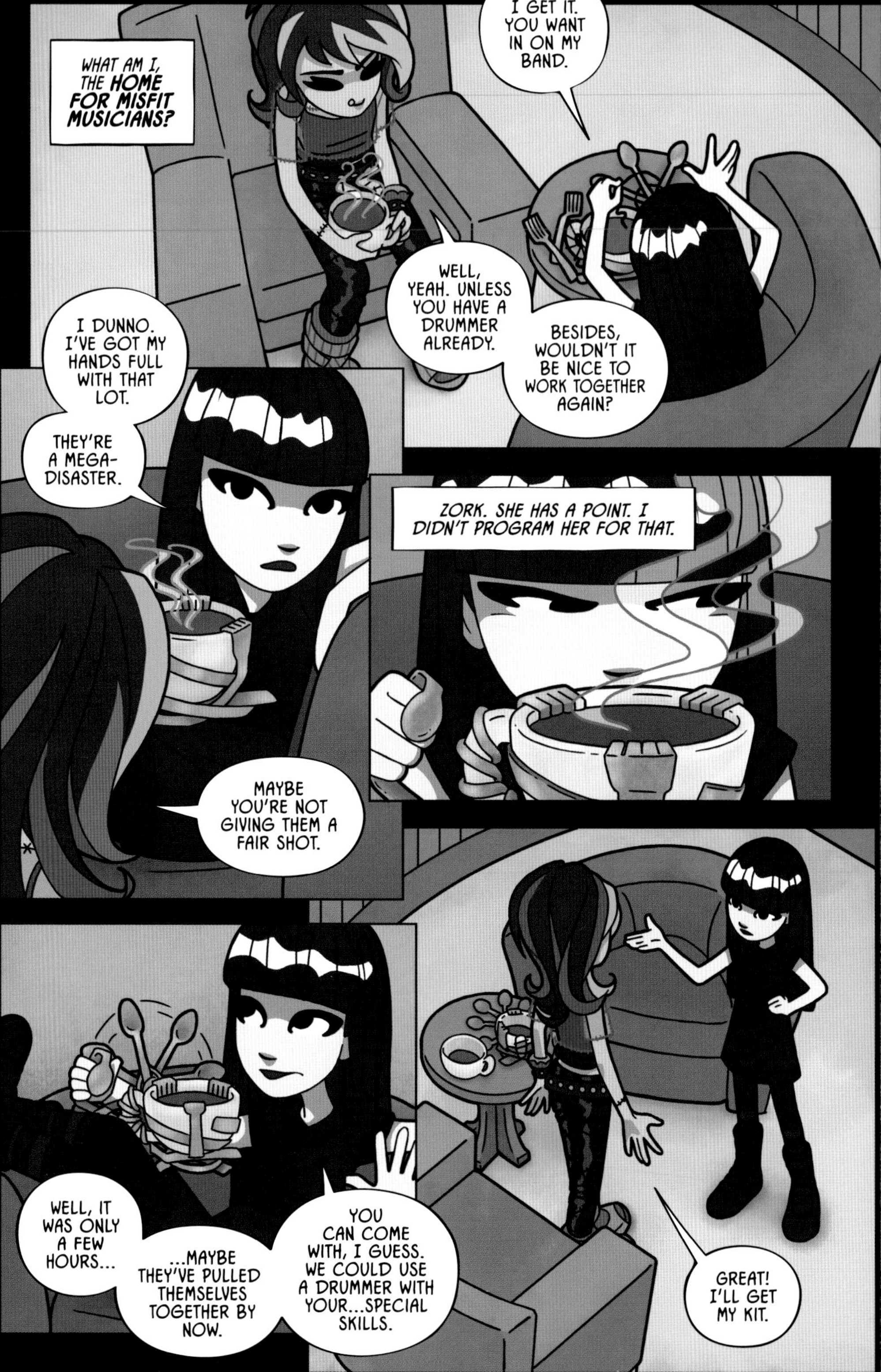
WHAT AM I, THE **HOME FOR MISFIT MUSICIANS?**
I GET IT. YOU WANT IN ON MY BAND.
WELL, YEAH. UNLESS YOU HAVE A DRUMMER ALREADY.
BESIDES, WOULDN'T IT BE NICE TO WORK TOGETHER AGAIN?
I DUNNO. I'VE GOT MY HANDS FULL WITH THAT LOT.
THEY'RE A MEGA-DISASTER.
MAYBE YOU'RE NOT GIVING THEM A FAIR SHOT.
ZORK. SHE HAS A POINT. I DIDN'T PROGRAM HER FOR THAT.
WELL, IT WAS ONLY A FEW HOURS...
...MAYBE THEY'VE PULLED THEMSELVES TOGETHER BY NOW.
YOU CAN COME WITH, I GUESS. WE COULD USE A DRUMMER WITH YOUR...SPECIAL SKILLS.
GREAT! I'LL GET MY KIT.

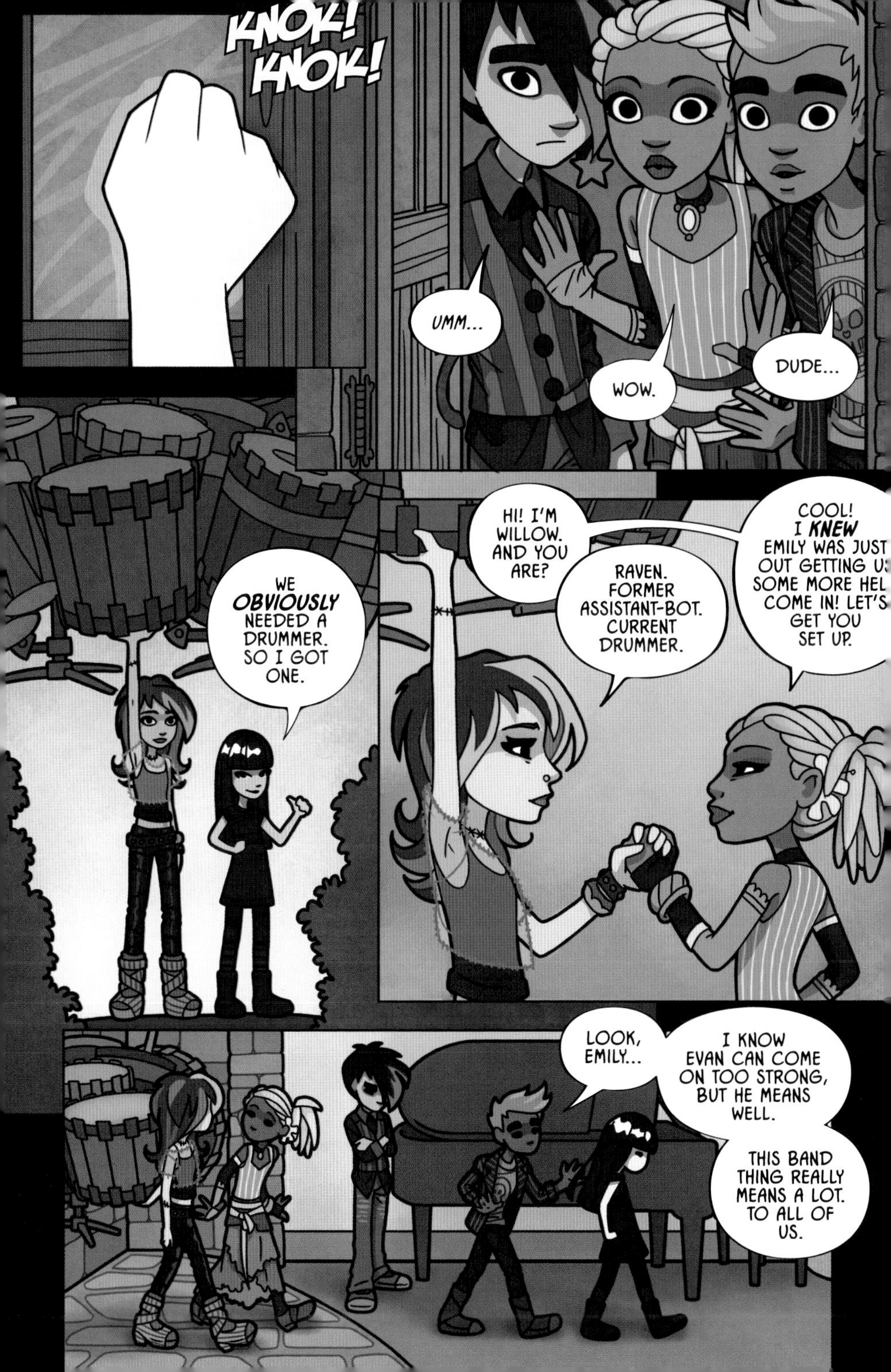
KNOK! KNOK!
UMM...
WOW.
DUDE...
WE OBVIOUSLY NEEDED A DRUMMER. SO I GOT ONE.
HI! I'M WILLOW. AND YOU ARE?
RAVEN. FORMER ASSISTANT-BOT. CURRENT DRUMMER.
COOL! I KNEW EMILY WAS JUST OUT GETTING US SOME MORE HELP. COME IN! LET'S GET YOU SET UP.
LOOK, EMILY...
I KNOW EVAN CAN COME ON TOO STRONG, BUT HE MEANS WELL.
THIS BAND THING REALLY MEANS A LOT. TO ALL OF US.

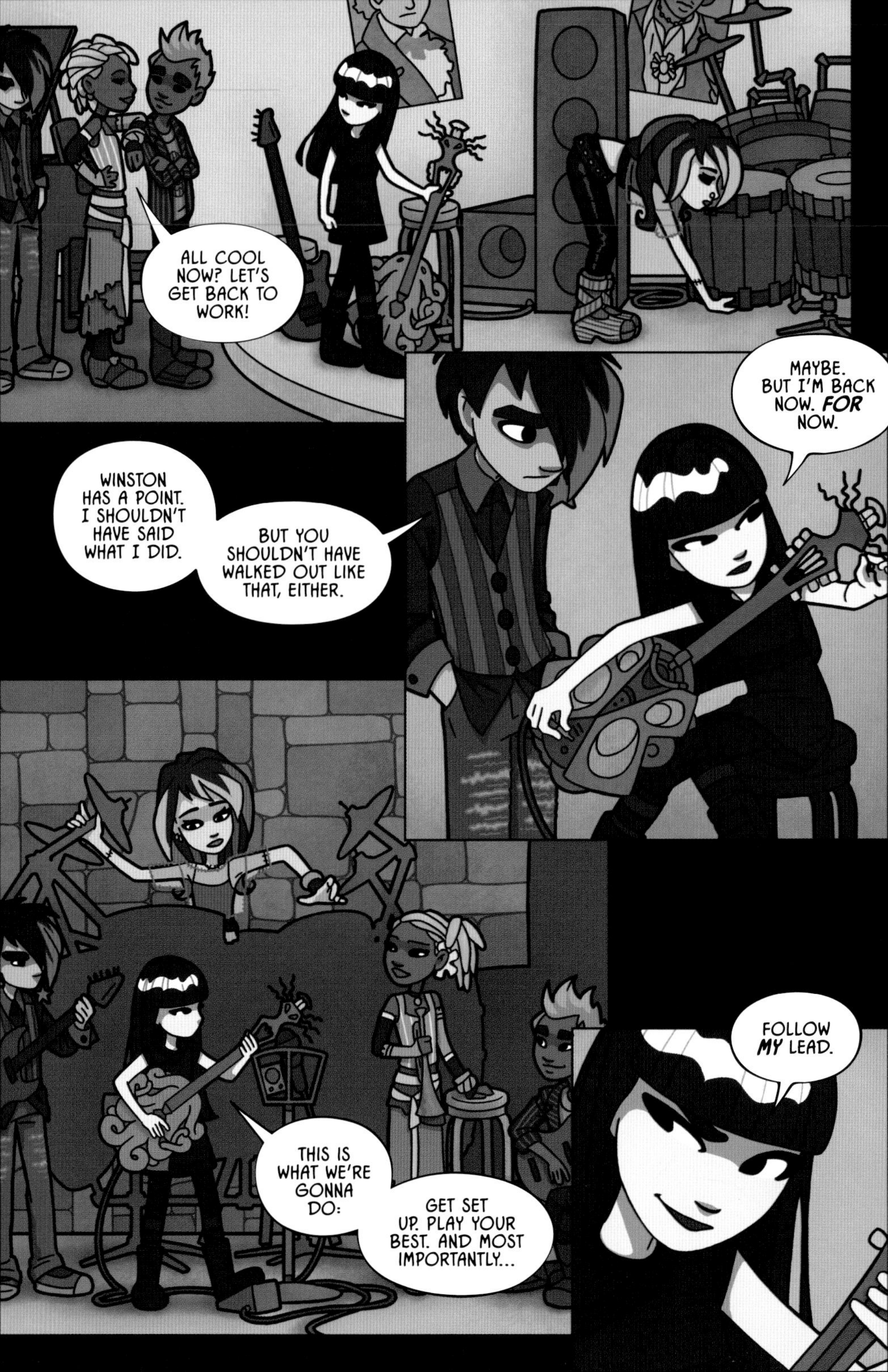
ALL COOL NOW? LET'S GET BACK TO WORK!
MAYBE. BUT I'M BACK NOW. *FOR* NOW.
WINSTON HAS A POINT. I SHOULDN'T HAVE SAID WHAT I DID.
BUT YOU SHOULDN'T HAVE WALKED OUT LIKE THAT, EITHER.
THIS IS WHAT WE'RE GONNA DO:
GET SET UP. PLAY YOUR BEST. AND MOST IMPORTANTLY...
FOLLOW *MY* LEAD.

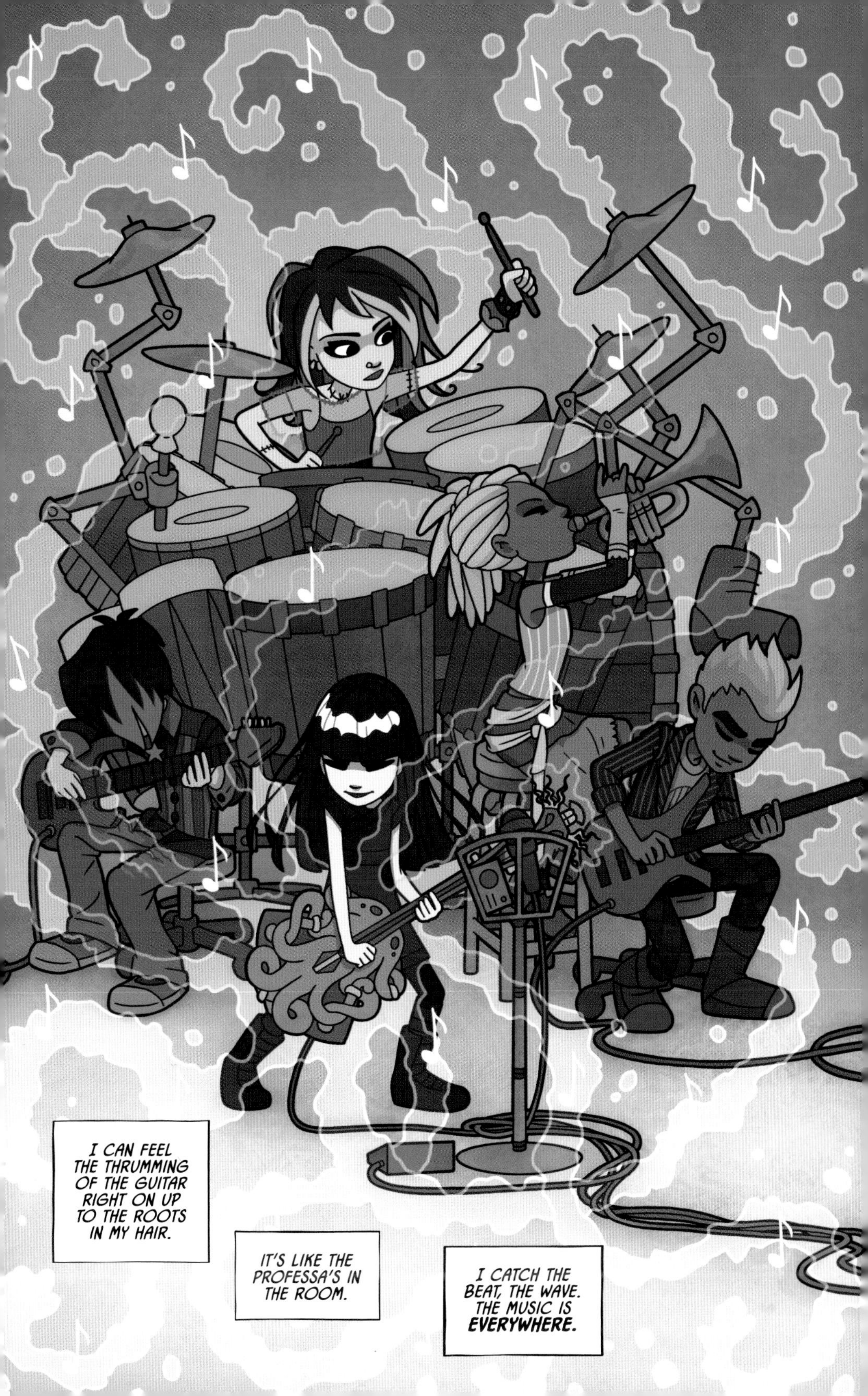
I CAN FEEL THE THRUMMING OF THE GUITAR RIGHT ON UP TO THE ROOTS IN MY HAIR.
IT'S LIKE THE PROFESSA'S IN THE ROOM.
I CATCH THE BEAT, THE WAVE. THE MUSIC IS **EVERYWHERE.**

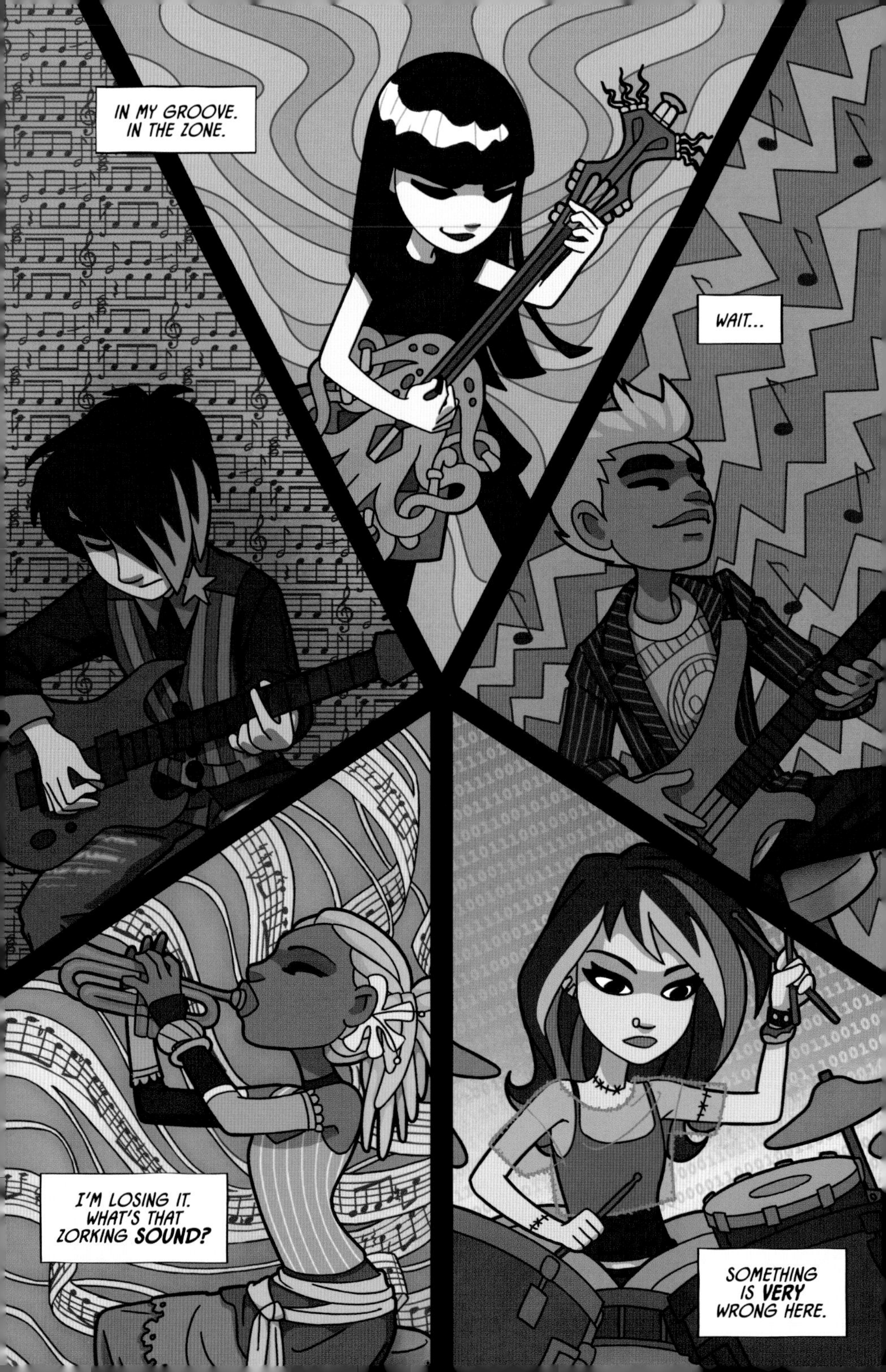
IN MY GROOVE. IN THE ZONE.
WAIT...
I'M LOSING IT. WHAT'S THAT ZORKING **SOUND?**
SOMETHING IS **VERY** WRONG HERE.

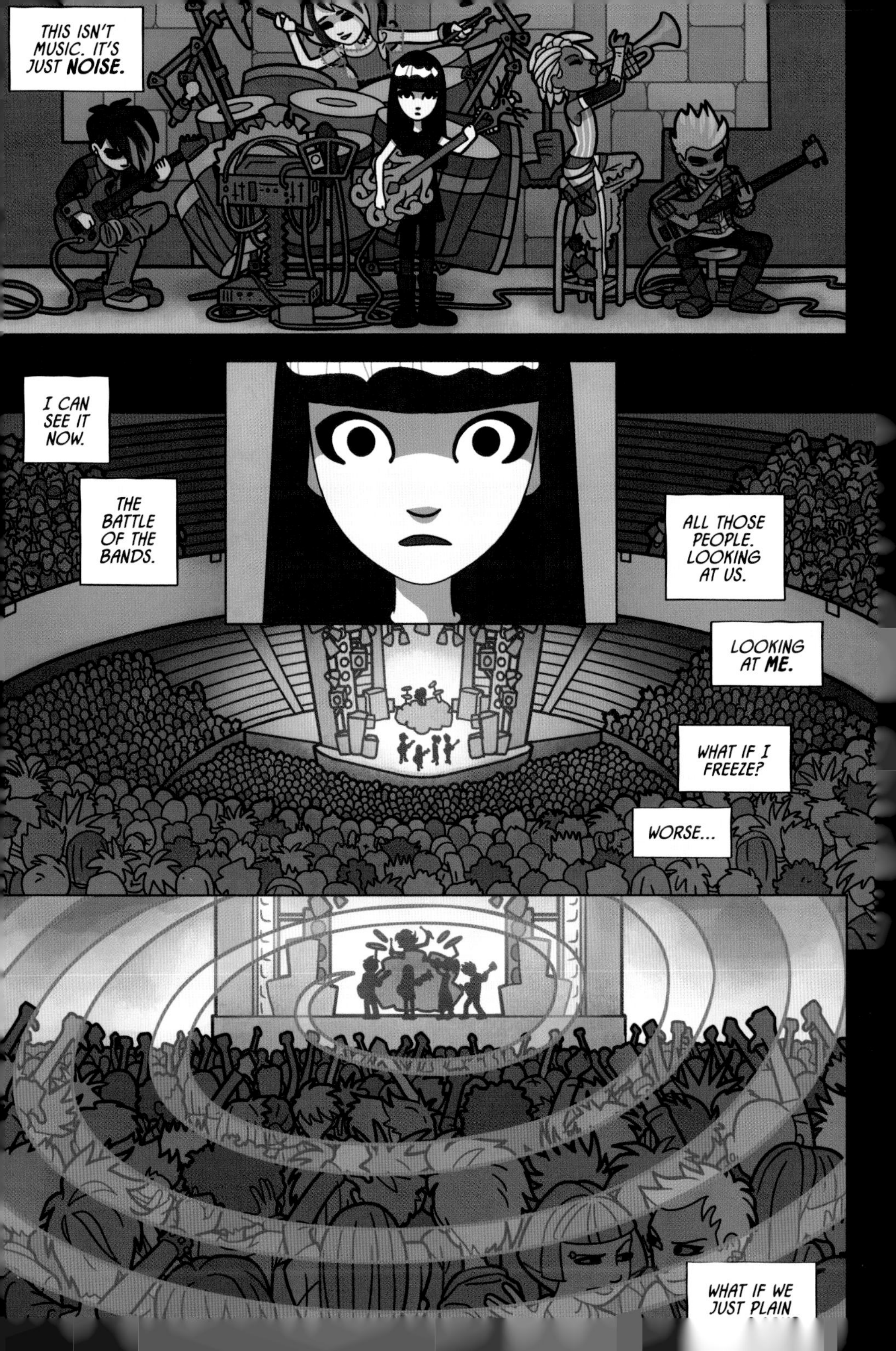
THIS ISN'T MUSIC. IT'S JUST NOISE.
I CAN SEE IT NOW.
THE BATTLE OF THE BANDS.
ALL THOSE PEOPLE. LOOKING AT US.
LOOKING AT ME.
WHAT IF I FREEZE?
WORSE...
WHAT IF WE JUST PLAIN

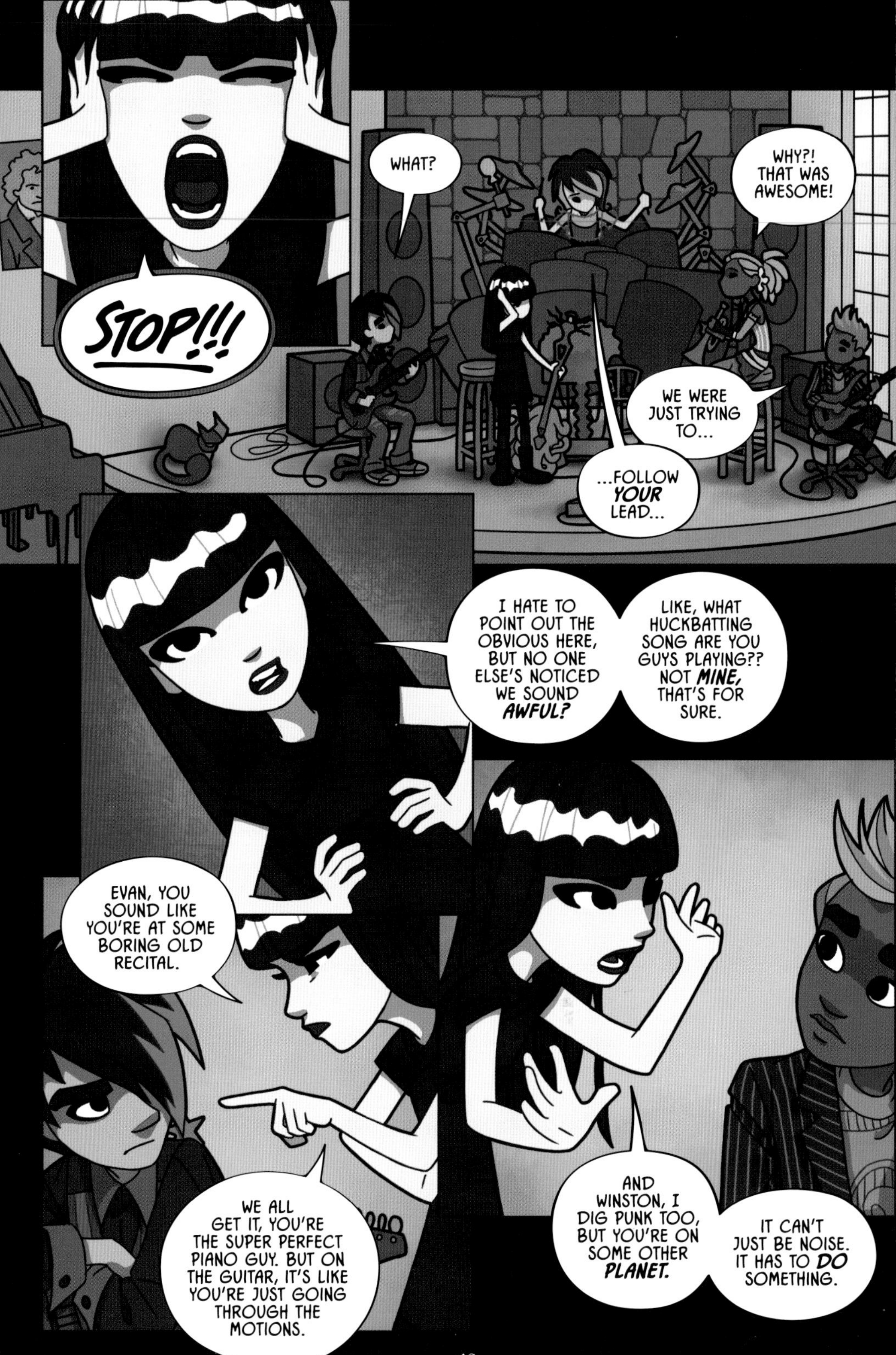
STOP!!!
WHAT?
WHY?! THAT WAS AWESOME!
WE WERE JUST TRYING TO...
...FOLLOW YOUR LEAD...
I HATE TO POINT OUT THE OBVIOUS HERE, BUT NO ONE ELSE'S NOTICED WE SOUND AWFUL?
LIKE, WHAT HUCKBATTING SONG ARE YOU GUYS PLAYING?? NOT MINE, THAT'S FOR SURE.
EVAN, YOU SOUND LIKE YOU'RE AT SOME BORING OLD RECITAL.
WE ALL GET IT, YOU'RE THE SUPER PERFECT PIANO GUY. BUT ON THE GUITAR, IT'S LIKE YOU'RE JUST GOING THROUGH THE MOTIONS.
AND WINSTON, I DIG PUNK TOO, BUT YOU'RE ON SOME OTHER PLANET.
IT CAN'T JUST BE NOISE. IT HAS TO DO SOMETHING.

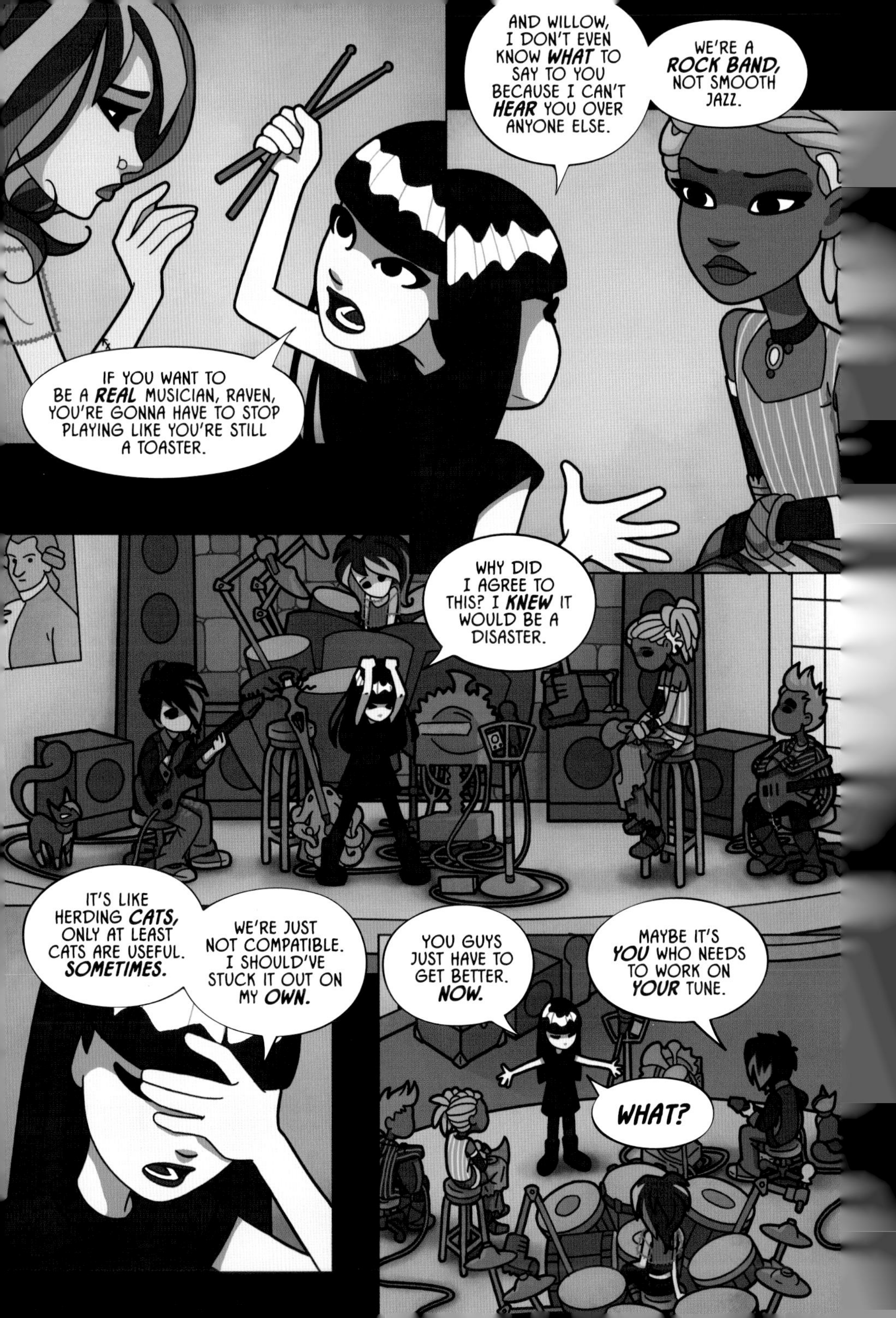
IF YOU WANT TO BE A REAL MUSICIAN, RAVEN, YOU'RE GONNA HAVE TO STOP PLAYING LIKE YOU'RE STILL A TOASTER.
AND WILLOW, I DON'T EVEN KNOW WHAT TO SAY TO YOU BECAUSE I CAN'T HEAR YOU OVER ANYONE ELSE.
WE'RE A ROCK BAND, NOT SMOOTH JAZZ.
WHY DID I AGREE TO THIS? I KNEW IT WOULD BE A DISASTER.
IT'S LIKE HERDING CATS, ONLY AT LEAST CATS ARE USEFUL. SOMETIMES.
WE'RE JUST NOT COMPATIBLE. I SHOULD'VE STUCK IT OUT ON MY OWN.
YOU GUYS JUST HAVE TO GET BETTER. NOW.
MAYBE IT'S YOU WHO NEEDS TO WORK ON YOUR TUNE.
WHAT?

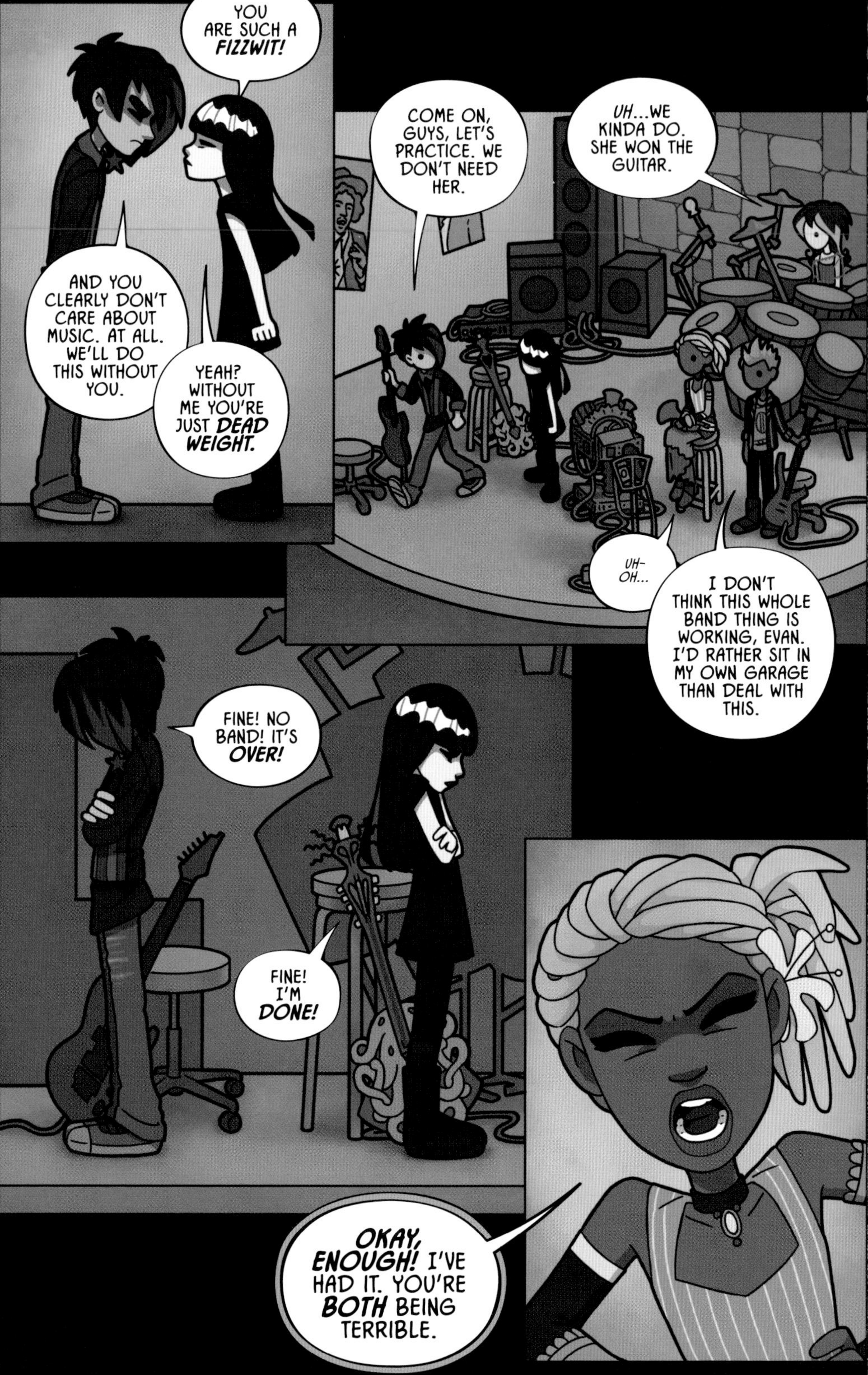
YOU ARE SUCH A FIZZWIT!
AND YOU CLEARLY DON'T CARE ABOUT MUSIC. AT ALL. WE'LL DO THIS WITHOUT YOU.
YEAH? WITHOUT ME YOU'RE JUST DEAD WEIGHT.
COME ON, GUYS, LET'S PRACTICE. WE DON'T NEED HER.
UH...WE KINDA DO. SHE WON THE GUITAR.
UH-OH...
I DON'T THINK THIS WHOLE BAND THING IS WORKING, EVAN. I'D RATHER SIT IN MY OWN GARAGE THAN DEAL WITH THIS.
FINE! NO BAND! IT'S OVER!
FINE! I'M DONE!
OKAY, ENOUGH! I'VE HAD IT. YOU'RE BOTH BEING TERRIBLE.

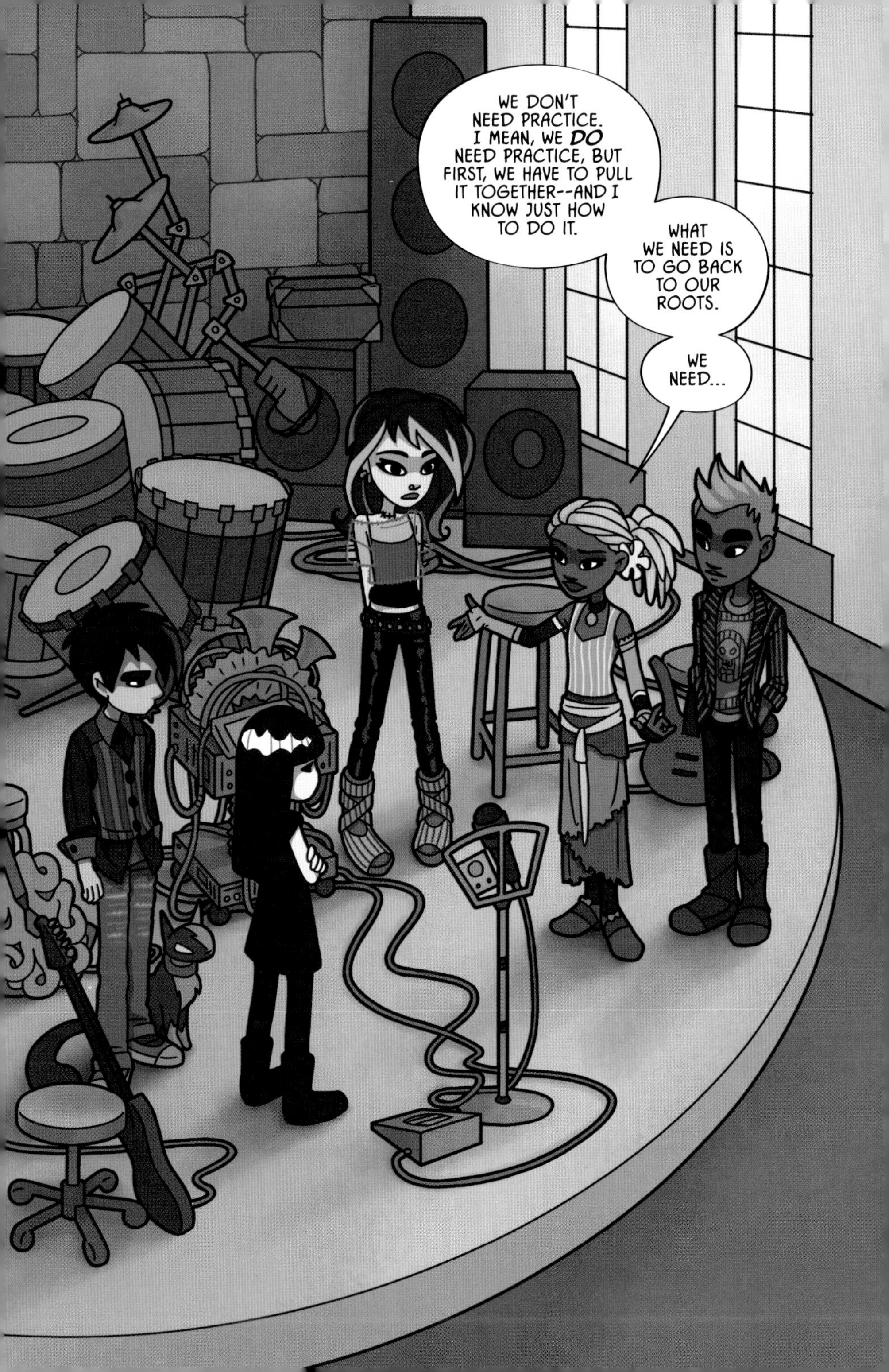
WE DON'T NEED PRACTICE. I MEAN, WE *DO* NEED PRACTICE, BUT FIRST, WE HAVE TO PULL IT TOGETHER--AND I KNOW JUST HOW TO DO IT.
WHAT WE NEED IS TO GO BACK TO OUR ROOTS.
WE NEED...

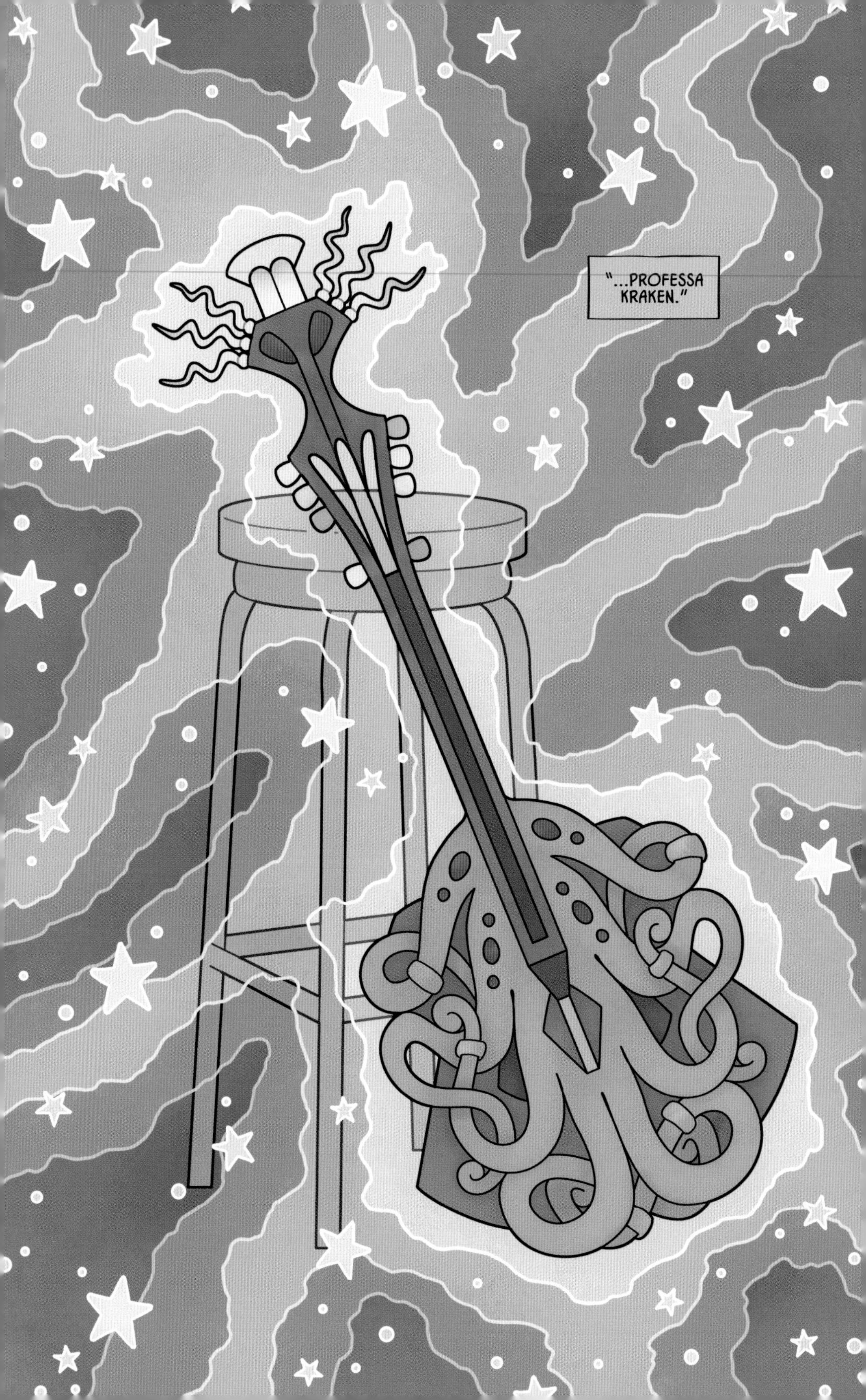
"...PROFESSA KRAKEN."

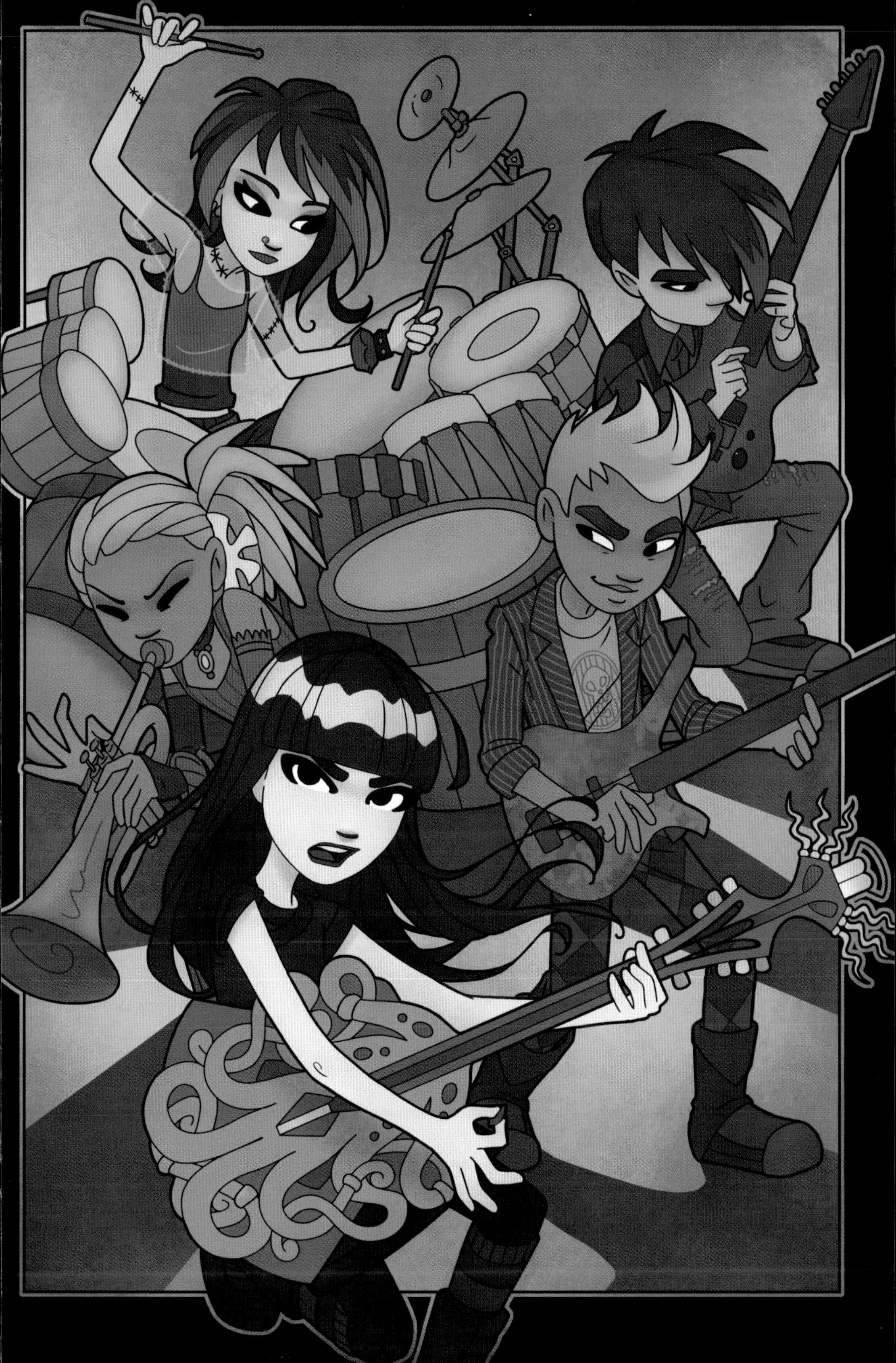

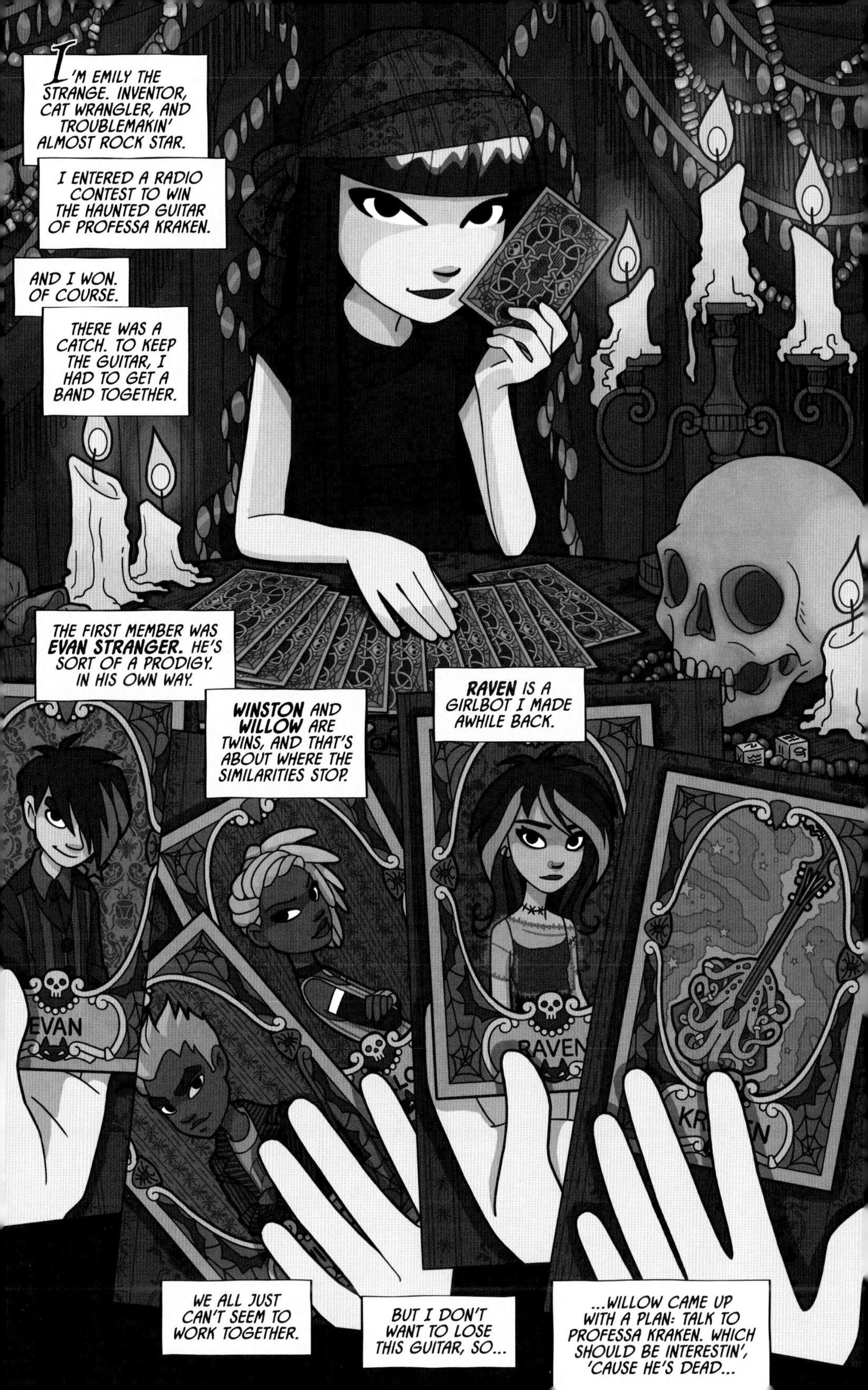
I'M EMILY THE STRANGE. INVENTOR, CAT WRANGLER, AND TROUBLEMAKIN' ALMOST ROCK STAR.
I ENTERED A RADIO CONTEST TO WIN THE HAUNTED GUITAR OF PROFESSA KRAKEN.
AND I WON. OF COURSE.
THERE WAS A CATCH. TO KEEP THE GUITAR, I HAD TO GET A BAND TOGETHER.
THE FIRST MEMBER WAS EVAN STRANGER. HE'S SORT OF A PRODIGY. IN HIS OWN WAY.
WINSTON AND WILLOW ARE TWINS, AND THAT'S ABOUT WHERE THE SIMILARITIES STOP.
RAVEN IS A GIRLBOT I MADE AWHILE BACK.
EVAN
RAVEN
WE ALL JUST CAN'T SEEM TO WORK TOGETHER.
BUT I DON'T WANT TO LOSE THIS GUITAR, SO...
...WILLOW CAME UP WITH A PLAN: TALK TO PROFESSA KRAKEN. WHICH SHOULD BE INTERESTIN', 'CAUSE HE'S DEAD...

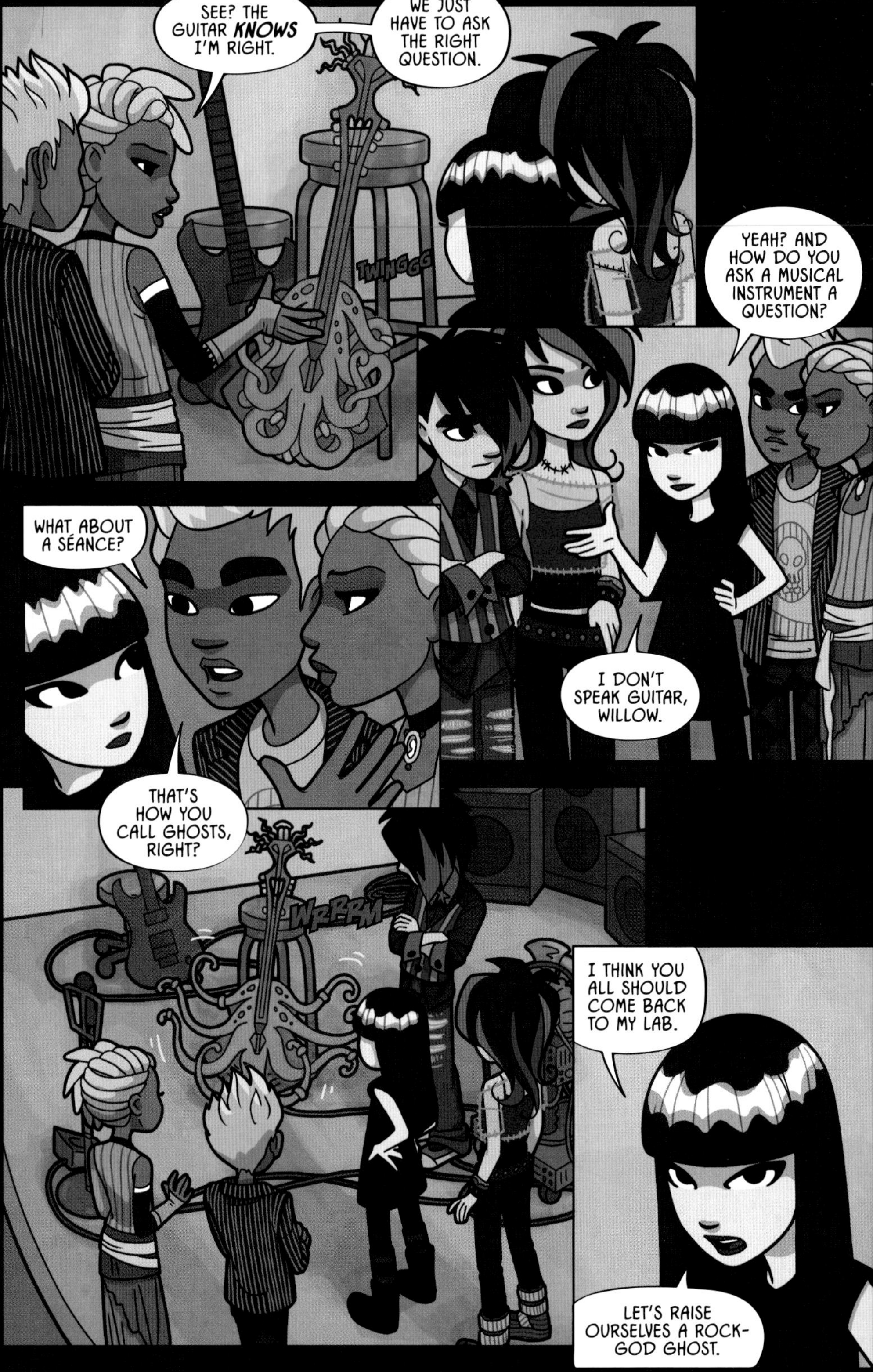
SEE? THE GUITAR KNOWS I'M RIGHT.
WE JUST HAVE TO ASK THE RIGHT QUESTION.
TWINGGG
YEAH? AND HOW DO YOU ASK A MUSICAL INSTRUMENT A QUESTION?
I DON'T SPEAK GUITAR, WILLOW.
WHAT ABOUT A SÉANCE?
THAT'S HOW YOU CALL GHOSTS, RIGHT?
WRRRM
I THINK YOU ALL SHOULD COME BACK TO MY LAB.
LET'S RAISE OURSELVES A ROCK-GOD GHOST.

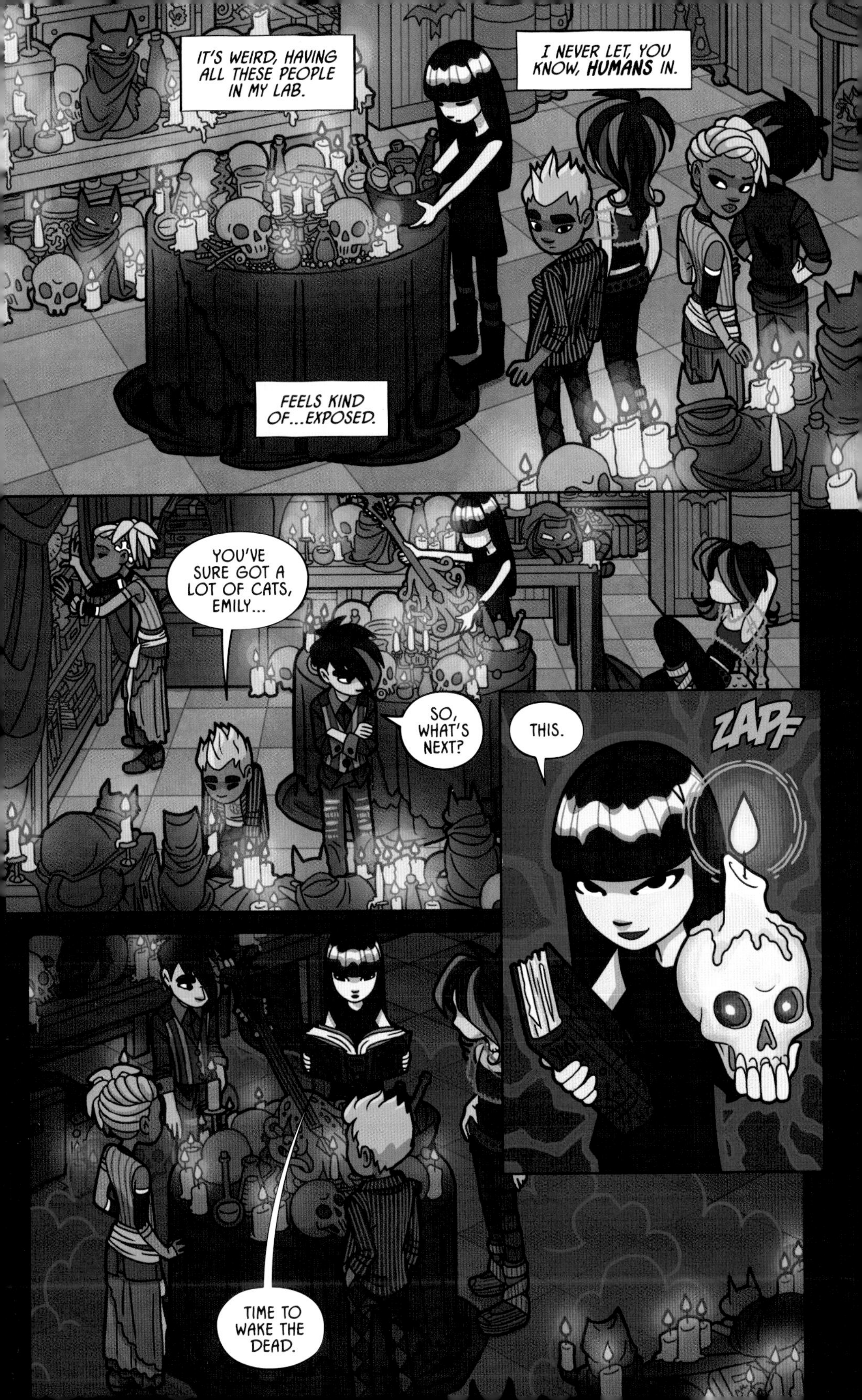
IT'S WEIRD, HAVING ALL THESE PEOPLE IN MY LAB.
I NEVER LET, YOU KNOW, **HUMANS** IN.
FEELS KIND OF...EXPOSED.
YOU'VE SURE GOT A LOT OF CATS, EMILY...
SO, WHAT'S NEXT?
THIS.
ZAP
TIME TO WAKE THE DEAD.

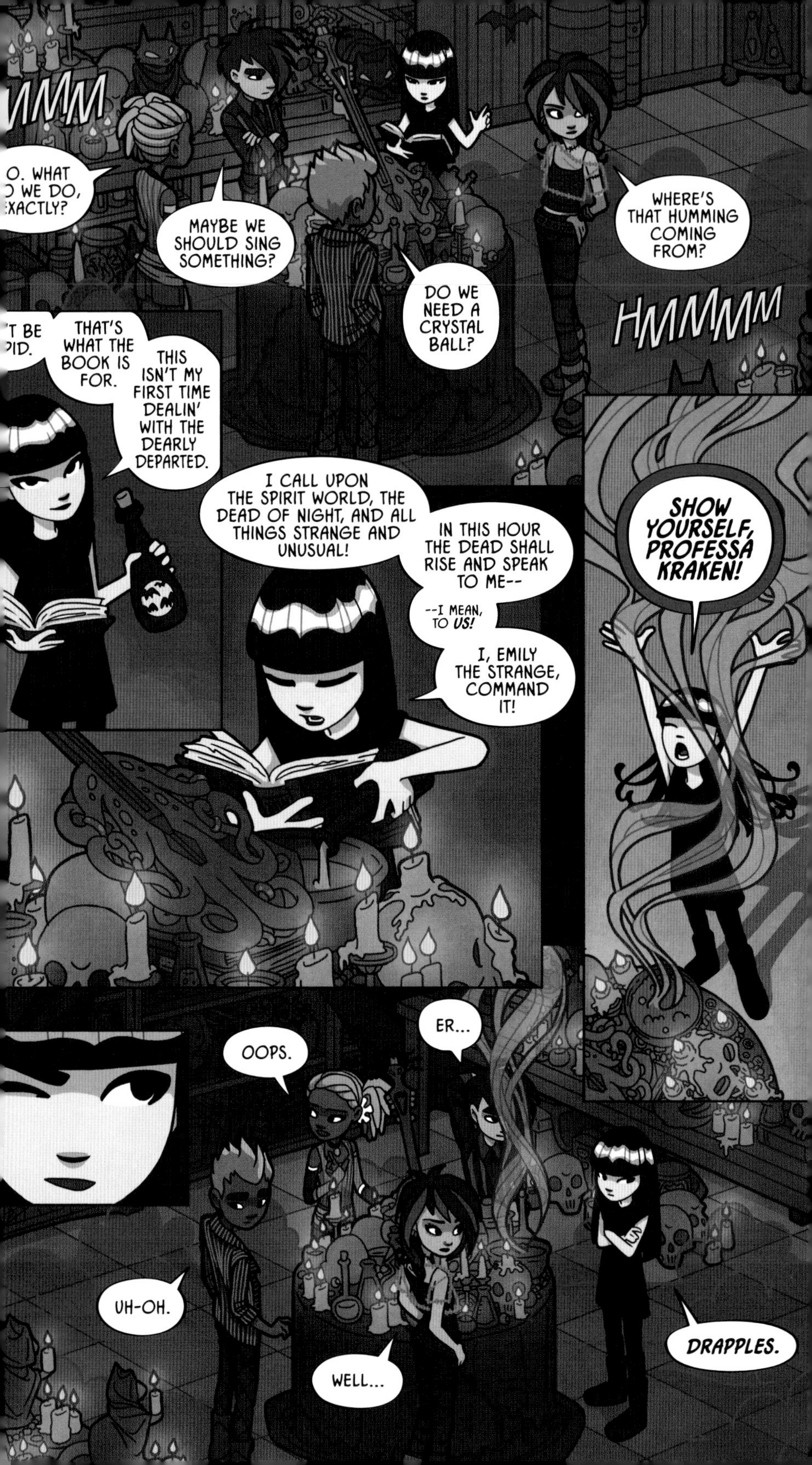
MMM
O. WHAT
D WE DO,
EXACTLY?
MAYBE WE SHOULD SING SOMETHING?
DO WE NEED A CRYSTAL BALL?
WHERE'S THAT HUMMING COMING FROM?
HMMMM
'T BE
PID.
THAT'S WHAT THE BOOK IS FOR.
THIS ISN'T MY FIRST TIME DEALIN' WITH THE DEARLY DEPARTED.
I CALL UPON THE SPIRIT WORLD, THE DEAD OF NIGHT, AND ALL THINGS STRANGE AND UNUSUAL!
IN THIS HOUR THE DEAD SHALL RISE AND SPEAK TO ME--
--I MEAN, TO *US!*
I, EMILY THE STRANGE, COMMAND IT!
SHOW YOURSELF, PROFESSA KRAKEN!
OOPS.
ER...
UH-OH.
WELL...
DRAPPLES.

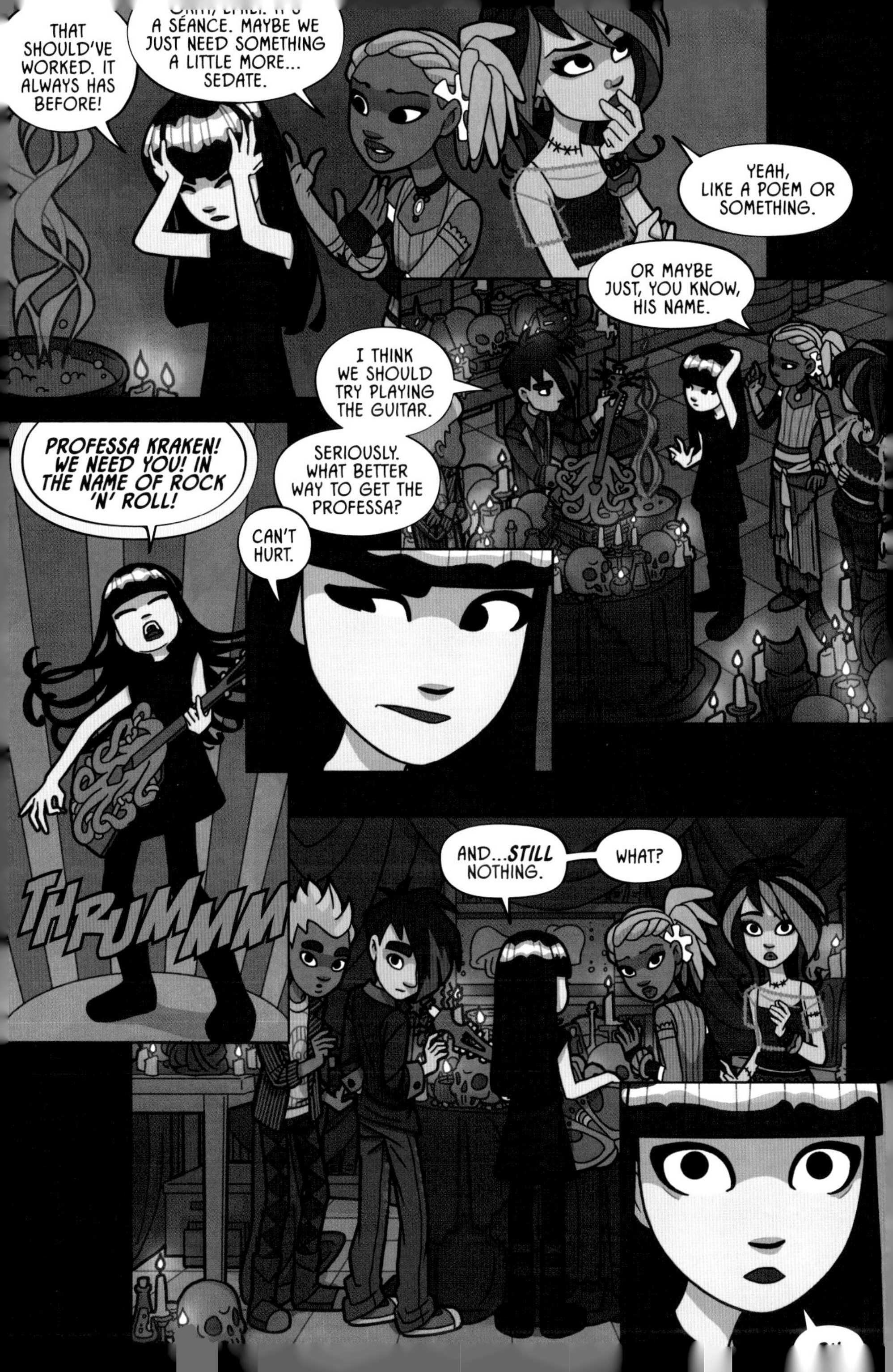
THAT SHOULD'VE WORKED. IT ALWAYS HAS BEFORE!
A SÉANCE. MAYBE WE JUST NEED SOMETHING A LITTLE MORE... SEDATE.
YEAH, LIKE A POEM OR SOMETHING.
OR MAYBE JUST, YOU KNOW, HIS NAME.
I THINK WE SHOULD TRY PLAYING THE GUITAR.
SERIOUSLY. WHAT BETTER WAY TO GET THE PROFESSA?
CAN'T HURT.
PROFESSA KRAKEN! WE NEED YOU! IN THE NAME OF ROCK 'N' ROLL!
THRUMMMM
AND...***STILL*** NOTHING.
WHAT?

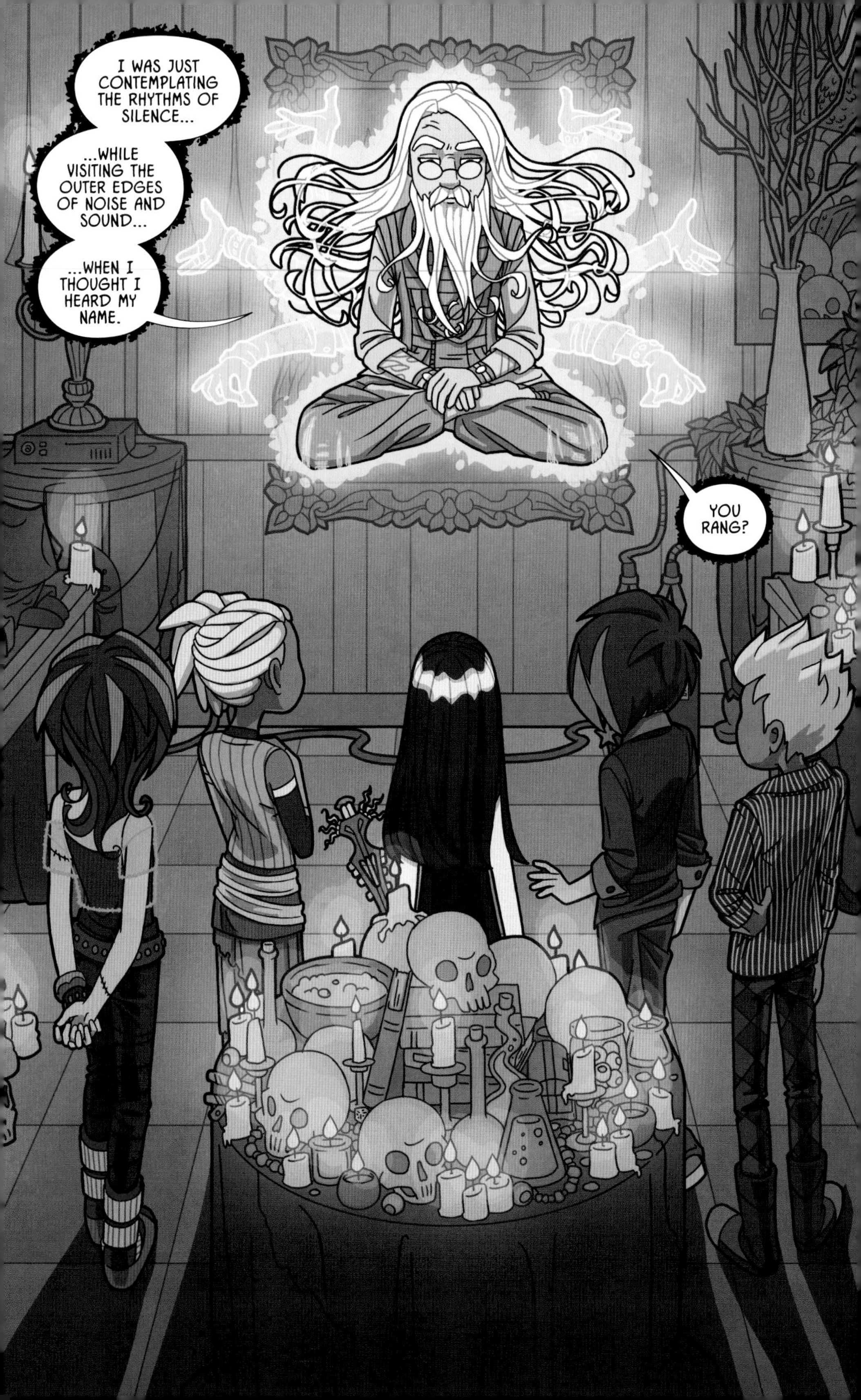
I WAS JUST CONTEMPLATING THE RHYTHMS OF SILENCE...
...WHILE VISITING THE OUTER EDGES OF NOISE AND SOUND...
...WHEN I THOUGHT I HEARD MY NAME.
YOU RANG?

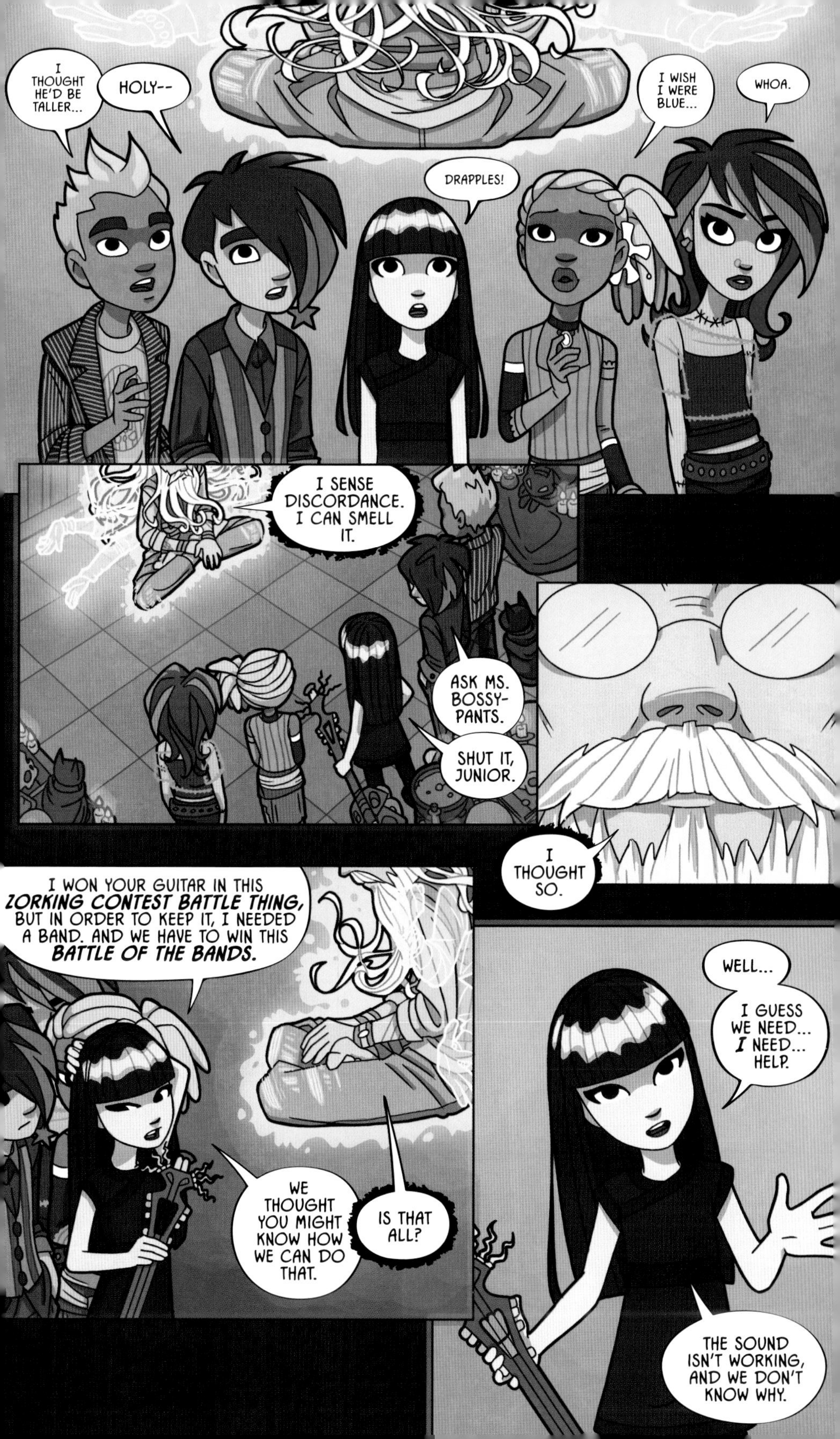

I THOUGHT HE'D BE TALLER...
HOLY--
DRAPPLES!
I WISH I WERE BLUE...
WHOA.
I SENSE DISCORDANCE. I CAN SMELL IT.
ASK MS. BOSSY-PANTS.
SHUT IT, JUNIOR.
I THOUGHT SO.
I WON YOUR GUITAR IN THIS ZORKING CONTEST BATTLE THING, BUT IN ORDER TO KEEP IT, I NEEDED A BAND. AND WE HAVE TO WIN THIS BATTLE OF THE BANDS.
WE THOUGHT YOU MIGHT KNOW HOW WE CAN DO THAT.
IS THAT ALL?
WELL...
I GUESS WE NEED... I NEED... HELP.
THE SOUND ISN'T WORKING, AND WE DON'T KNOW WHY.

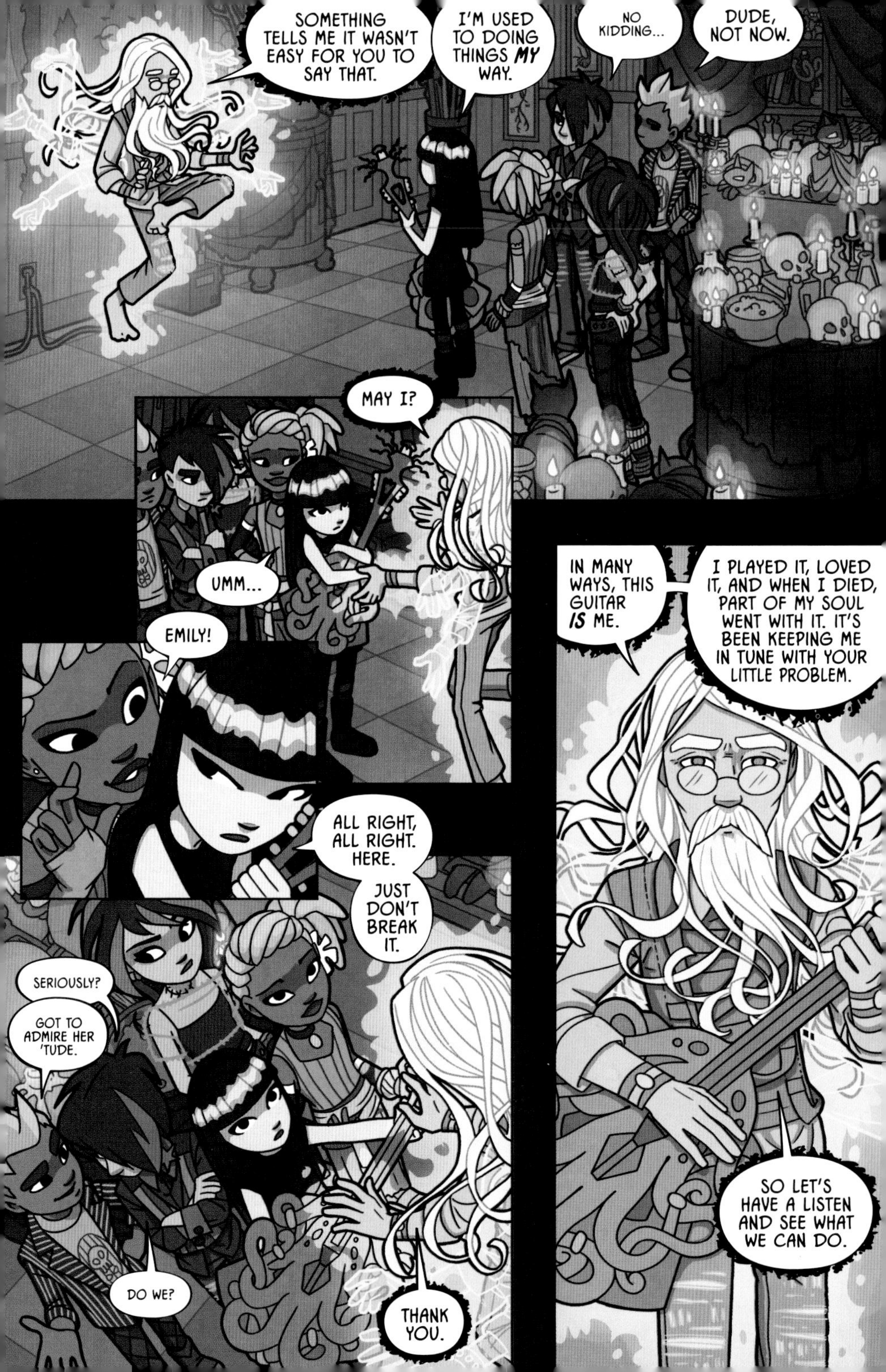

SOMETHING TELLS ME IT WASN'T EASY FOR YOU TO SAY THAT.
I'M USED TO DOING THINGS MY WAY.
NO KIDDING...
DUDE, NOT NOW.
MAY I?
UMM...
EMILY!
ALL RIGHT, ALL RIGHT. HERE.
JUST DON'T BREAK IT.
SERIOUSLY?
GOT TO ADMIRE HER 'TUDE.
DO WE?
THANK YOU.
IN MANY WAYS, THIS GUITAR IS ME.
I PLAYED IT, LOVED IT, AND WHEN I DIED, PART OF MY SOUL WENT WITH IT. IT'S BEEN KEEPING ME IN TUNE WITH YOUR LITTLE PROBLEM.
SO LET'S HAVE A LISTEN AND SEE WHAT WE CAN DO.

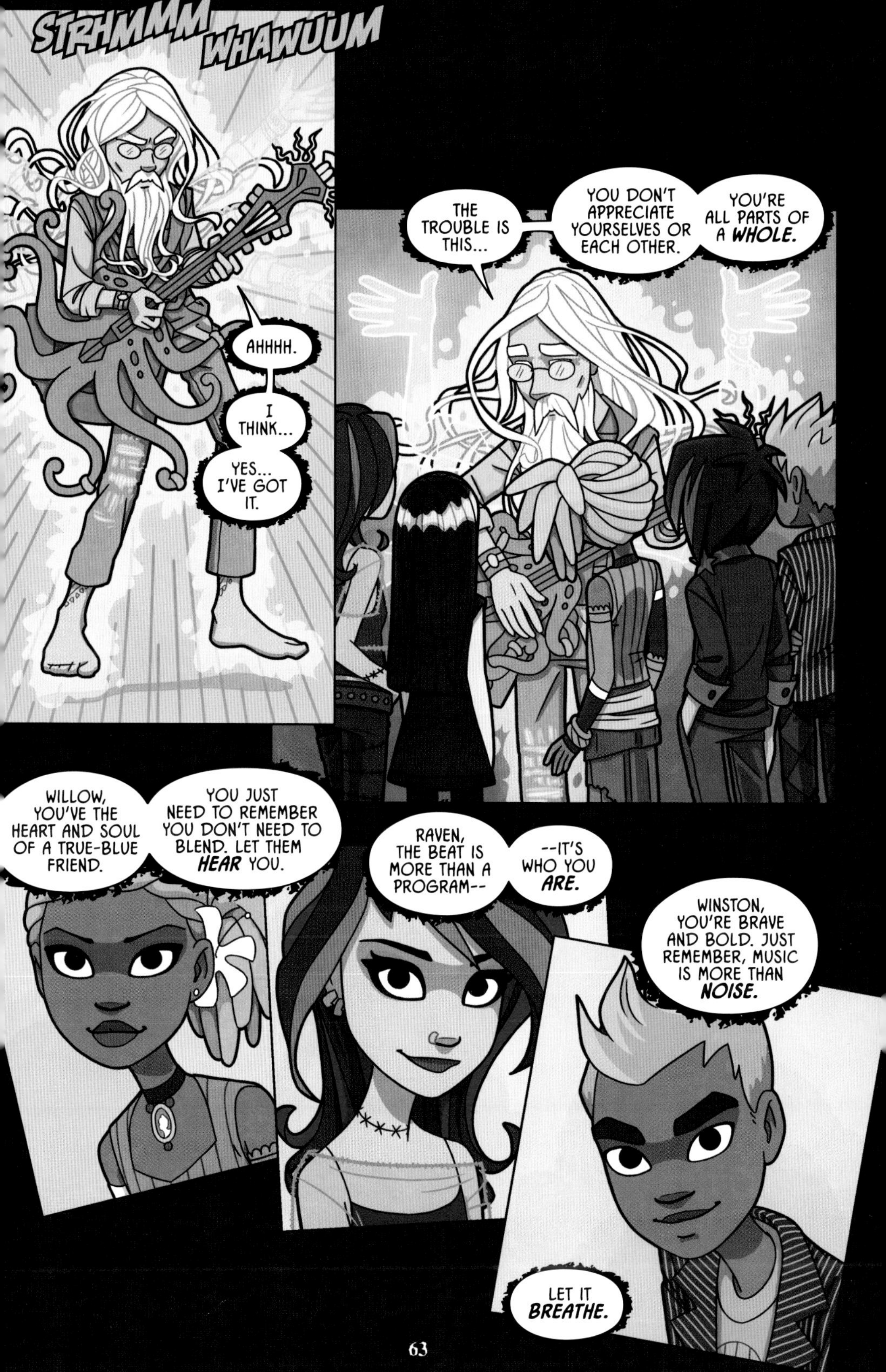
STRHMMM WHAWUUM
AHHHH.
I THINK...
YES... I'VE GOT IT.
THE TROUBLE IS THIS...
YOU DON'T APPRECIATE YOURSELVES OR EACH OTHER.
YOU'RE ALL PARTS OF A **WHOLE.**
WILLOW, YOU'VE THE HEART AND SOUL OF A TRUE-BLUE FRIEND.
YOU JUST NEED TO REMEMBER YOU DON'T NEED TO BLEND. LET THEM **HEAR** YOU.
RAVEN, THE BEAT IS MORE THAN A PROGRAM--
--IT'S WHO YOU **ARE.**
WINSTON, YOU'RE BRAVE AND BOLD. JUST REMEMBER, MUSIC IS MORE THAN **NOISE.**
LET IT **BREATHE.**

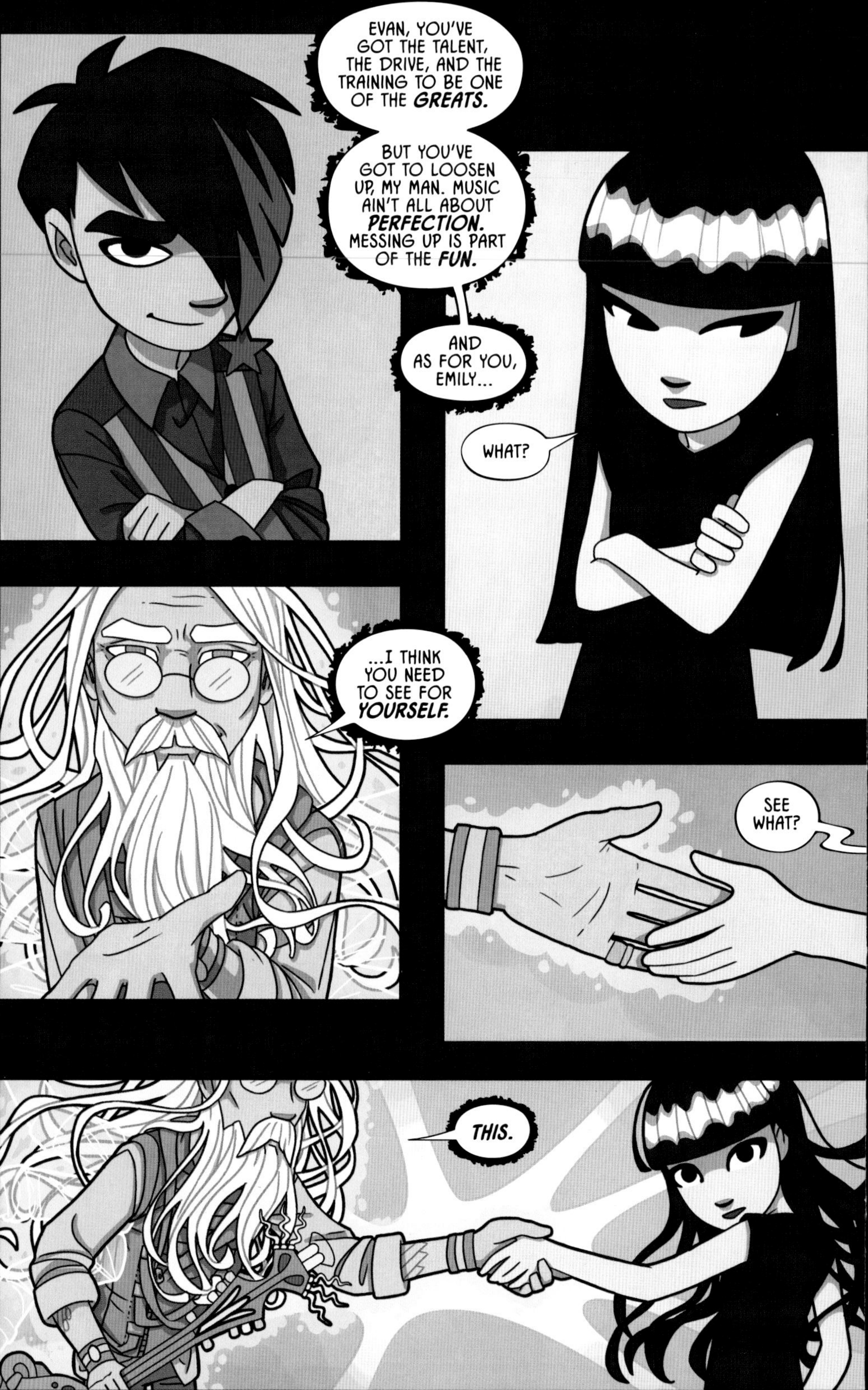
EVAN, YOU'VE GOT THE TALENT, THE DRIVE, AND THE TRAINING TO BE ONE OF THE *GREATS.*
BUT YOU'VE GOT TO LOOSEN UP, MY MAN. MUSIC AIN'T ALL ABOUT *PERFECTION.* MESSING UP IS PART OF THE *FUN.*
AND AS FOR YOU, EMILY...
WHAT?
...I THINK YOU NEED TO SEE FOR *YOURSELF.*
SEE WHAT?
THIS.

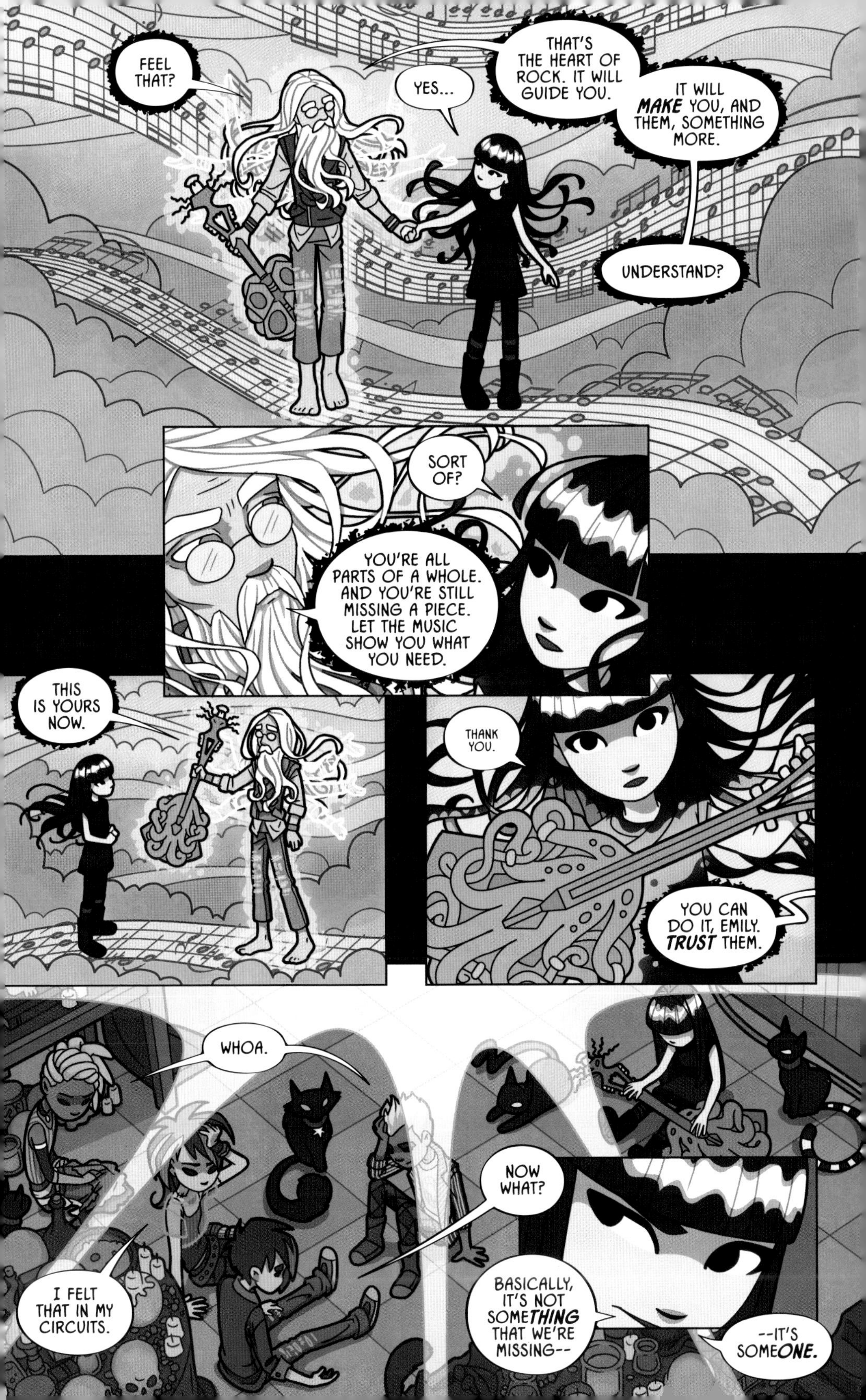
FEEL THAT?
YES...
THAT'S THE HEART OF ROCK. IT WILL GUIDE YOU.
IT WILL **MAKE** YOU, AND THEM, SOMETHING MORE.
UNDERSTAND?
SORT OF?
YOU'RE ALL PARTS OF A WHOLE. AND YOU'RE STILL MISSING A PIECE. LET THE MUSIC SHOW YOU WHAT YOU NEED.
THIS IS YOURS NOW.
THANK YOU.
YOU CAN DO IT, EMILY. ***TRUST*** THEM.
WHOA.
I FELT THAT IN MY CIRCUITS.
NOW WHAT?
BASICALLY, IT'S NOT SOME***THING*** THAT WE'RE MISSING--
--IT'S SOME***ONE***.

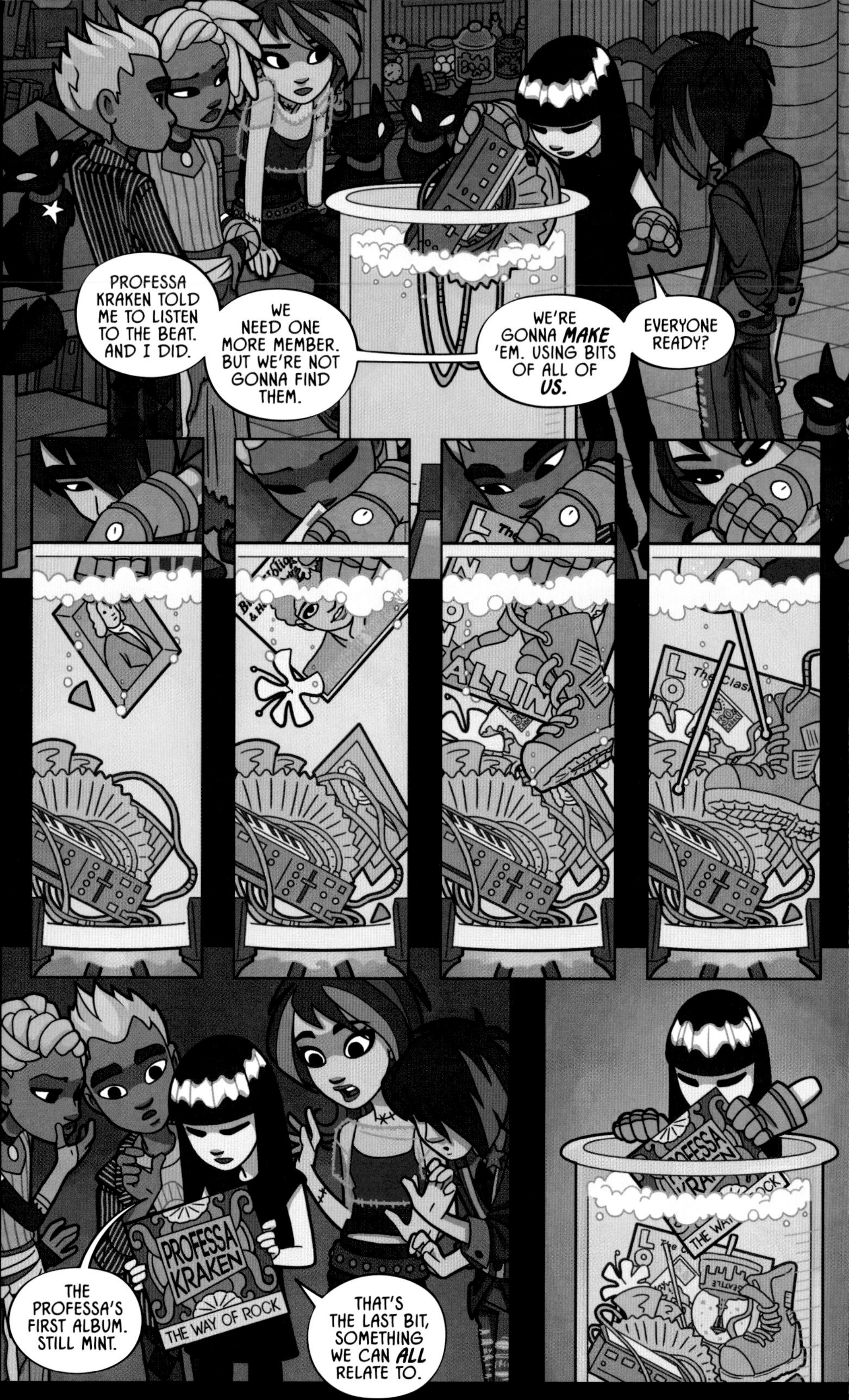
PROFESSA KRAKEN TOLD ME TO LISTEN TO THE BEAT. AND I DID.
WE NEED ONE MORE MEMBER. BUT WE'RE NOT GONNA FIND THEM.
WE'RE GONNA MAKE 'EM. USING BITS OF ALL OF US.
EVERYONE READY?
PROFESSA KRAKEN
THE WAY OF ROCK
THE PROFESSA'S FIRST ALBUM. STILL MINT.
THAT'S THE LAST BIT, SOMETHING WE CAN ALL RELATE TO.

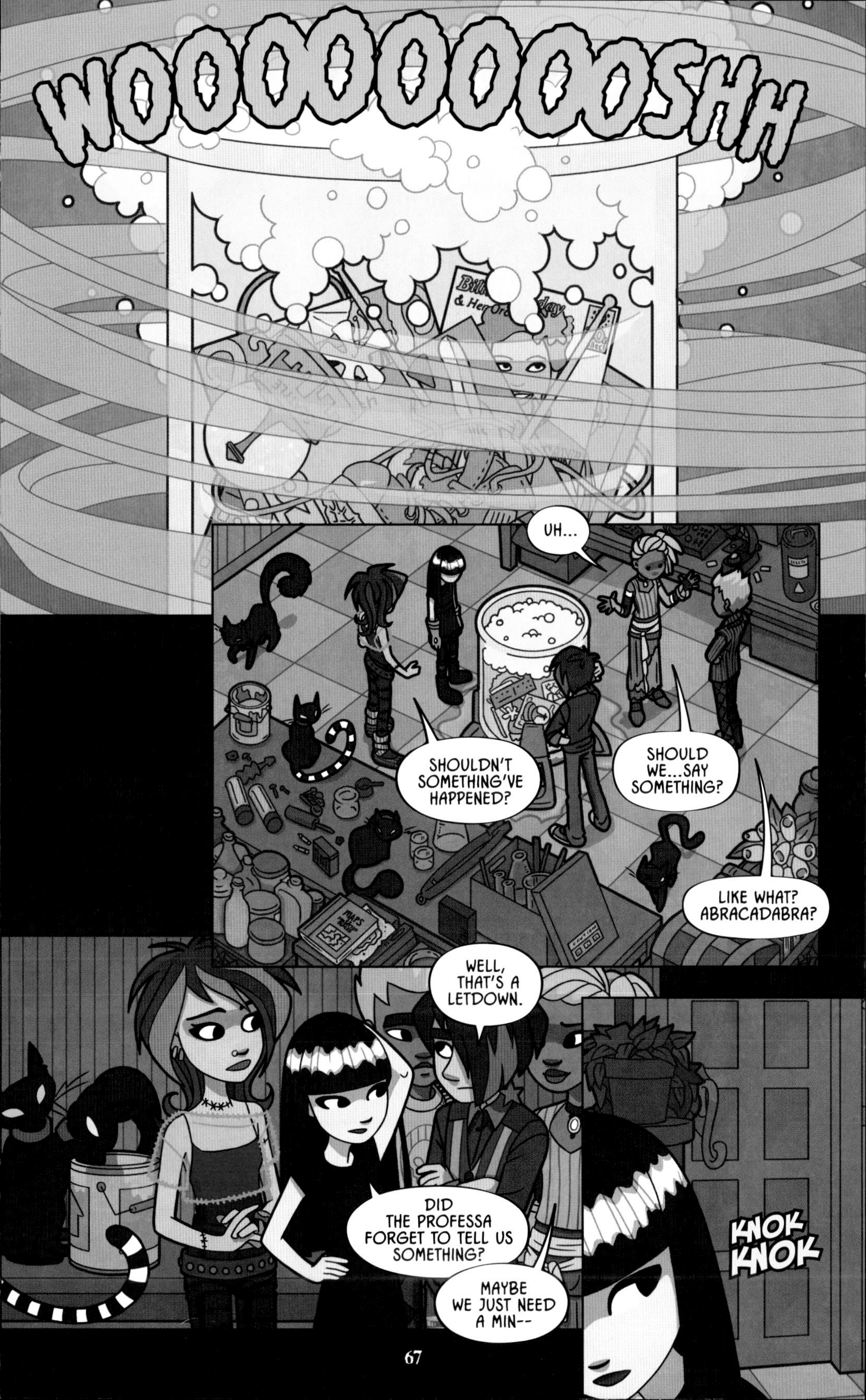
WOOOOOOOOSHH
UH...
SHOULDN'T SOMETHING'VE HAPPENED?
SHOULD WE...SAY SOMETHING?
LIKE WHAT? ABRACADABRA?
WELL, THAT'S A LETDOWN.
DID THE PROFESSA FORGET TO TELL US SOMETHING?
MAYBE WE JUST NEED A MIN--
KNOK KNOK

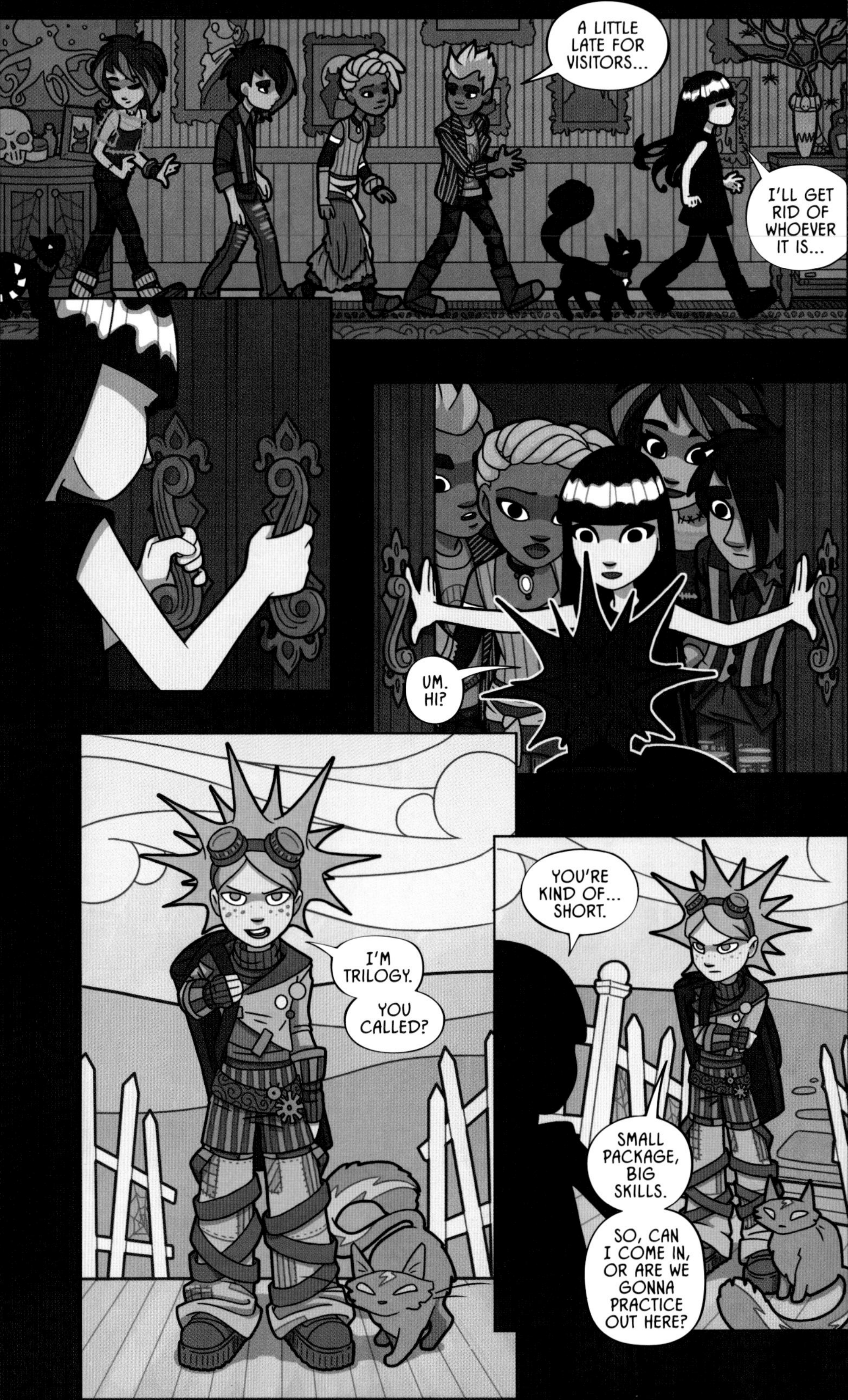
A LITTLE LATE FOR VISITORS...
I'LL GET RID OF WHOEVER IT IS...
UM. HI?
I'M TRILOGY.
YOU CALLED?
YOU'RE KIND OF... SHORT.
SMALL PACKAGE, BIG SKILLS.
SO, CAN I COME IN, OR ARE WE GONNA PRACTICE OUT HERE?

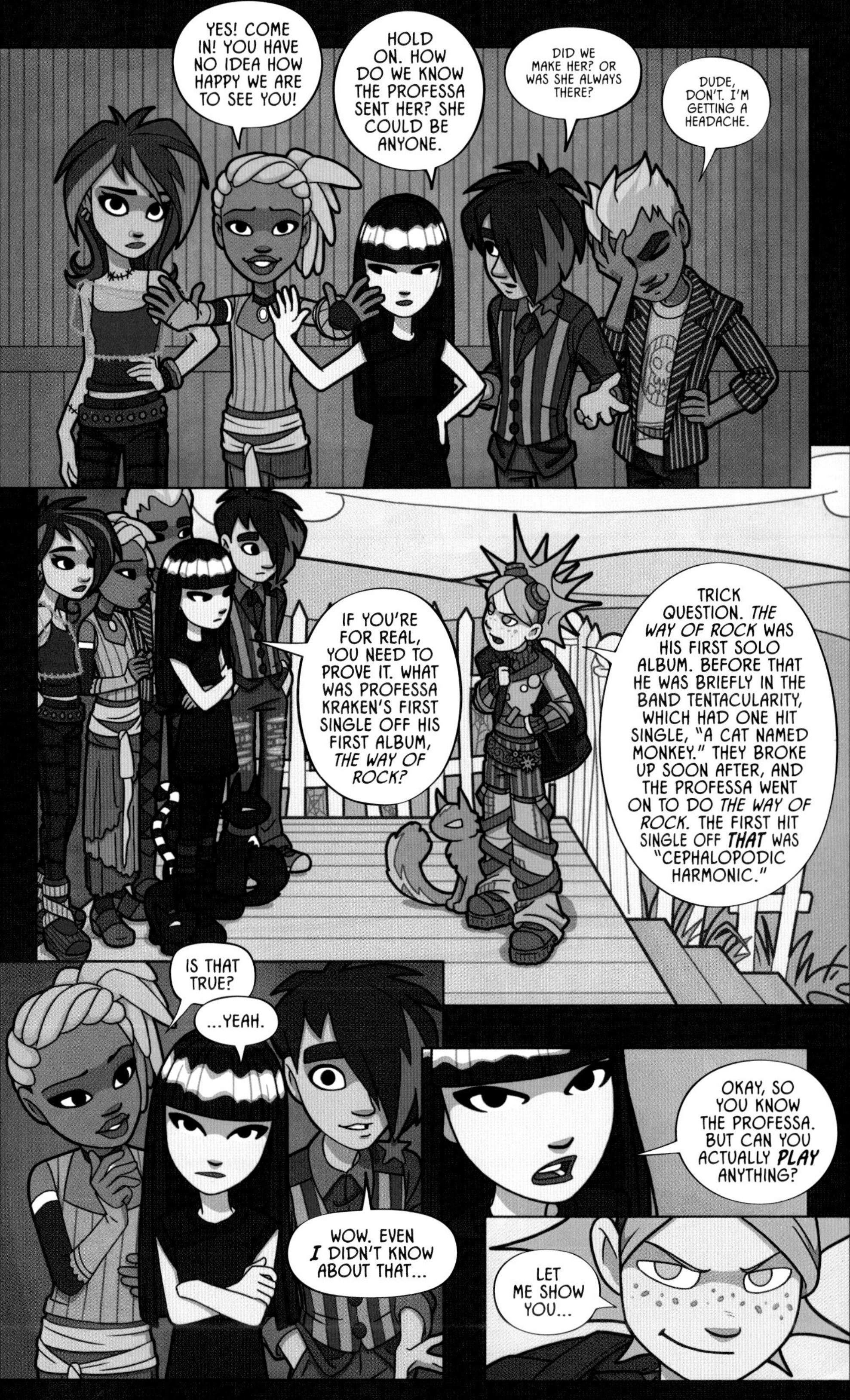
YES! COME IN! YOU HAVE NO IDEA HOW HAPPY WE ARE TO SEE YOU!
HOLD ON. HOW DO WE KNOW THE PROFESSA SENT HER? SHE COULD BE ANYONE.
DID WE MAKE HER? OR WAS SHE ALWAYS THERE?
DUDE, DON'T. I'M GETTING A HEADACHE.
IF YOU'RE FOR REAL, YOU NEED TO PROVE IT. WHAT WAS PROFESSA KRAKEN'S FIRST SINGLE OFF HIS FIRST ALBUM, *THE WAY OF ROCK*?
TRICK QUESTION. *THE WAY OF ROCK* WAS HIS FIRST SOLO ALBUM. BEFORE THAT HE WAS BRIEFLY IN THE BAND TENTACULARITY, WHICH HAD ONE HIT SINGLE, "A CAT NAMED MONKEY." THEY BROKE UP SOON AFTER, AND THE PROFESSA WENT ON TO DO *THE WAY OF ROCK*. THE FIRST HIT SINGLE OFF ***THAT*** WAS "CEPHALOPODIC HARMONIC."
IS THAT TRUE?
...YEAH.
WOW. EVEN ***I*** DIDN'T KNOW ABOUT THAT...
OKAY, SO YOU KNOW THE PROFESSA. BUT CAN YOU ACTUALLY ***PLAY*** ANYTHING?
LET ME SHOW YOU...

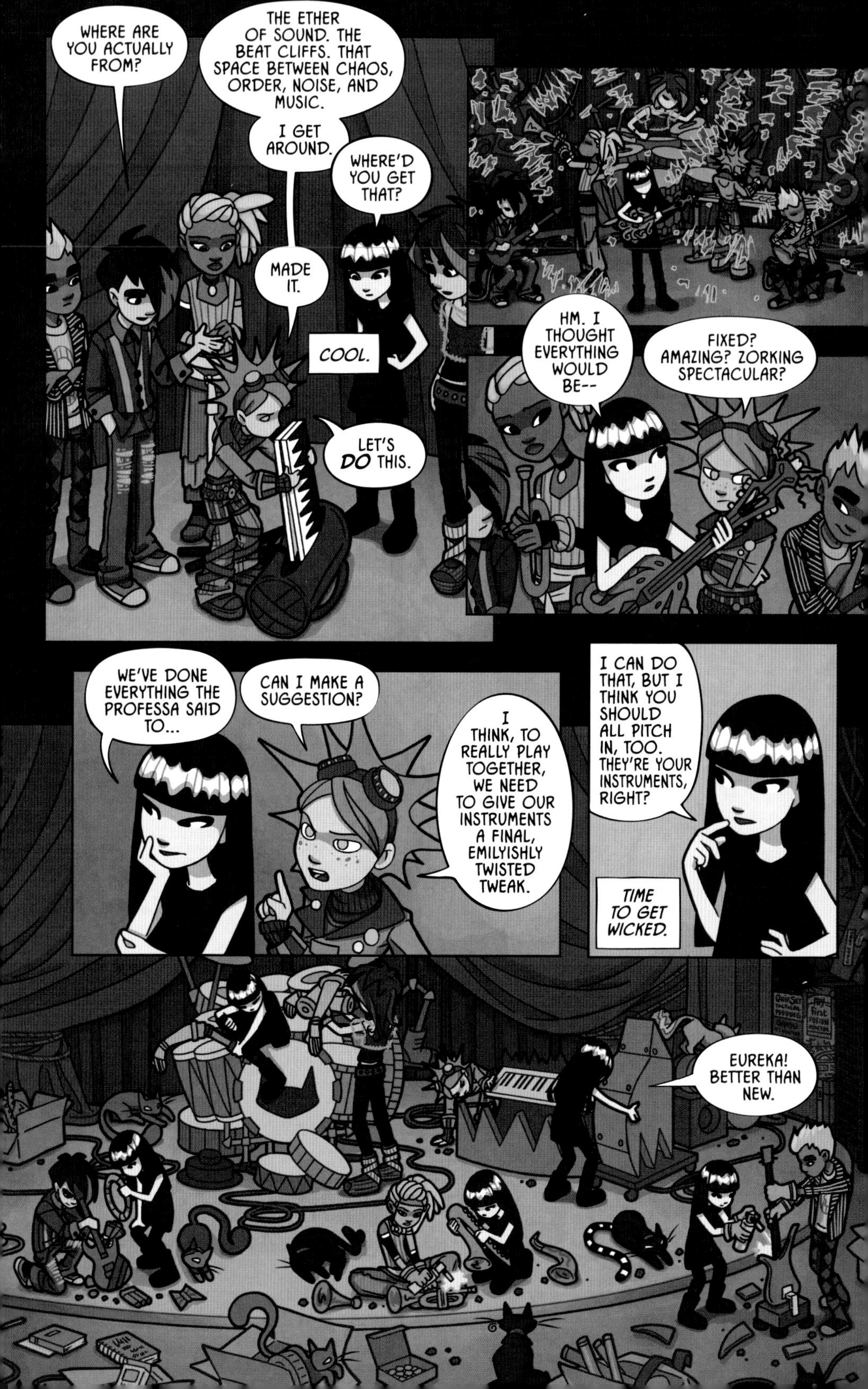
WHERE ARE YOU ACTUALLY FROM?
THE ETHER OF SOUND. THE BEAT CLIFFS. THAT SPACE BETWEEN CHAOS, ORDER, NOISE, AND MUSIC.
I GET AROUND.
WHERE'D YOU GET THAT?
MADE IT.
COOL.
LET'S DO THIS.
HM. I THOUGHT EVERYTHING WOULD BE--
FIXED? AMAZING? ZORKING SPECTACULAR?
WE'VE DONE EVERYTHING THE PROFESSA SAID TO...
CAN I MAKE A SUGGESTION?
I THINK, TO REALLY PLAY TOGETHER, WE NEED TO GIVE OUR INSTRUMENTS A FINAL, EMILYISHLY TWISTED TWEAK.
I CAN DO THAT, BUT I THINK YOU SHOULD ALL PITCH IN, TOO. THEY'RE YOUR INSTRUMENTS, RIGHT?
TIME TO GET WICKED.
EUREKA! BETTER THAN NEW.

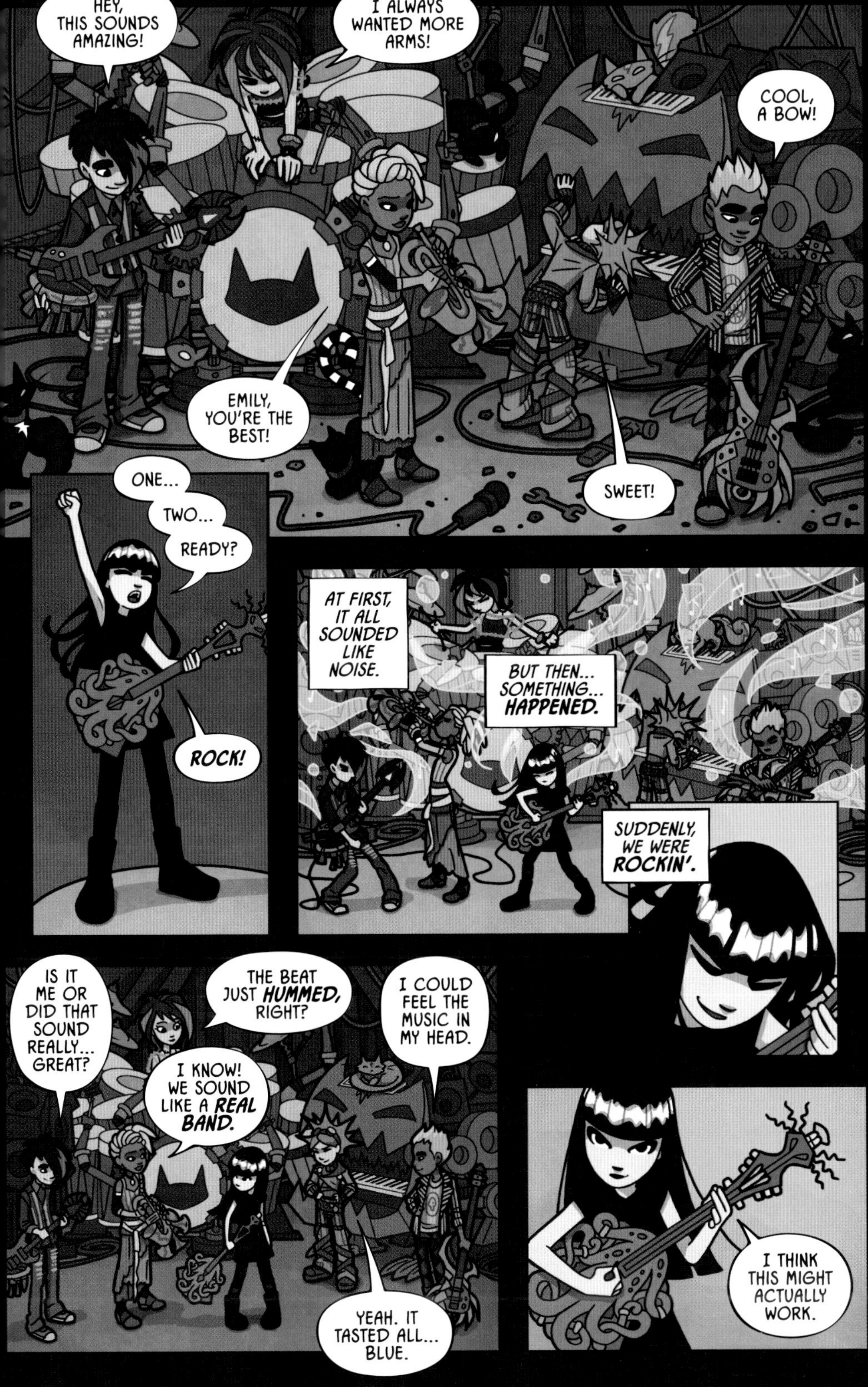
HEY, THIS SOUNDS AMAZING!
I ALWAYS WANTED MORE ARMS!
COOL, A BOW!
EMILY, YOU'RE THE BEST!
SWEET!
ONE...
TWO...
READY?
ROCK!
AT FIRST, IT ALL SOUNDED LIKE NOISE.
BUT THEN... SOMETHING... HAPPENED.
SUDDENLY, WE WERE ROCKIN'.
IS IT ME OR DID THAT SOUND REALLY... GREAT?
THE BEAT JUST HUMMED, RIGHT?
I COULD FEEL THE MUSIC IN MY HEAD.
I KNOW! WE SOUND LIKE A REAL BAND.
YEAH. IT TASTED ALL... BLUE.
I THINK THIS MIGHT ACTUALLY WORK.

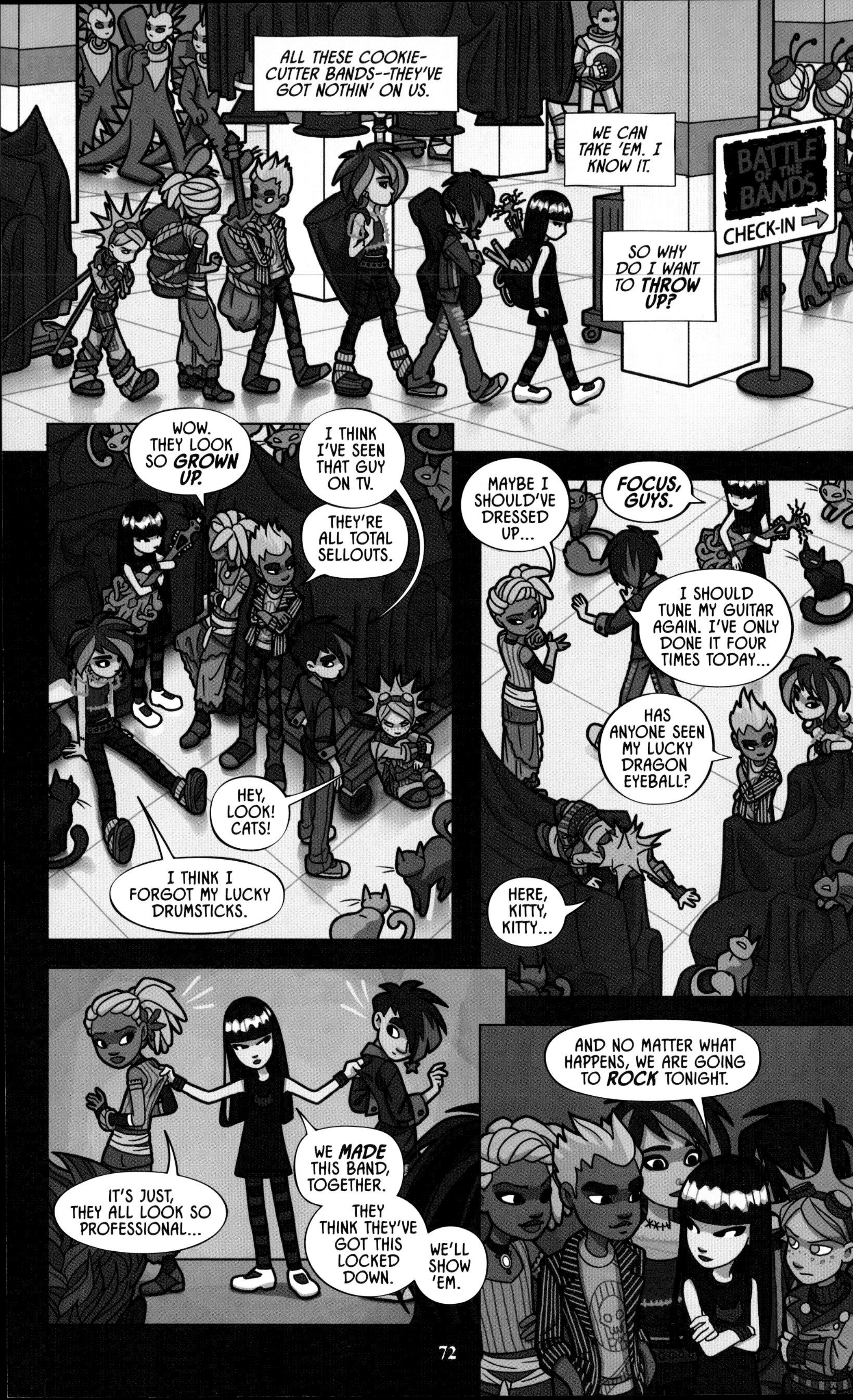

ALL THESE COOKIE-CUTTER BANDS--THEY'VE GOT NOTHIN' ON US.
WE CAN TAKE 'EM. I KNOW IT.
BATTLE OF THE BANDS
CHECK-IN
SO WHY DO I WANT TO THROW UP?
WOW. THEY LOOK SO GROWN UP.
I THINK I'VE SEEN THAT GUY ON TV.
THEY'RE ALL TOTAL SELLOUTS.
HEY, LOOK! CATS!
I THINK I FORGOT MY LUCKY DRUMSTICKS.
MAYBE I SHOULD'VE DRESSED UP...
FOCUS, GUYS.
I SHOULD TUNE MY GUITAR AGAIN. I'VE ONLY DONE IT FOUR TIMES TODAY...
HAS ANYONE SEEN MY LUCKY DRAGON EYEBALL?
HERE, KITTY, KITTY...
IT'S JUST, THEY ALL LOOK SO PROFESSIONAL...
WE MADE THIS BAND, TOGETHER.
THEY THINK THEY'VE GOT THIS LOCKED DOWN.
WE'LL SHOW 'EM.
AND NO MATTER WHAT HAPPENS, WE ARE GOING TO ROCK TONIGHT.

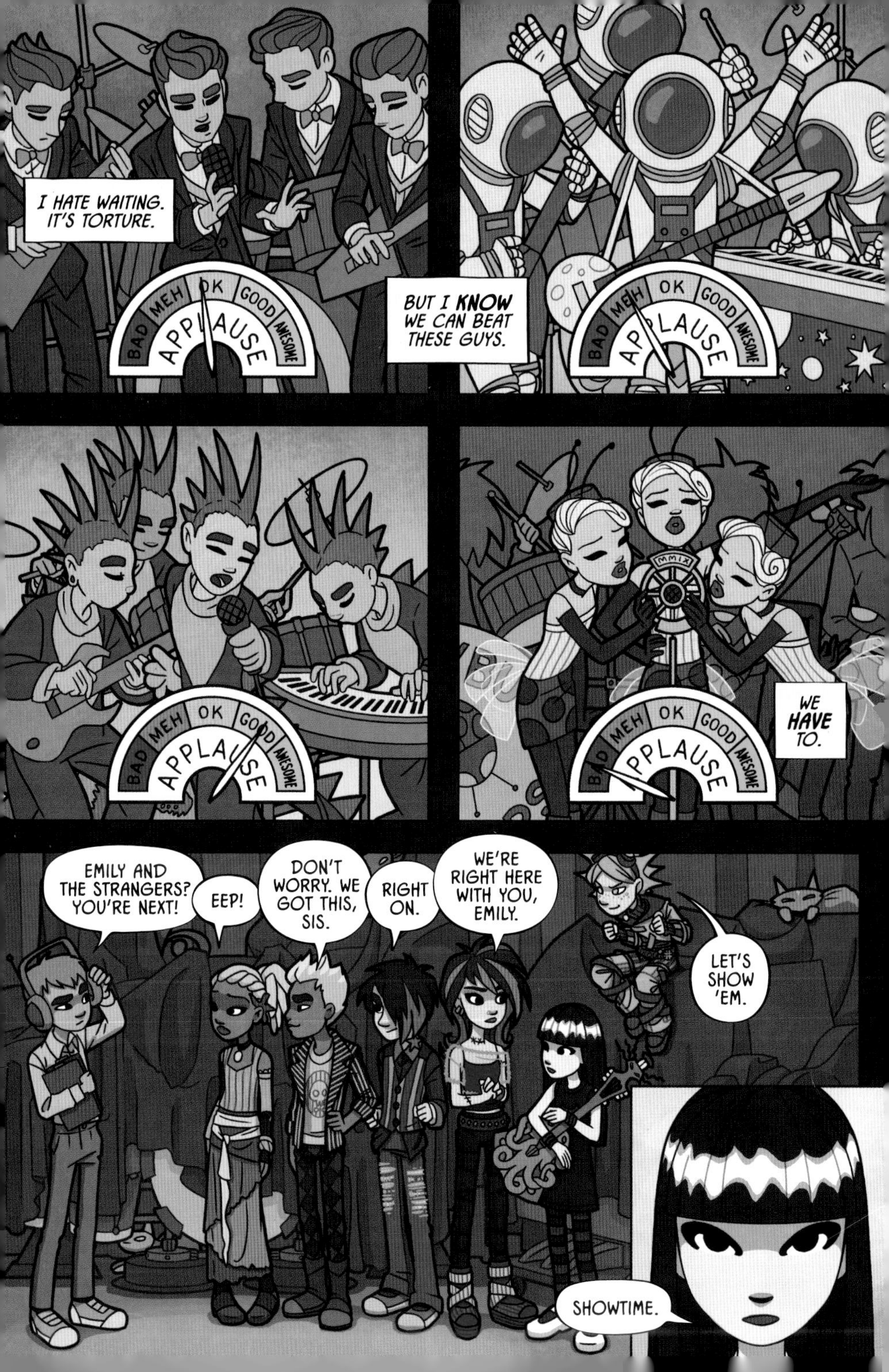
I HATE WAITING. IT'S TORTURE.
BAD MEH OK GOOD AWESOME
APPLAUSE
BUT I **KNOW** WE CAN BEAT THESE GUYS.
BAD MEH OK GOOD AWESOME
APPLAUSE
BAD MEH OK GOOD AWESOME
APPLAUSE
MMIX
BAD MEH OK GOOD AWESOME
APPLAUSE
WE **HAVE** TO.
EMILY AND THE STRANGERS? YOU'RE NEXT!
EEP!
DON'T WORRY. WE GOT THIS, SIS.
RIGHT ON.
WE'RE RIGHT HERE WITH YOU, EMILY.
LET'S SHOW 'EM.
SHOWTIME.

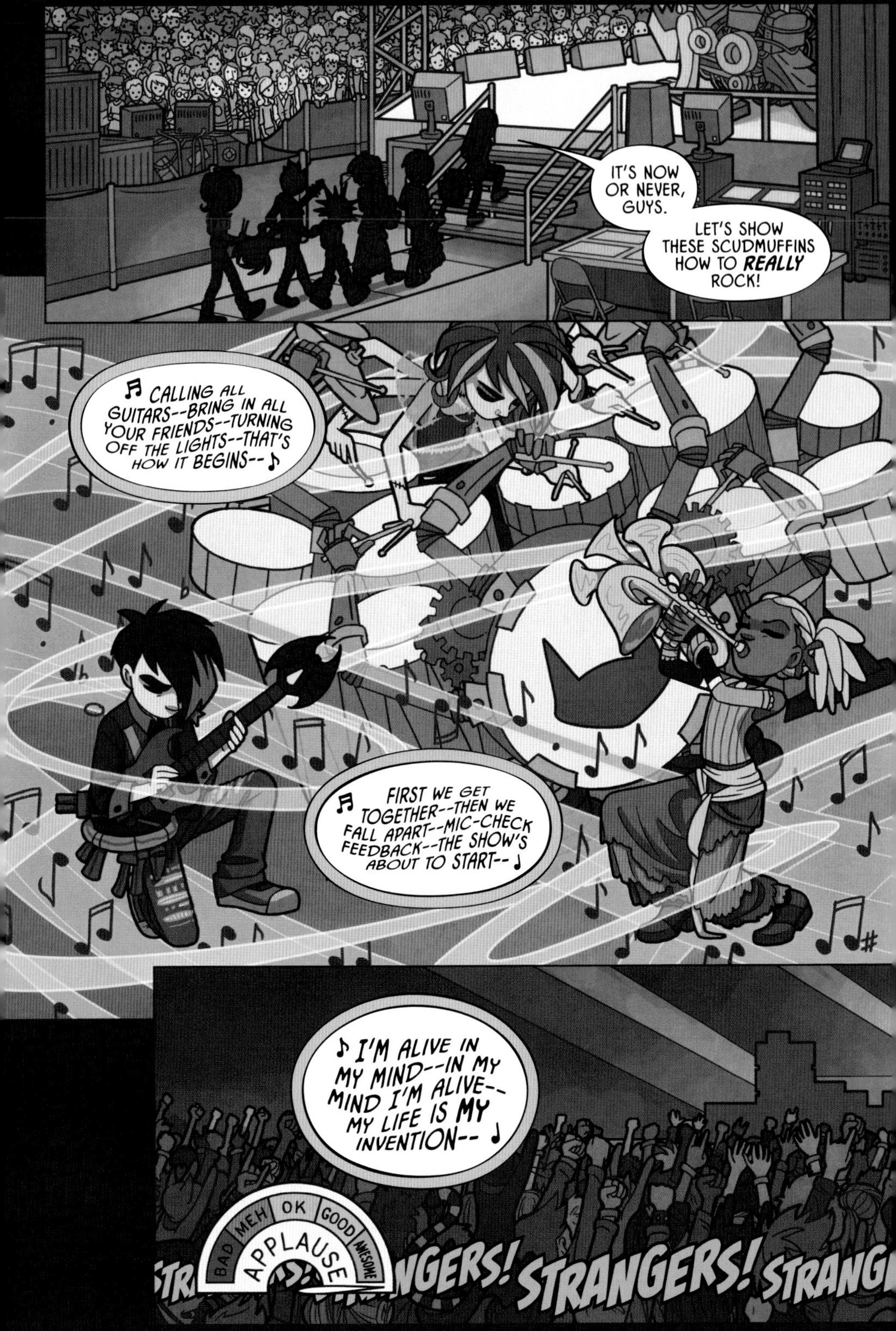
IT'S NOW OR NEVER, GUYS.
LET'S SHOW THESE SCUDMUFFINS HOW TO **REALLY** ROCK!
♬ CALLING ALL GUITARS--BRING IN ALL YOUR FRIENDS--TURNING OFF THE LIGHTS--THAT'S HOW IT BEGINS-- ♪
♬ FIRST WE GET TOGETHER--THEN WE FALL APART--MIC-CHECK FEEDBACK--THE SHOW'S ABOUT TO START-- ♩
♪ I'M ALIVE IN MY MIND--IN MY MIND I'M ALIVE--MY LIFE IS MY INVENTION-- ♩
BAD MEH OK GOOD AWESOME
APPLAUSE
STRANGERS! STRANGERS!

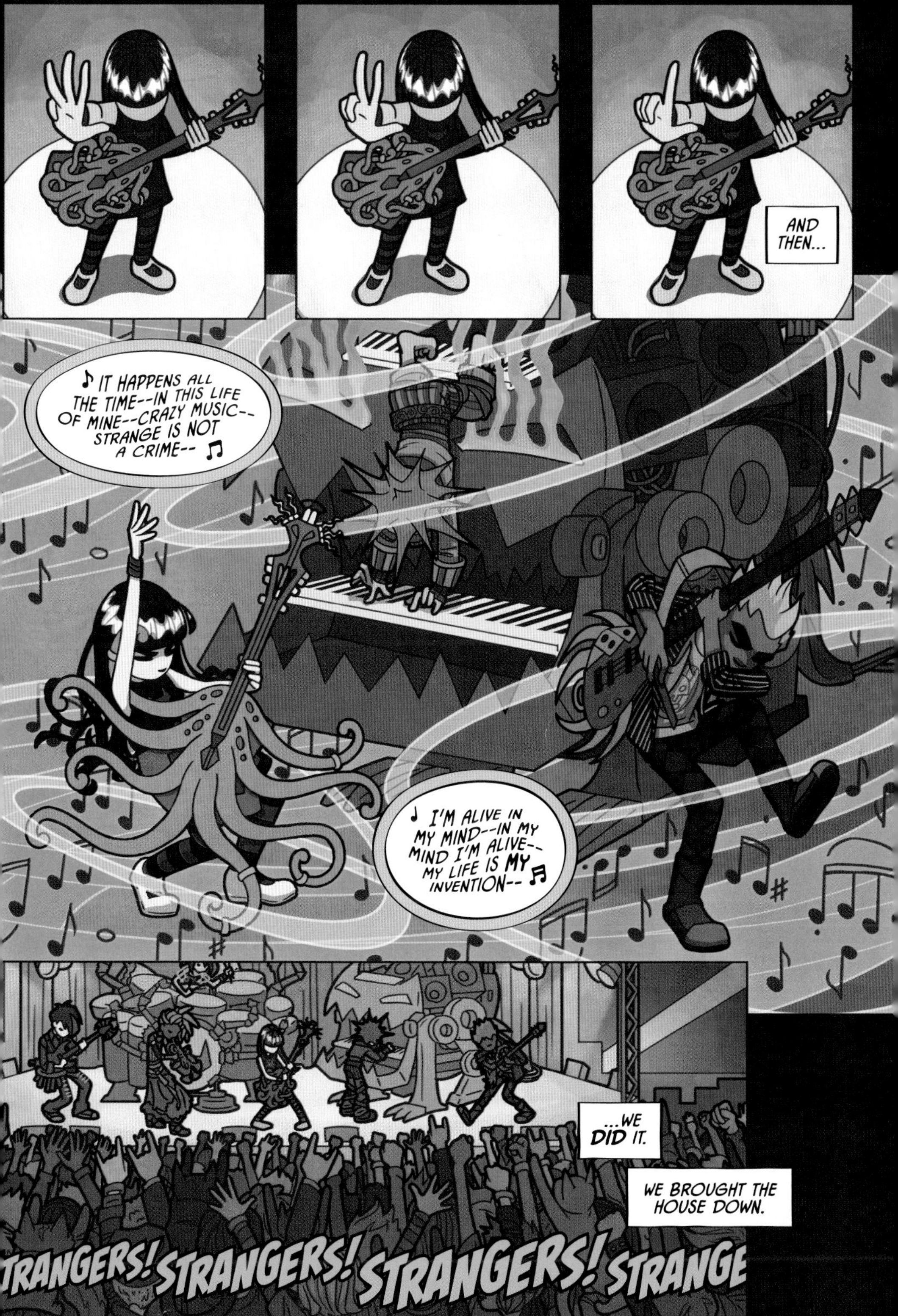
AND THEN...
♪ IT HAPPENS ALL THE TIME--IN THIS LIFE OF MINE--CRAZY MUSIC--STRANGE IS NOT A CRIME-- ♫
♩ I'M ALIVE IN MY MIND--IN MY MIND I'M ALIVE--MY LIFE IS MY INVENTION-- ♬
...WE DID IT.
WE BROUGHT THE HOUSE DOWN.
TRANGERS! STRANGERS! STRANGERS! STRANGE

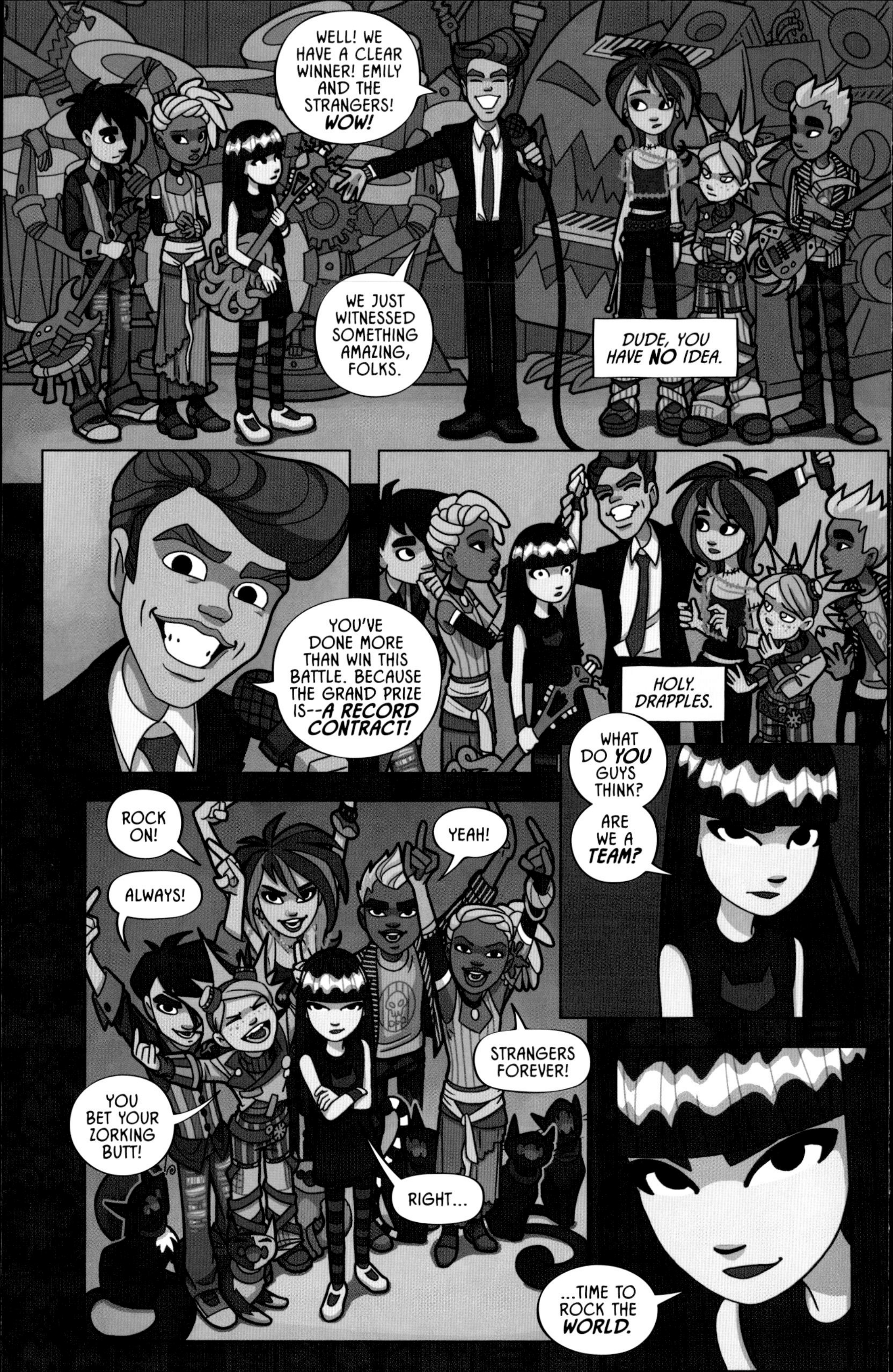
WELL! WE HAVE A CLEAR WINNER! EMILY AND THE STRANGERS! WOW!
WE JUST WITNESSED SOMETHING AMAZING, FOLKS.
DUDE, YOU HAVE NO IDEA.
YOU'VE DONE MORE THAN WIN THIS BATTLE. BECAUSE THE GRAND PRIZE IS--A RECORD CONTRACT!
HOLY. DRAPPLES.
WHAT DO YOU GUYS THINK?
ARE WE A TEAM?
ROCK ON!
YEAH!
ALWAYS!
STRANGERS FOREVER!
YOU BET YOUR ZORKING BUTT!
RIGHT...
...TIME TO ROCK THE WORLD.

EMILY AND THE STRANGERS

GIG POSTERS

BY

RICH BLACK | WINSTON SMITH

AND CYNTHIA VON BUHLER

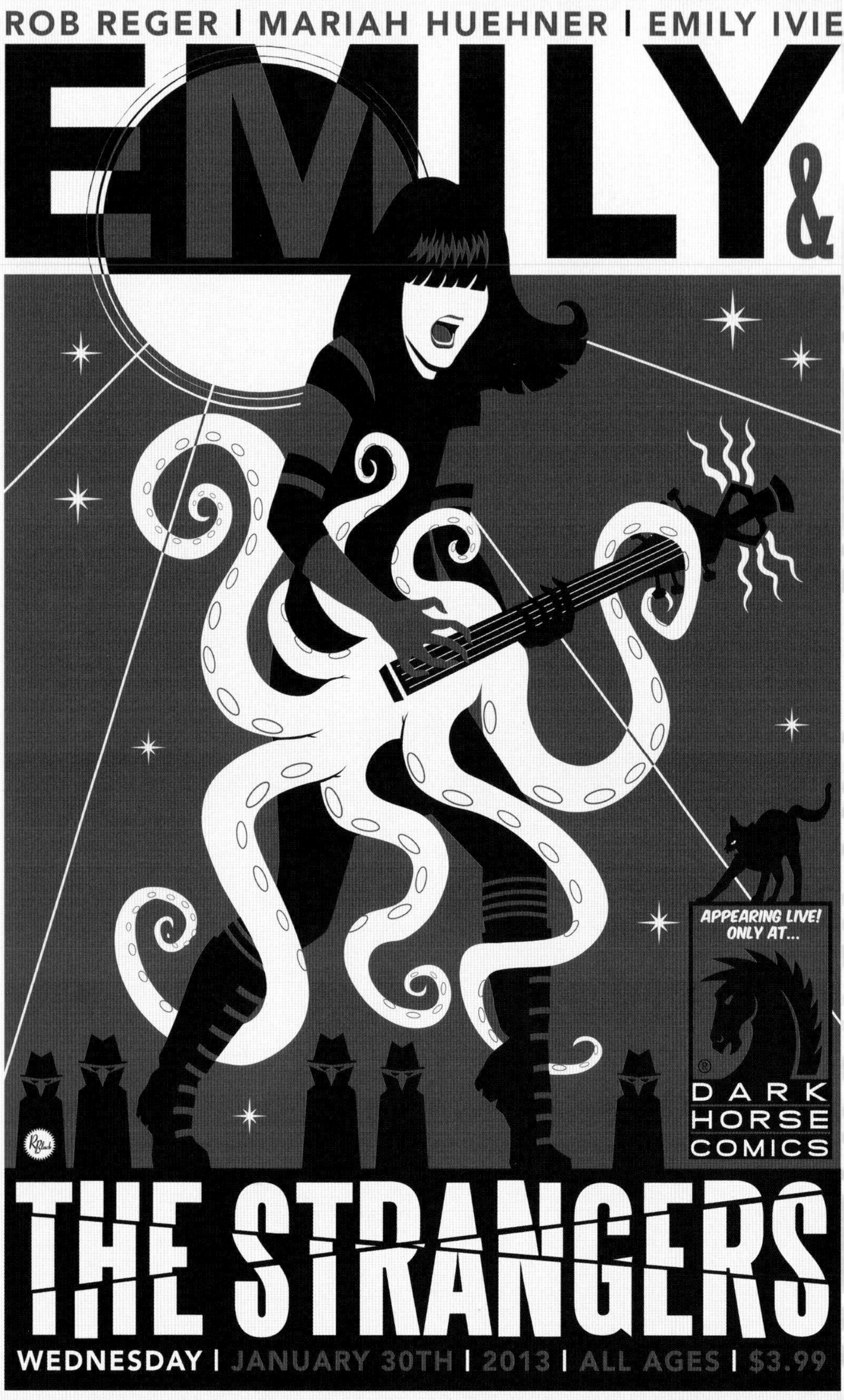
ROB REGER | MARIAH HUEHNER | EMILY IVIE
EMILY&
APPEARING LIVE! ONLY AT...
DARK HORSE COMICS
THE STRANGERS
WEDNESDAY | JANUARY 30TH | 2013 | ALL AGES | $3.99

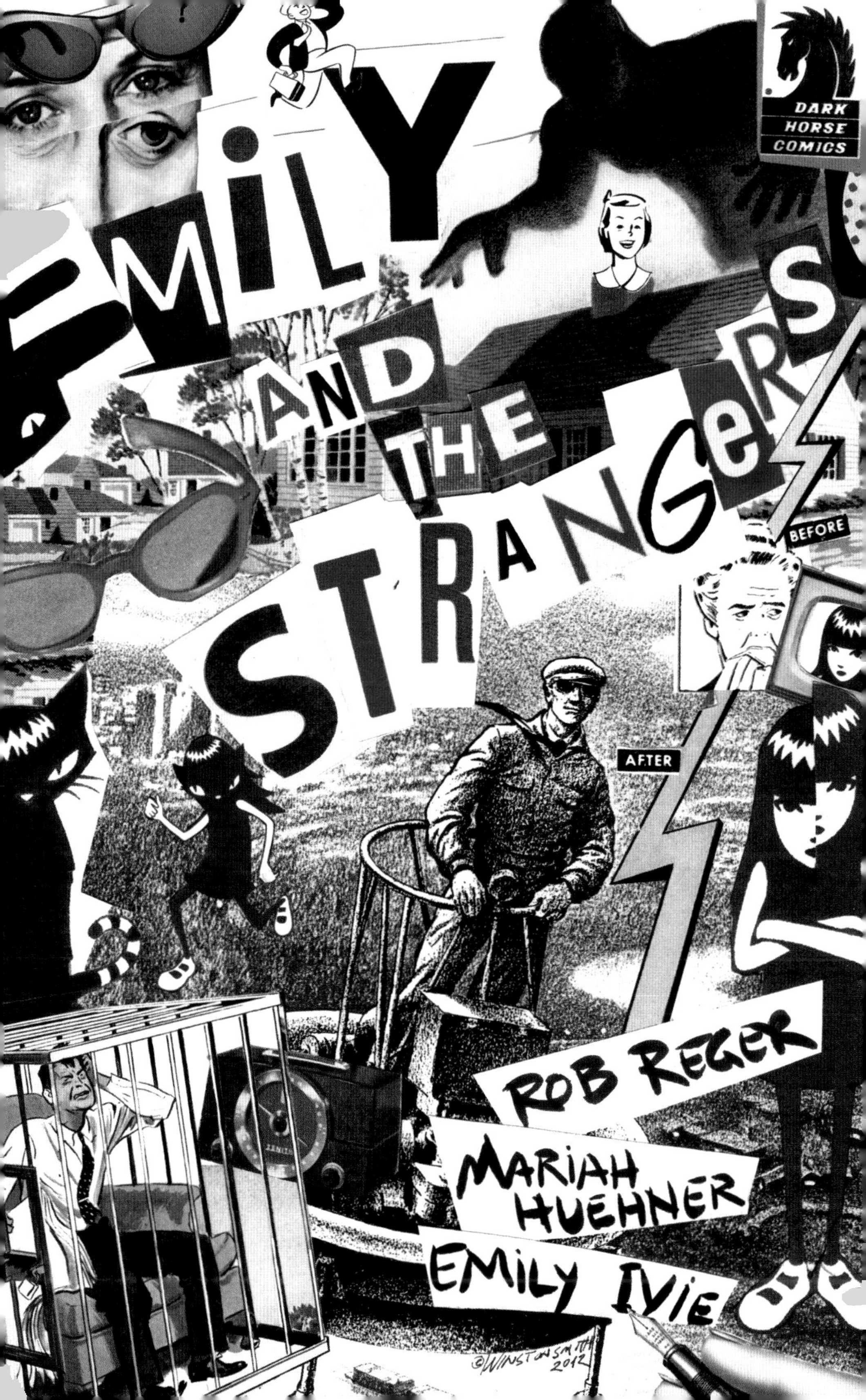
DARK HORSE COMICS
EMILY AND THE STRANGERS
BEFORE
AFTER
ROB REGER
MARIAH HUEHNER
EMILY IVIE
©WINSTON SMITH 2012

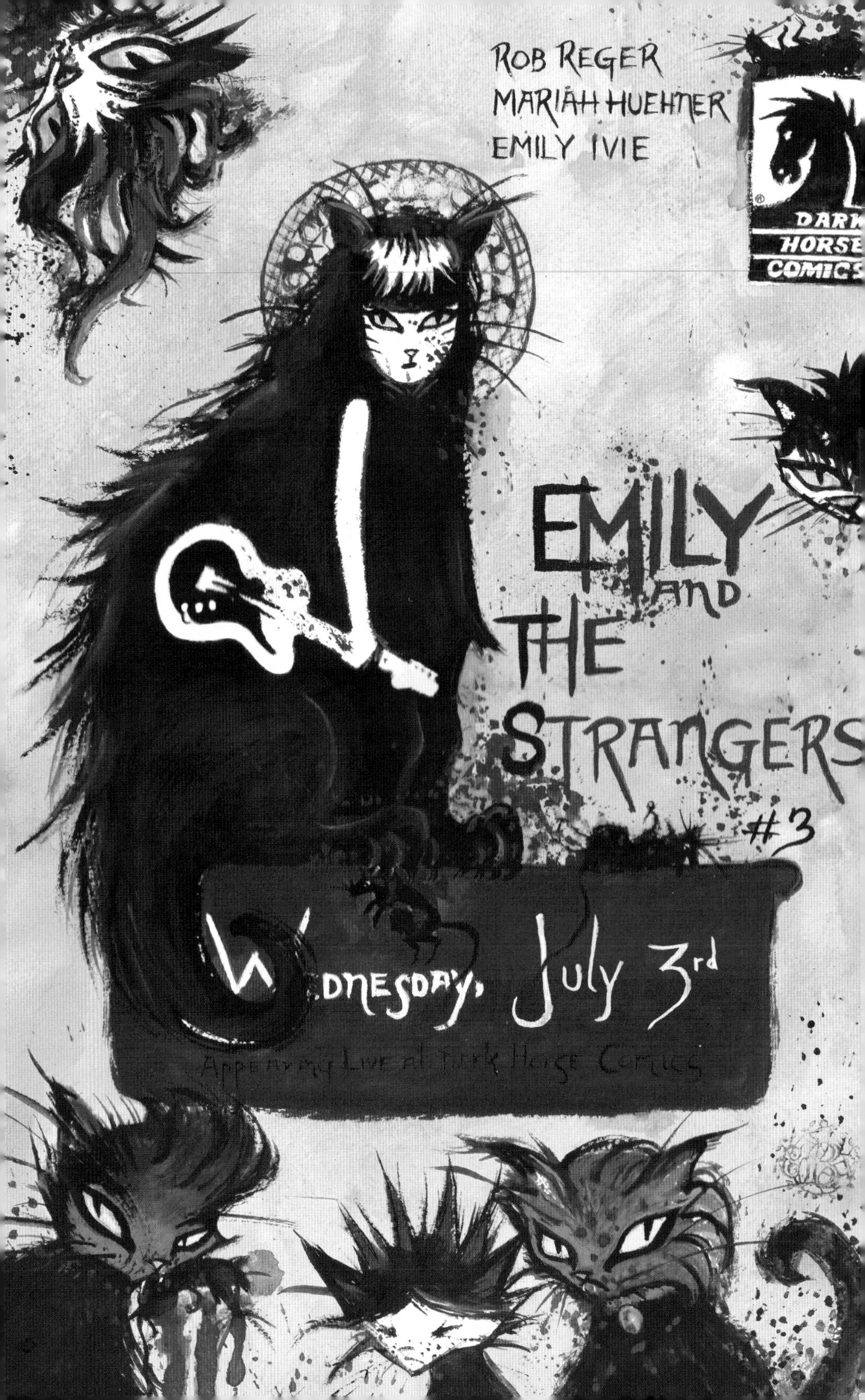
ROB REGER
MARIAH HUEHNER
EMILY IVIE
EMILY AND THE STRANGERS
#3
Wednesday, July 3rd
Appearing Live at Dark Horse Comics

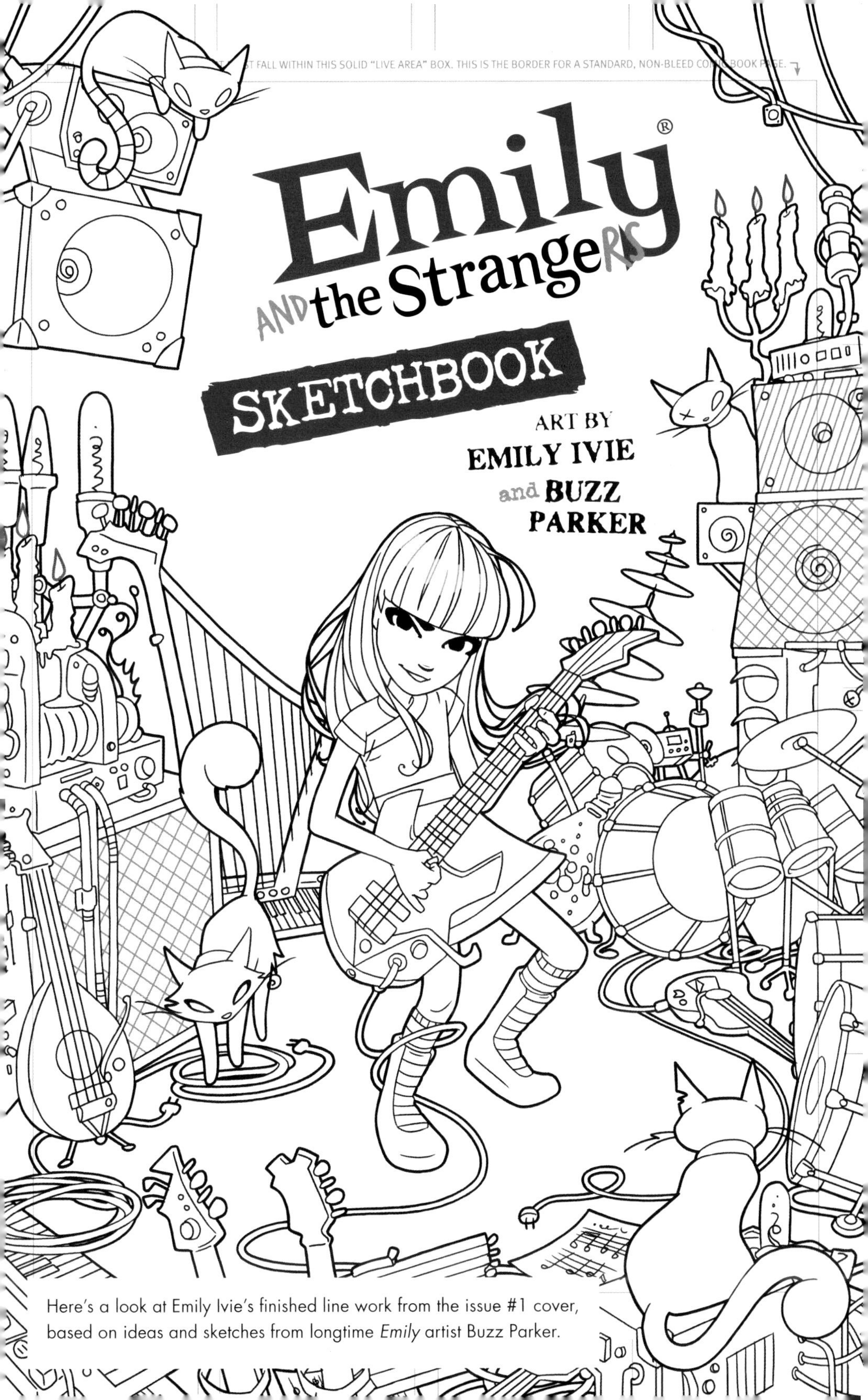
FALL WITHIN THIS SOLID "LIVE AREA" BOX. THIS IS THE BORDER FOR A STANDARD, NON-BLEED
Emily®
AND the StrangeRS
SKETCHBOOK
ART BY
EMILY IVIE
and BUZZ
PARKER

Here's a look at Emily Ivie's finished line work from the issue #1 cover, based on ideas and sketches from longtime *Emily* artist Buzz Parker.

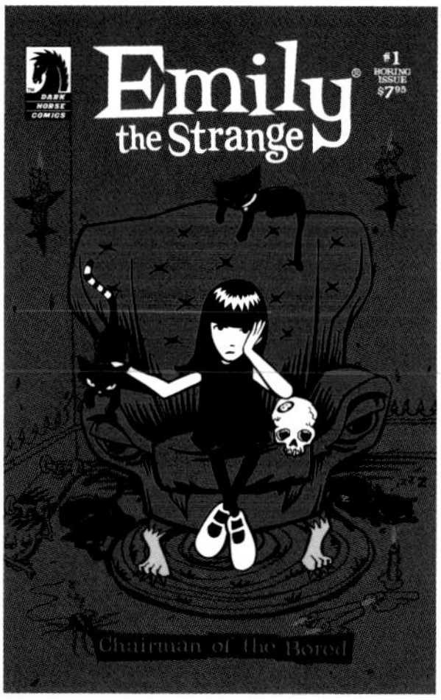
Emily the Strange
#1 BORING ISSUE $7.95
Chairman of the Bored

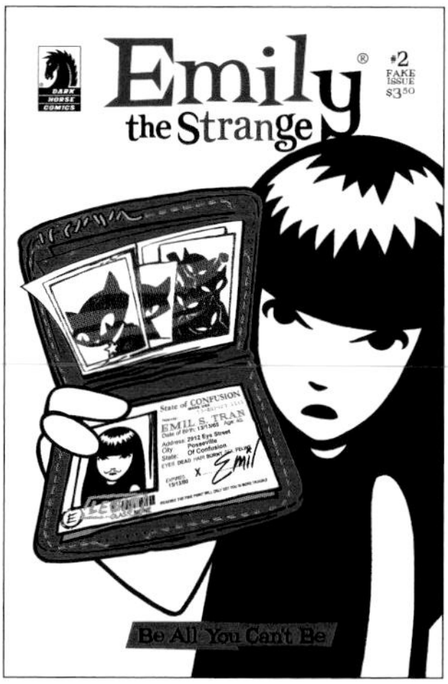
Emily the Strange
#2 FAKE ISSUE $3.50
Be All You Can't Be

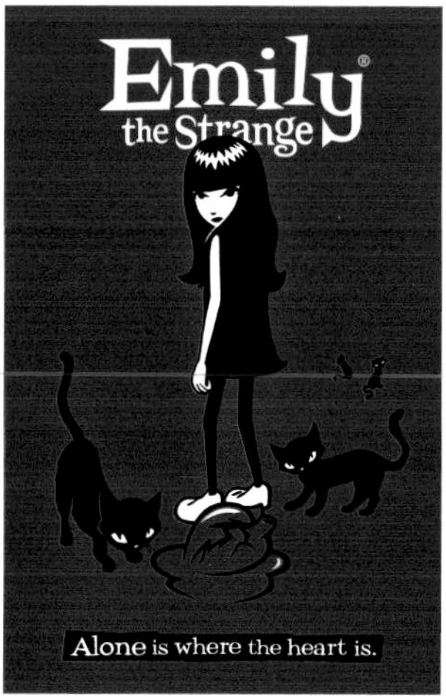
Emily the Strange
Alone is where the heart is.

First appearing in 1991, Emily the Strange made her way to comics in 2005. The above covers, by Buzz Parker, showcase Emily's classic look.

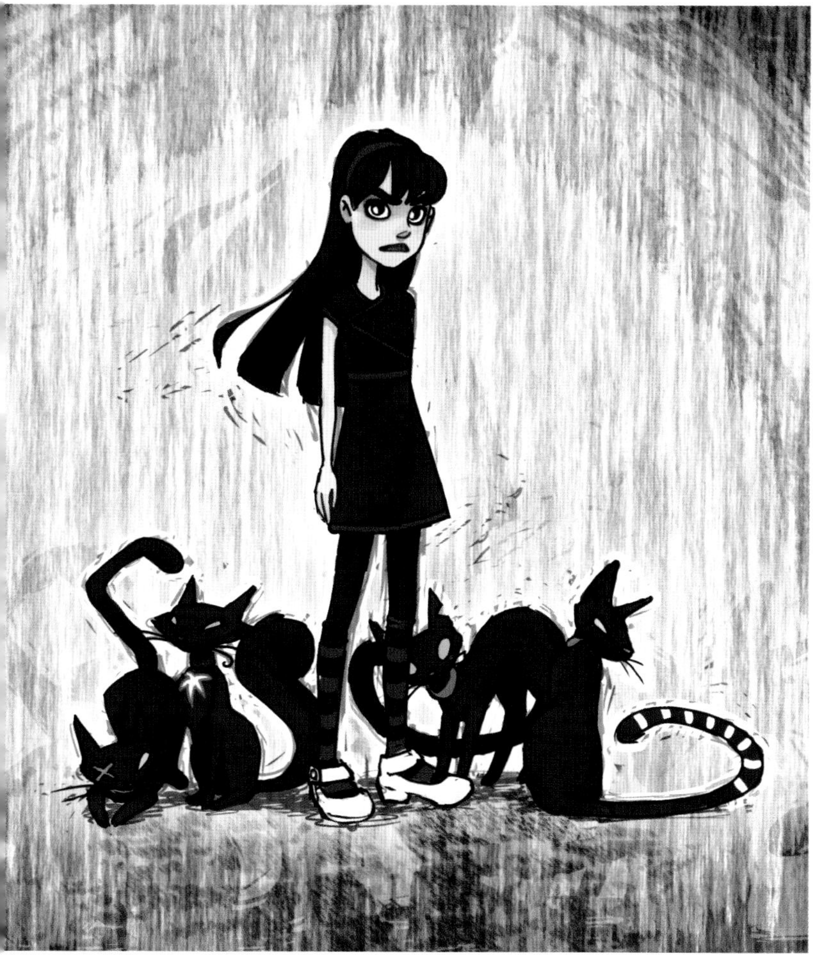

On the left, you can see Emily Ivie's original sketch for the *Emily and the Strangers* update of our restless heroine.

On the next page is Emily's final look for this new series in the finished colored cover of issue #1 by Ivie, which is also the cover of this collection.

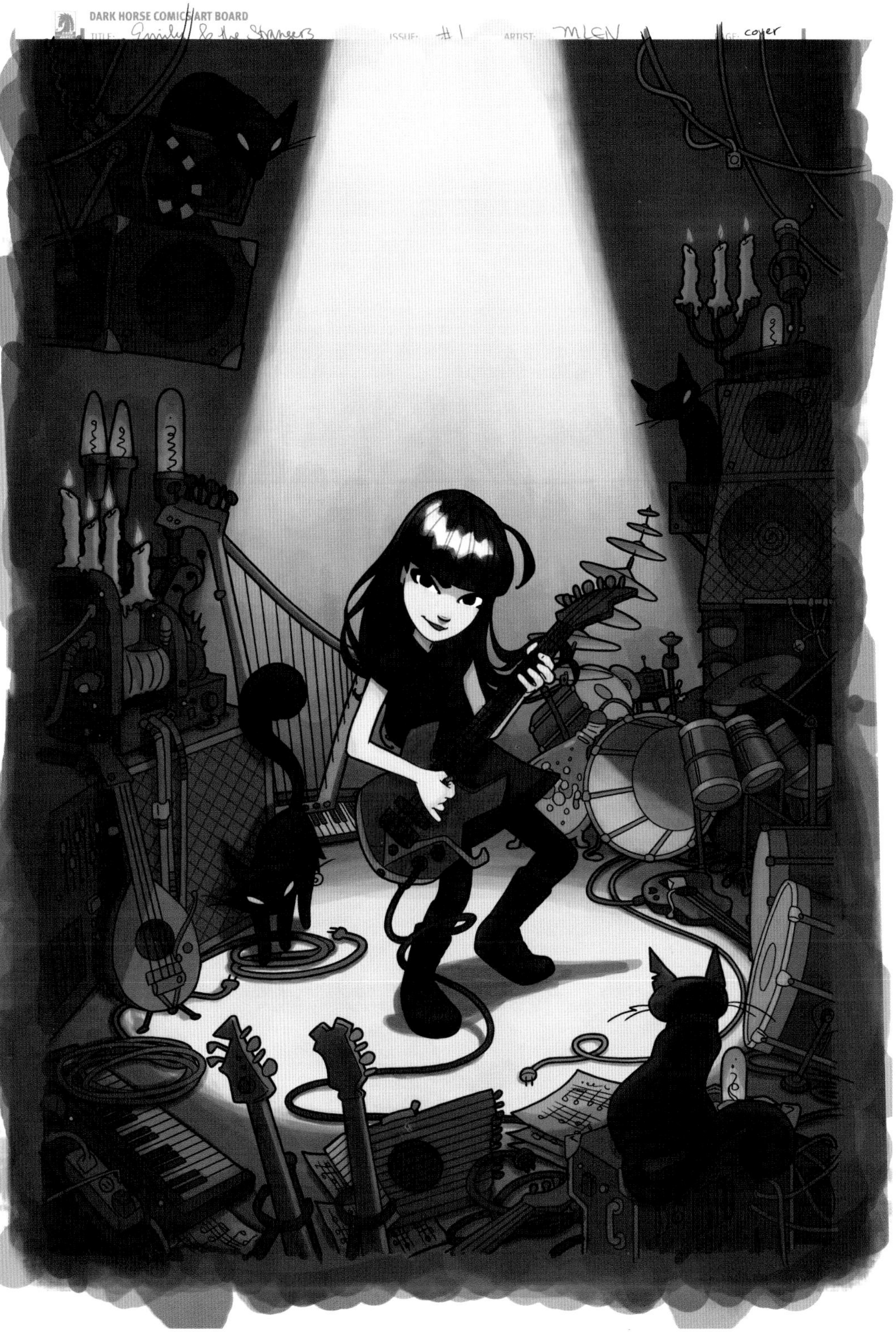
DARK HORSE COMICS ART BOARD
TITLE: Emily & the Strangers
ISSUE: #1
ARTIST: MLEN
cover

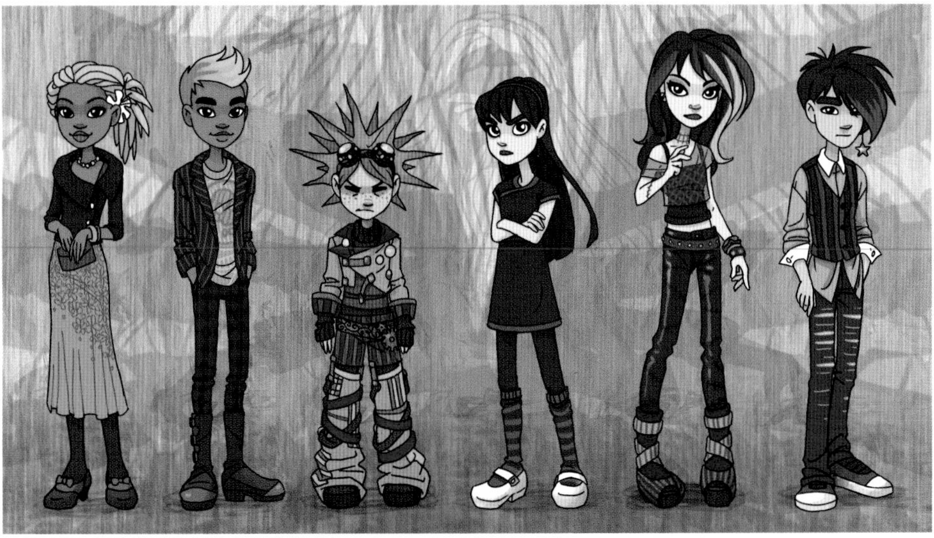

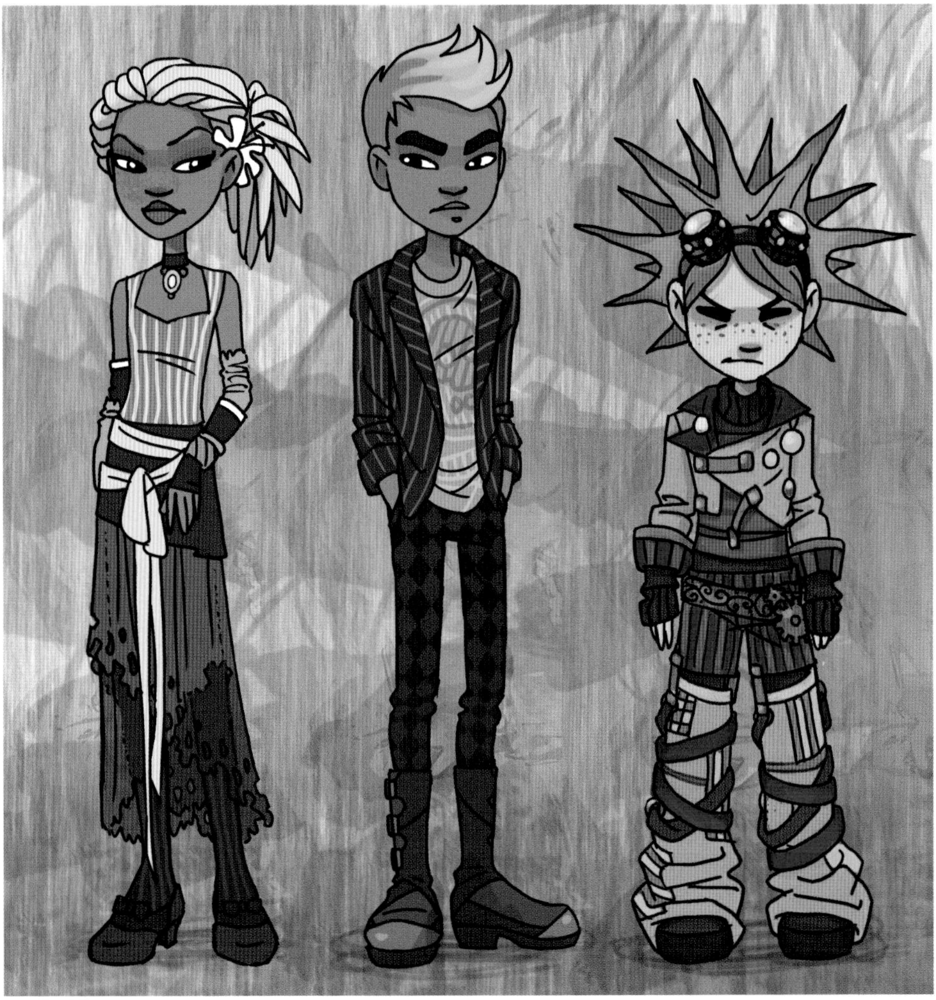

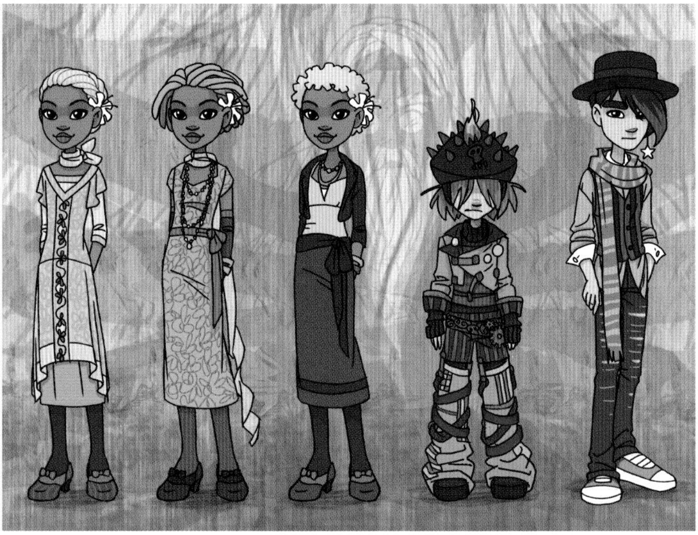

Not too far off the mark from the get-go, here are Ivie's initial designs (top left) for Emily and her band and the minor alterations that led to their final look (below), as well as a few funky alternatives for Willow, Trilogy, and Evan.

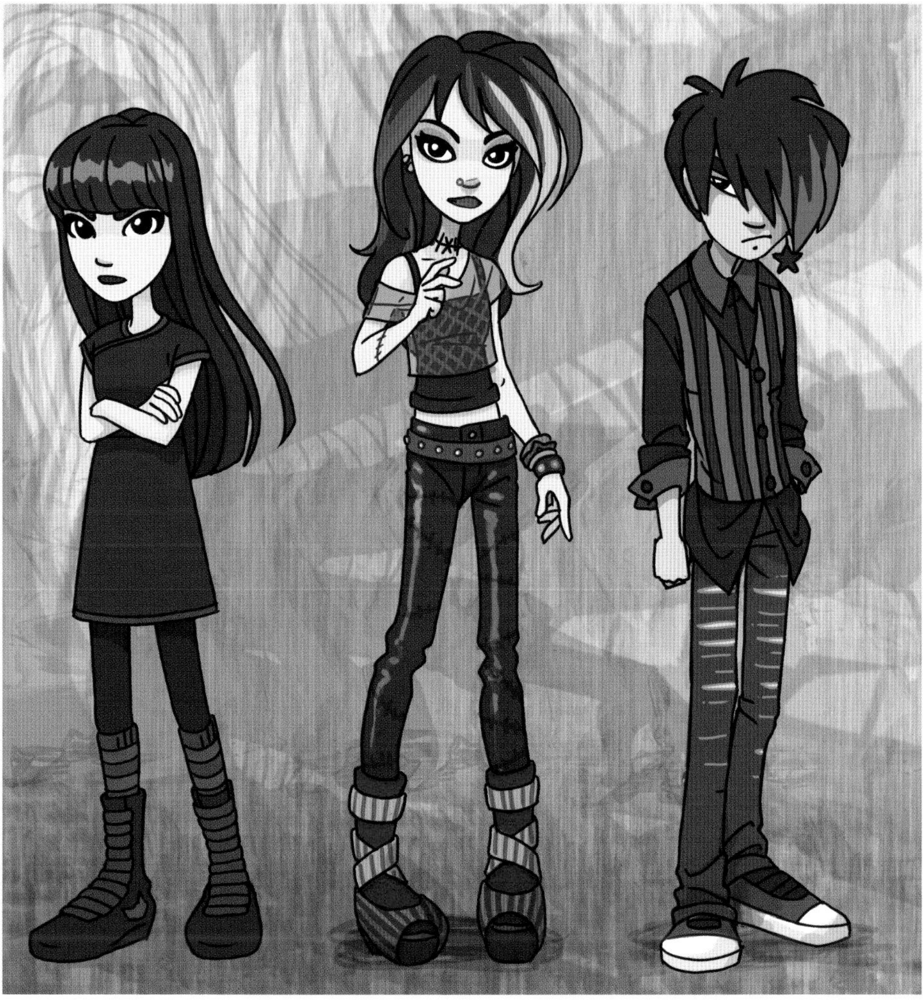

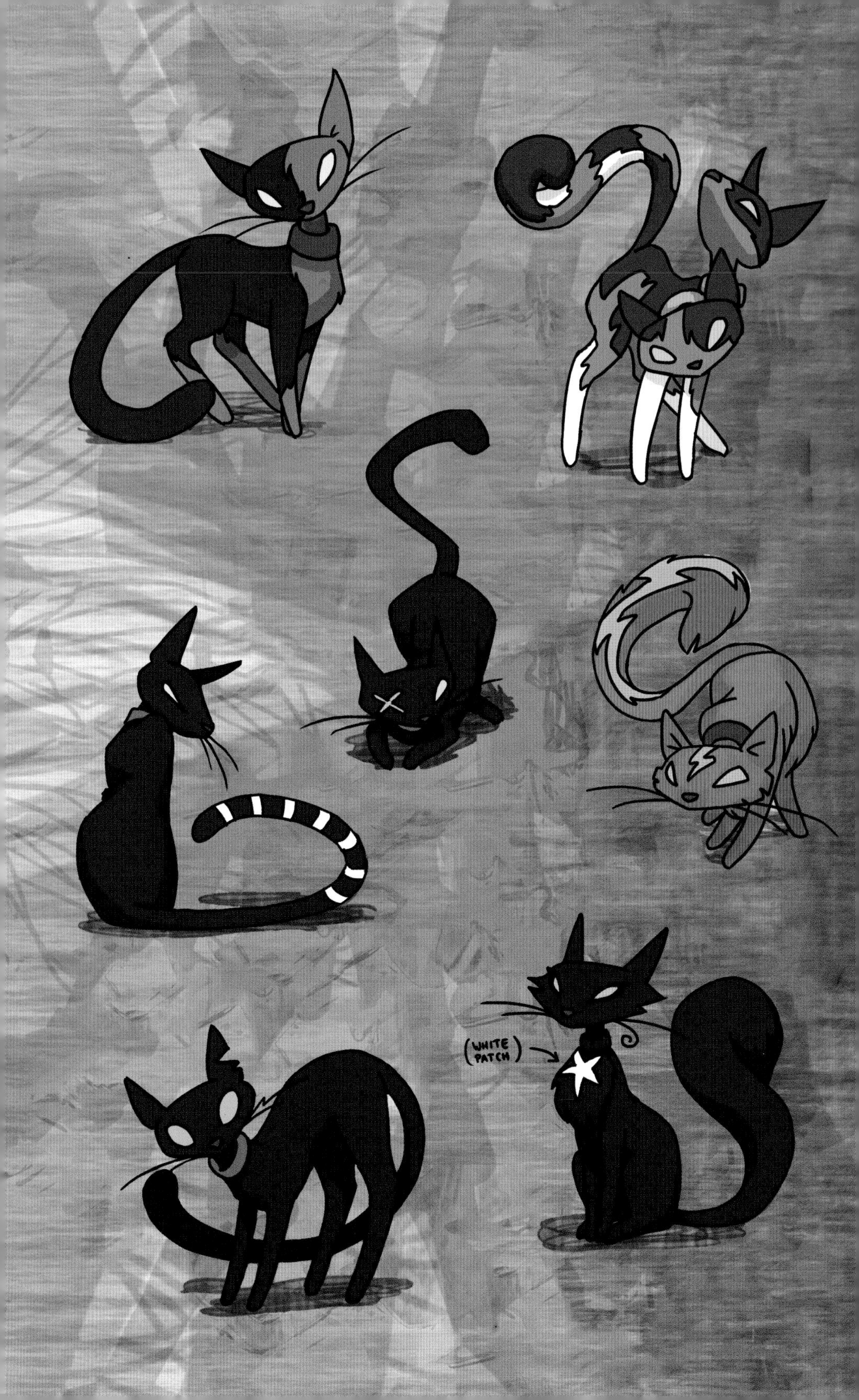
(WHITE PATCH)

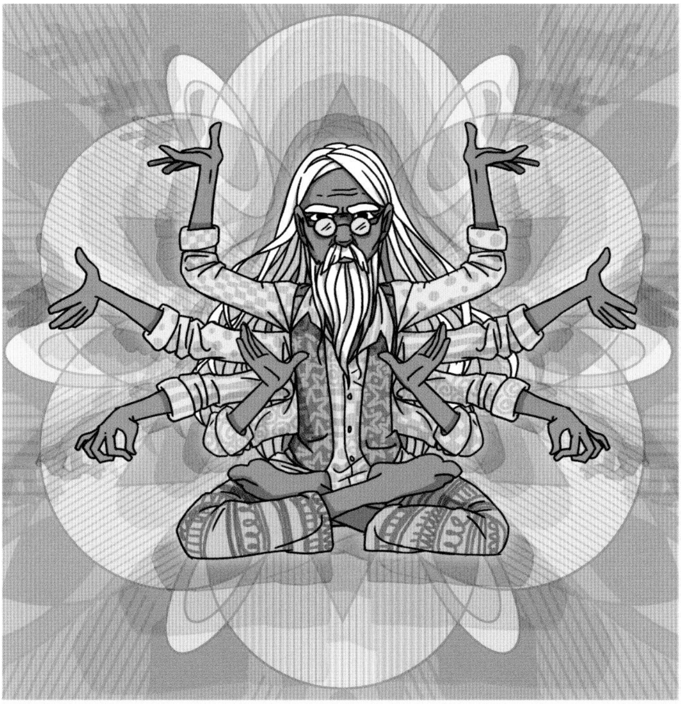

As cats have always been an important part of the *Emily the Strange* comics, of course there needed to be cats in this new series. Take a look at Ivie's designs for the cats in *Emily and the Strangers* and see if you can guess which cat matches up with each band member!

To the right, check out the first take on Professa Kraken (top), as well as his final design.

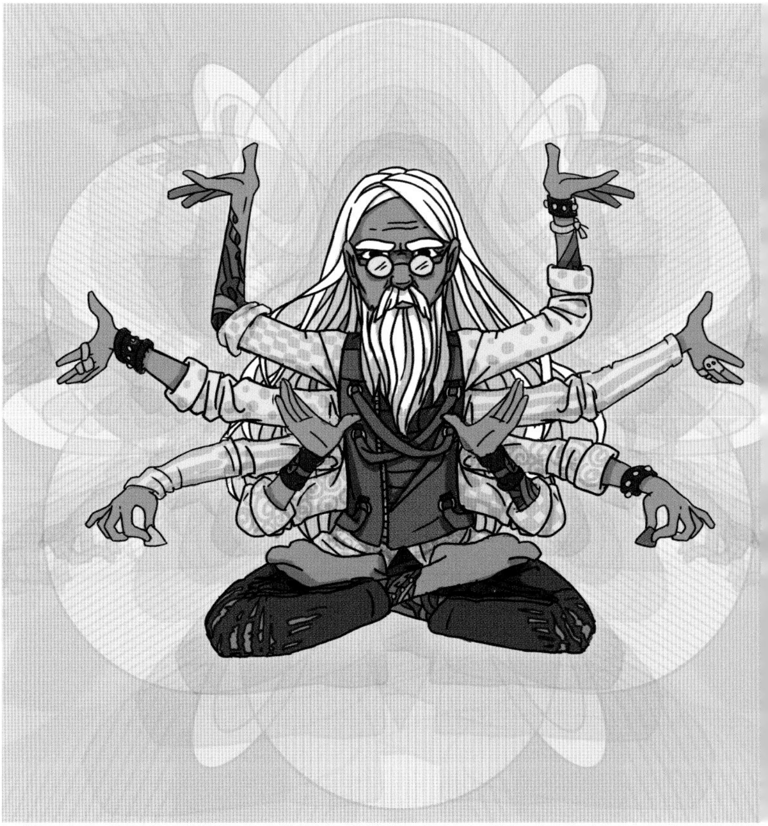

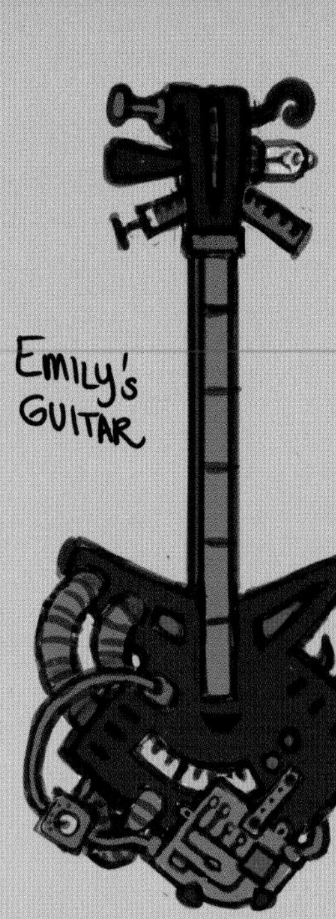
EMILY'S
GUITAR

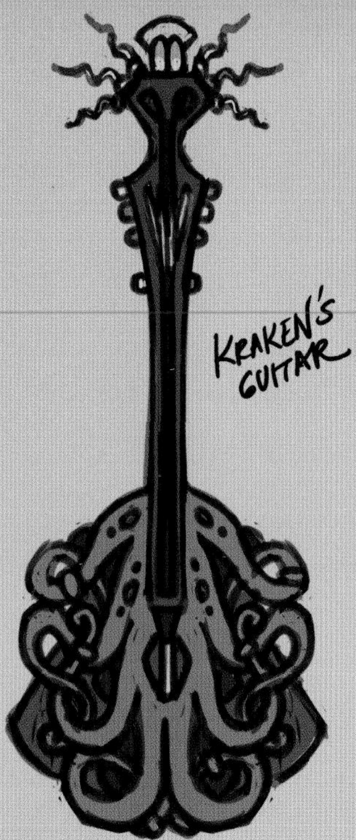
KRAKEN'S
GUITAR

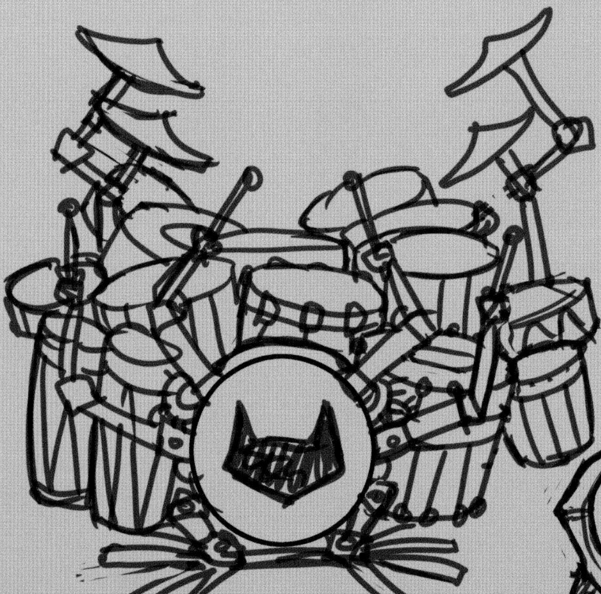

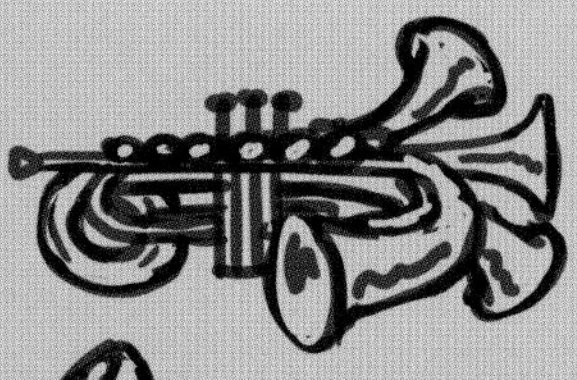

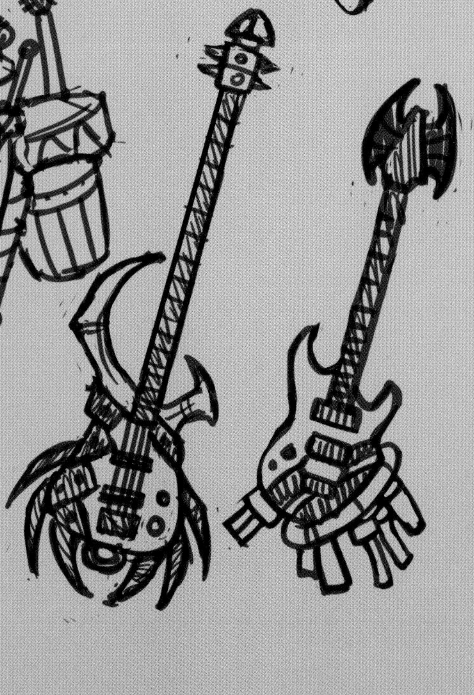

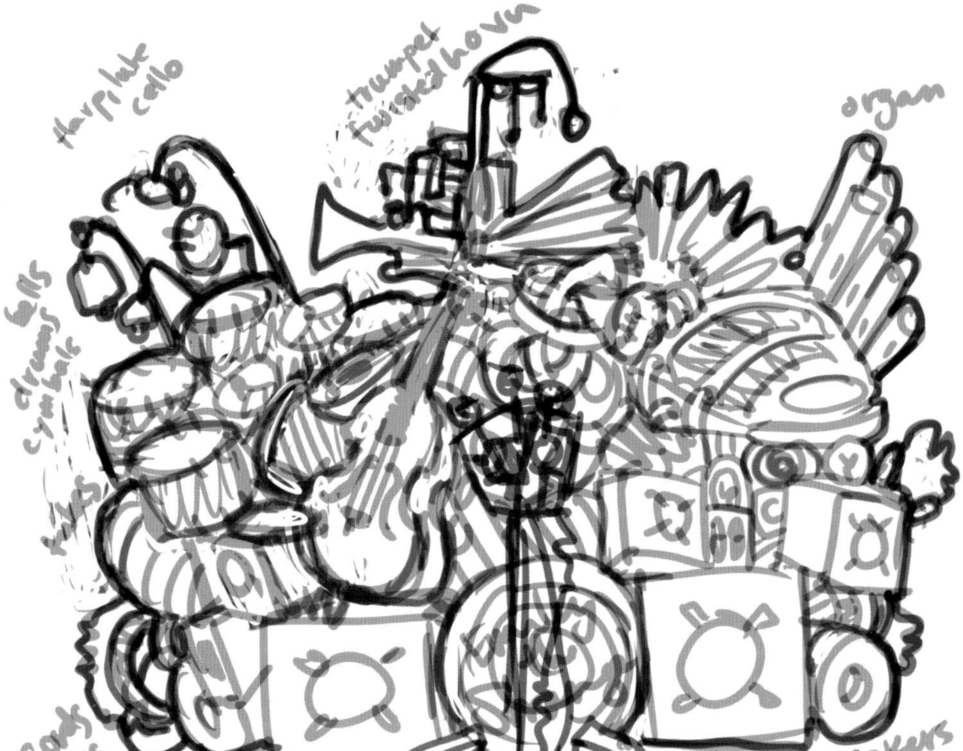
cello
trumpet
twisted horn
organ
bells
drums
cymbals
cords
wires
speakers
bass

When it comes to instruments, Emily's taste is as far out as the ideas she uses to create her other inventions. So, naturally, the Strangers couldn't play with just any ol' instruments! Here are some initial designs of the rad music makers the band uses through this first volume of *Emily and the Strangers*!

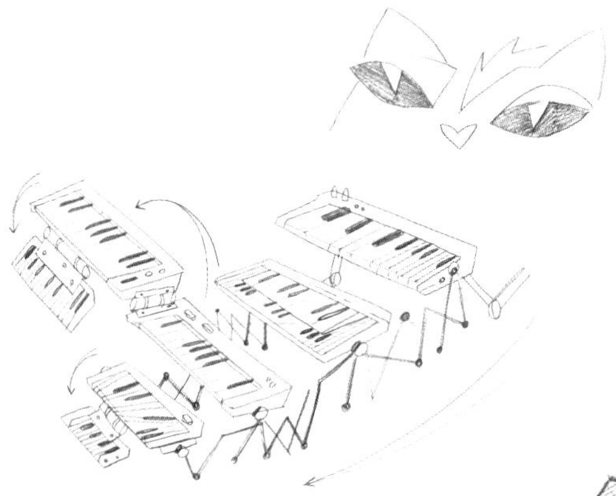

Additional funky instrument designs by Buzz Parker for Trilogy's piano, Raven's drums, and Emily's mic.

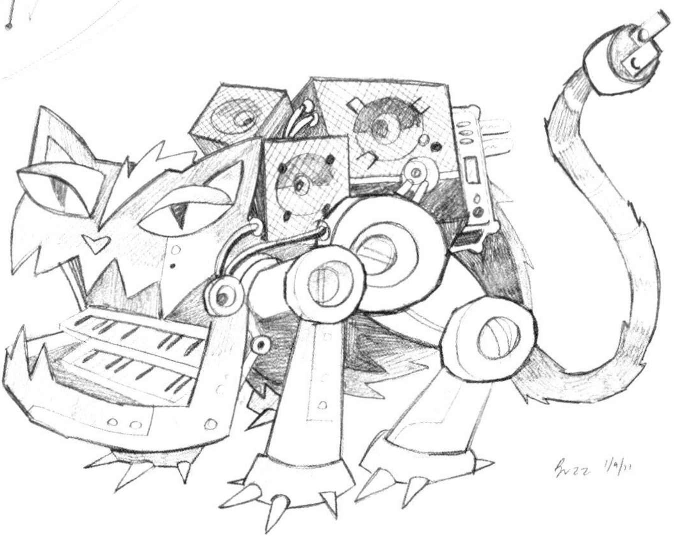

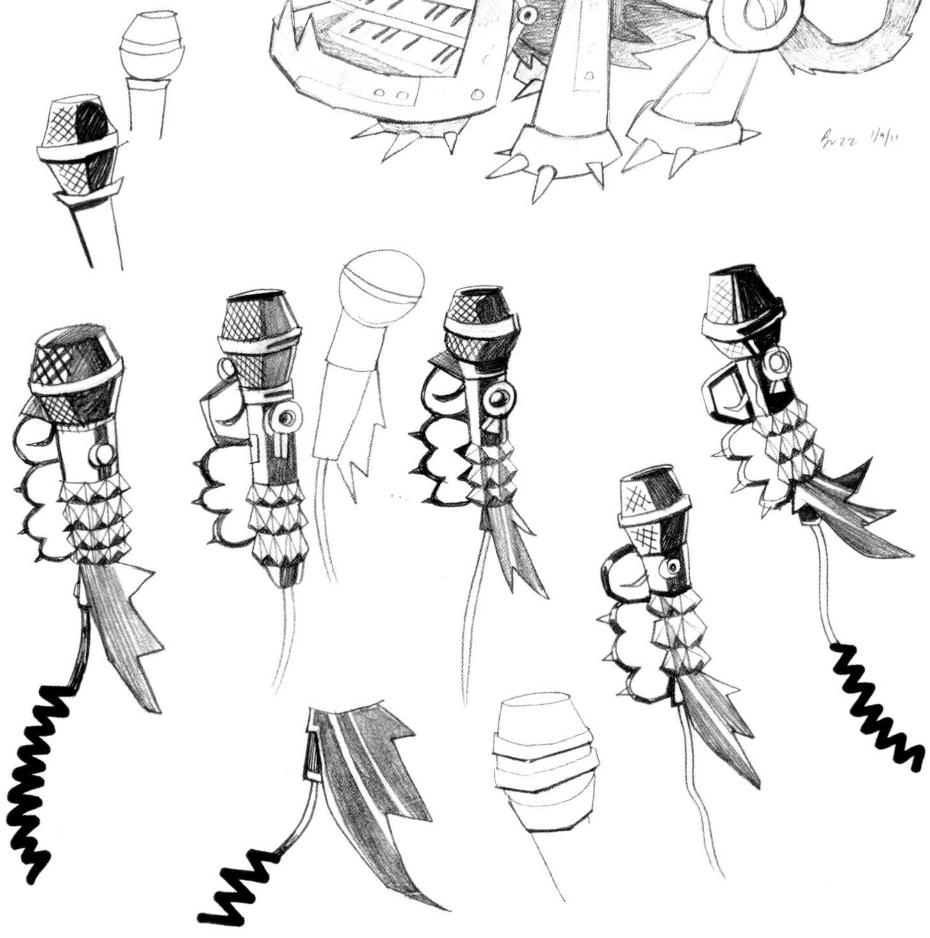

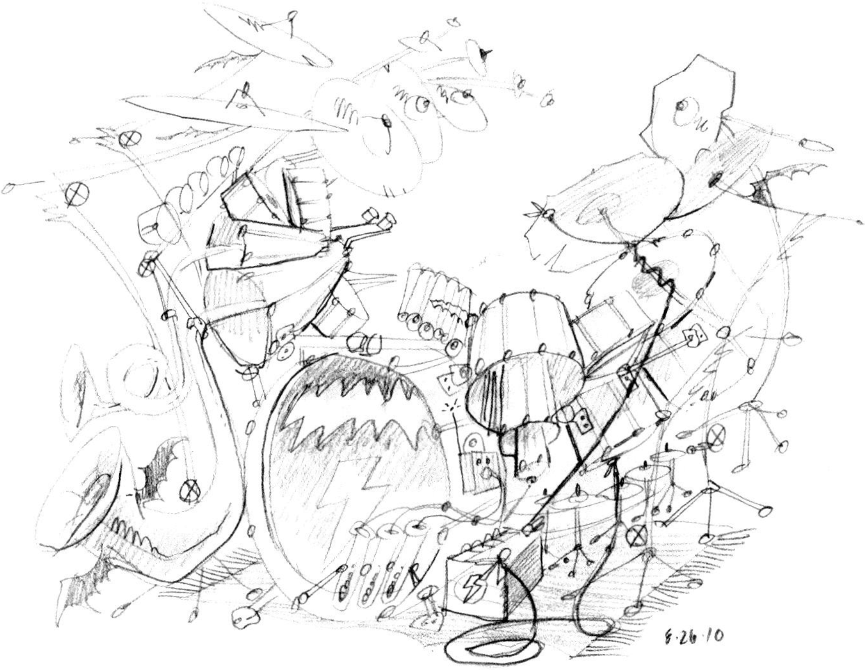
8·26·10

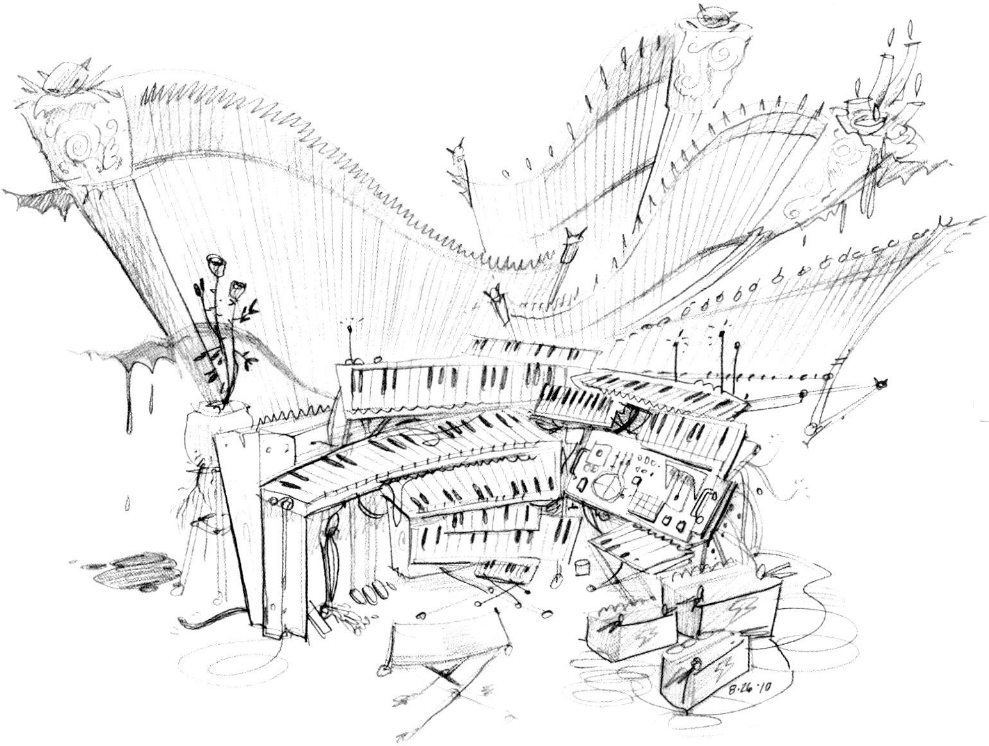
8·26·10

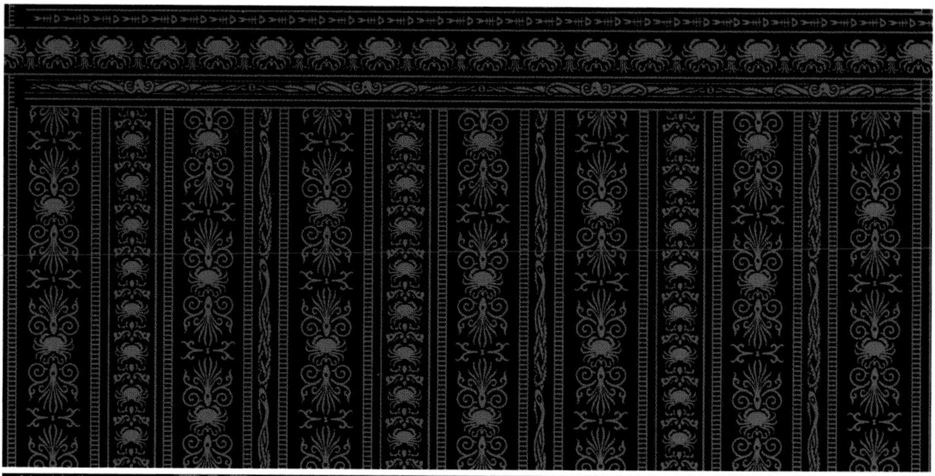

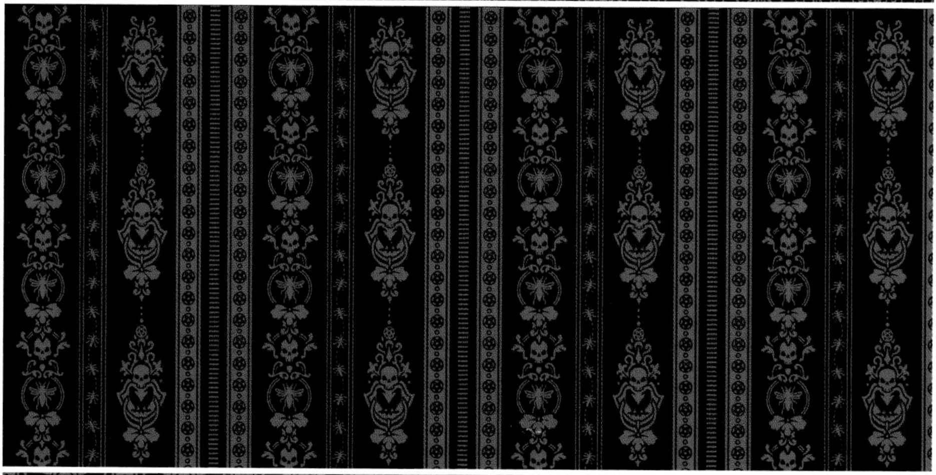

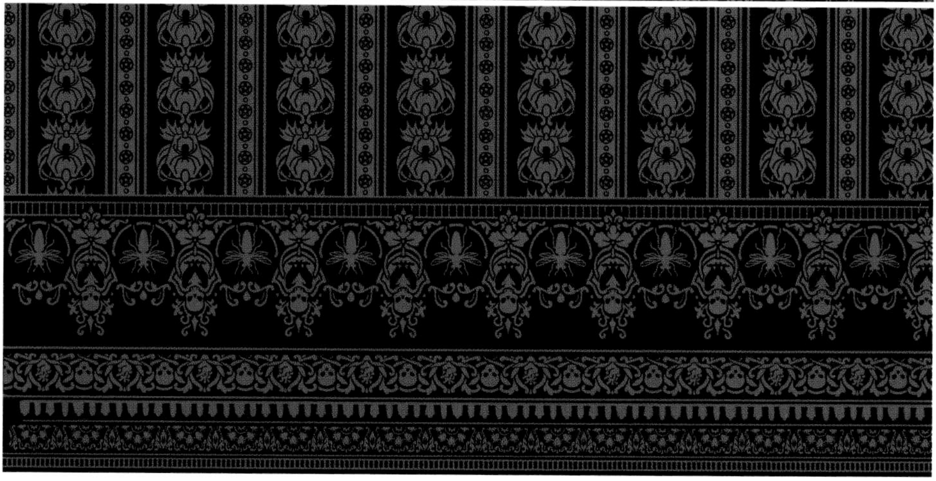

Ivie created a series of Emily-inspired wallpapers, utilized throughout the series as backdrops to her art, to give each page depth and—for eagle-eyed readers—something exciting to look at in the black bit between panels. Take a look at six of these intricate pieces.

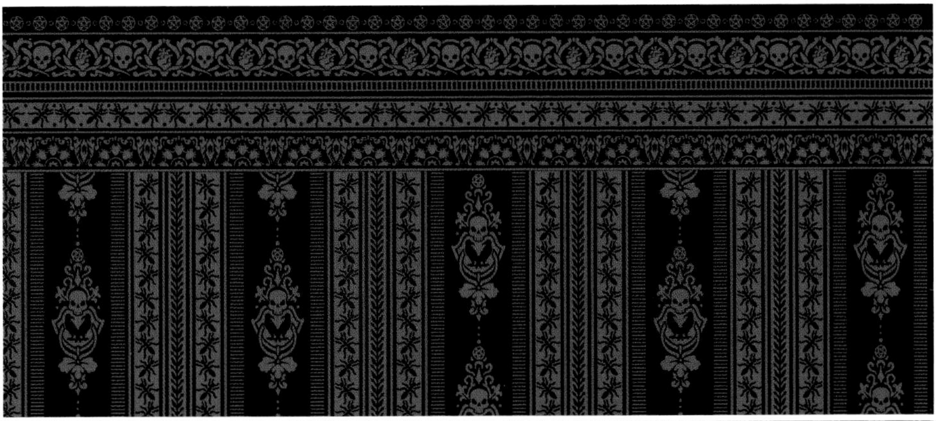

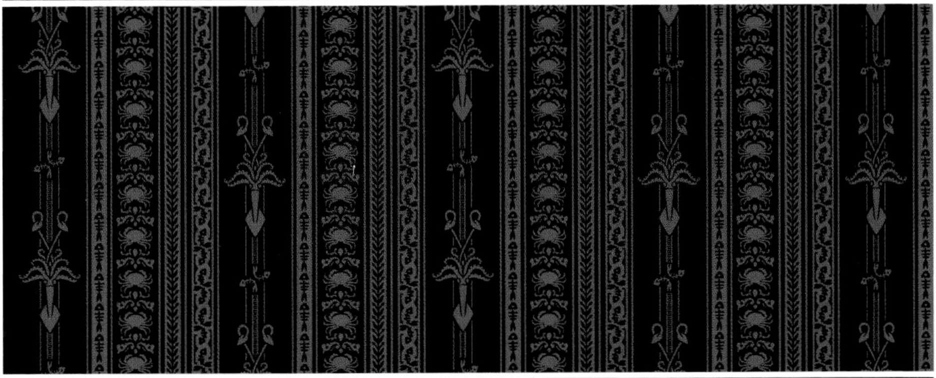

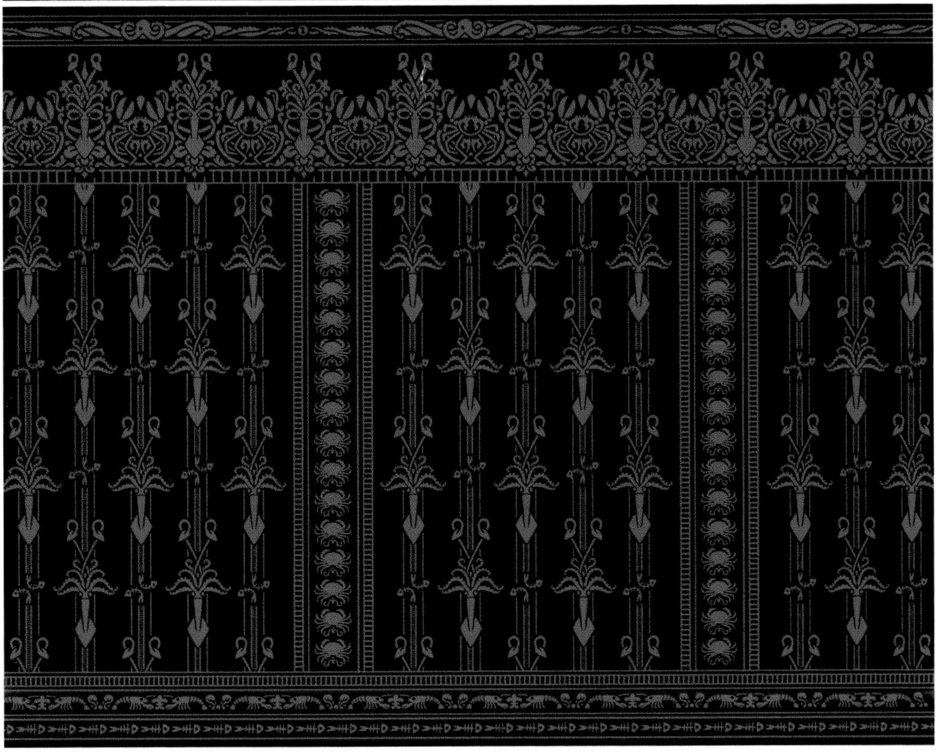

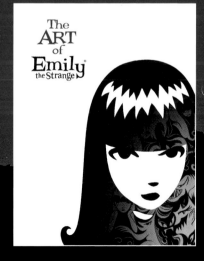

DISCOVER THE ADVENTURE!

Explore these beloved books for the entire family.